Luke pulled away from Julia.

When he looked at her, he found her watching him with equal parts desire and fear in her eyes. Her emotions so closely matched his own that he closed his eyes. He couldn't allow himself to want her this way.

"Reaction makes you do funny things, doesn't it?" Julia's voice was too bright, and she refused to meet his eyes. "Release of tension and all that, I guess."

"Right." He stared at her averted head and felt a perverse kick of anger. "God knows it would be completely unthinkable that you could actually want me."

"Just like you would rather die than want me," she agreed. Her cheeks still flamed, but she met his eyes squarely.

"I'm glad we have that straight." He stood up abruptly and moved away from her.

From now on he would damn well keep his hands to himself.

Dear Reader,

We've got six drop-dead-gorgeous and utterly irresistible heroes for you this month, starting with Marilyn Pappano's latest contribution to our HEARTBREAKERS program. Dillon Boone, in *Survive the Night,* is a man on the run—right into Ashley Benedict's arms. The only problem is, will they survive long enough to fulfill their promises of forever?

Our ROMANTIC TRADITIONS title is Judith Duncan's *Driven to Distraction,* a sexy take on the younger man/older woman theme. I promise you that Tony Parnelli will drive right into your heart. *A Cowboy's Heart,* Doreen Roberts' newest, features a one-time rodeo rider who's just come face-to-face with a woman—and a secret—from his past. Kay David's *Baby of the Bride* is a marriage-of-convenience story with an adorable little girl at its center—and a groom you'll fall for in a big, bad way. *Blackwood's Woman,* by Beverly Barton, is the last in her miniseries, THE PROTECTORS. And in J.T. Blackwood she's created yet another hero to remember. Finally, Margaret Watson returns with her second book, *An Honorable Man.* Watch as hero Luke McKinley is forced to confront the one woman he would like never to see again—the one woman who is fated to be his.

Enjoy them all, and come back next month for more great romantic reading—here in Silhouette Intimate Moments.

Yours,

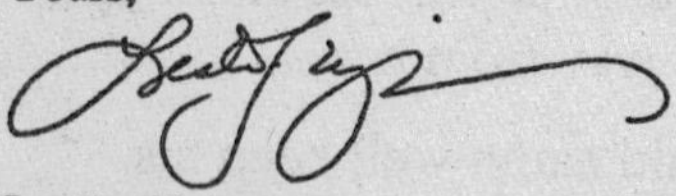

Leslie Wainger
Senior Editor and Editorial Coordinator

Please address questions and book requests to:
Silhouette Reader Service
U.S.: 3010 Walden Ave., P.O. Box 1325, Buffalo, NY 14269
Canadian: P.O. Box 609, Fort Erie, Ont. L2A 5X3

AN HONORABLE MAN

MARGARET WATSON

Silhouette® INTIMATE™ MOMENTS®
Published by Silhouette Books
America's Publisher of Contemporary Romance

SILHOUETTE BOOKS

ISBN 0-373-07708-4

AN HONORABLE MAN

This edition published by arrangement with Harlequin Books S.A.

Printed in U.S.A.

Books by Margaret Watson

Silhouette Intimate Moments

An Innocent Man #636
An Honorable Man #708

MARGARET WATSON

says that from the time she learned to read, she could usually be found with her nose in a book. Her lifelong passion for reading led to her interest in writing, and now she's happily writing exactly the kind of stories she likes to read. Margaret is a veterinarian who lives in the Chicago suburbs with her husband and their three daughters. In her spare time she enjoys in-line skating, birding and spending time with her family. Readers can write to Margaret at P.O. Box 2333, Naperville, IL 60567-2333.

For Katie, Chelsea and Meg. I'm so proud that you are my daughters. Thank you for all you give me and all the joy you add to my life.

Thanks to Tom Watson for his expertise on the city of Chicago and its neighborhoods.

Chapter 1

A sleepless night was a hell of a way to start the day. Lucas McKinley closed his eyes and leaned back in the creaking desk chair. It tipped to the side, as usual, and he propped his feet up on the scarred desk for balance.

An hour's sleep was all he needed. After that, coffee could get him through the rest of the day. As he slid lower in the chair, the weak morning light from the window next to him filtered through his eyelids, making his eyes burn. Someone had to turn down the sunlight, he thought drowsily, shifting to get into the shade. He thought longingly of the couch listing against the wall, but put it firmly out of his mind. He couldn't afford to sleep the day away.

Footsteps snapped on the linoleum outside his door, but he ignored them. No one ever came looking for him this early in the morning. His clientele tended to be creatures of the night. At this hour of the day, most of them would be getting into bed, not out of it. Just like he should be doing, he thought sourly as he adjusted his position again.

The footsteps stopped outside his door. When they didn't move on after a few moments, he groaned and pulled himself upright. Undoubtedly it was another newly arrived immigrant, speaking little or no English, looking for the podiatrist or the employment agency farther down the hall rather than his office, which offered private investigations. Maybe after he helped them find the right room, using the few words of Polish he'd learned in his last two years on the northwest side of Chicago, he'd stretch out on that couch after all.

The door swung slowly open and he let his feet drop to the floor, plastering what would have to pass for a pleasant smile on his face. When his visitor stepped into the sunlight streaming into the office, his smile froze and his face hardened until he thought it would crack.

She stood in the doorway for a moment, almost as if she were gathering her courage. Then, with a deep breath, she closed the door behind her and took two more steps toward him.

"Good morning, Mr. McKinley."

Her voice was low and pleasant, just like he remembered it. He'd thought at the time that anyone with such a sexy, husky voice shouldn't be capable of shattering his world so easily and so completely.

"May I come in?"

There was only polite inquiry in her voice, but a shadow, quickly hidden, flickered across her face. If he didn't know better, he'd say she looked uncomfortable.

But that was impossible. Julia Carleton, the queen of cool, was never uncomfortable. The ice princess of the Chicago Police Force's Internal Affairs Department never showed a crack in her marble facade.

"Of course," he said, waving his arm as he slouched in his chair and watched her warily. "Have a seat. Make yourself at home."

She looked around uncertainly at the dark red leather couch that leaned drunkenly against the wall, and opted instead for a battered wooden chair that stood in front of his desk. Setting her briefcase carefully on the floor, she smoothed the skirt of her dark blue suit and balanced herself on the edge of the chair.

As he watched her settle herself the old anger stirred, and he abruptly tipped the chair back to the floor. "What the hell are you doing here?"

Her hands clenched together a little more tightly in her lap. "I've come to offer you a job," she said, the words spilling out just a little too quickly.

For a moment he thought she meant his old job on the force, and he wanted to jump up with a shout of triumph. Then, as he looked at her sitting tense and wary on the edge of the chair, his elation dissipated abruptly. That wasn't what she'd meant at all.

"You want to hire me, you mean." His voice was flat.

"Of course." She seemed to gather her composure as she gave him a long, measuring look. "You are still accepting clients, aren't you?"

"I'm still accepting clients. When I'm in the mood for new clients," he said deliberately. He rubbed his hand over the sandpaper of his face and watched her steadily, not missing the tiny flare of embarrassment in her eyes. "What are you doing here?" he finally asked again, his words both harsh and unwelcoming.

He couldn't be sure, but he thought a faint wash of color came and went in her cheeks. "I need to hire a private investigator, and your... qualifications are perfect."

"My qualifications are perfect for a lot of things. That didn't make much difference two years ago."

He was right. There was color in her cheeks, but she didn't look away. "I didn't come here to rehash what happened two years ago. You know why you were dismissed. I had no choice, and you know that, too. As far as I'm concerned, that's a dead issue."

"Well, maybe it isn't a dead issue as far as I'm concerned. And maybe I don't need another client right now."

"I think you do," she said quietly. She looked away from him and let her gaze drift over the office, from the leather couch with the shine completely rubbed off by the countless rear ends that had sat on it, to the worn, faded carpet and battered-looking desk and chair. "I'm willing to pay you half of your fee up front and all expenses."

She was right, he needed the money. But he'd be damned if he'd crawl to Julia Carleton. "That's my usual arrangement," he drawled. "If you want me to work for you—" his voice emphasized the *you* ever so faintly "—you'll have to do a lot better than that."

"Just what would you require?" Her voice was cool and she raised her chin just a bit.

In spite of himself, he had to admire her composure. He was being about as rude as it was possible to be, but she wasn't turning tail and bolting. She had guts, he had to give her that.

"To begin with, I don't take any cases without knowing all the facts." He leaned back in his chair again. "So what do you have? A boyfriend that needs checking out? Someone who needs to be followed, maybe, to make sure he's not cheating on you?"

The quick flash of color came and went in her cheeks again. "This isn't personal." Her voice was tight. "It's police business."

He stood abruptly, towering over her. "Then have the police take care of it," he said harshly, unable to keep the bitterness out of his voice. "That's not my job anymore."

Instead of retreating, she drew herself straighter in her chair and looked him in the eye. "That's not possible. I need an outsider, someone who's not a part of the police department. With your skills and your police connections, you're the perfect person to help me."

"But what if I'm not interested in using my 'police connections' to help you?" he said, his voice soft. He didn't sit, but continued to stare down at her.

"It was my understanding that there was very little you refused to do these days, if the money was right," she said coolly. She leaned back in her chair and met his gaze without flinching.

He let his gaze travel slowly down her body, then up again. "Even I have my standards."

Holding her head just a fraction higher, she asked, "Aren't you even interested in the details?"

Again, he felt that unwilling surge of admiration for her. Julia Carleton was no coward. "All right," he said suddenly, sitting down and pulling his chair closer to his desk. "What are the details?"

In answer she leaned over and searched through her briefcase. Her curtain of heavy, dark red hair fell forward over her face. The jacket of her suit fell open, exposing the creamy white blouse beneath it. Perfectly ordinary, conservative business attire, except that when she bent over farther, the fabric tightened against her chest, outlining something lacy and delicate beneath the plain white blouse.

Unable to tear his gaze away from the lacy thing she wore next to her skin, he stared at her chest and his body tightened. He'd have bet a hundred dollars that Julia Carleton wore plain, functional white cotton underwear. The lace that strained against her blouse couldn't belong to the buttoned-up, straight-as-an-arrow, go-by-the-book investigator that he'd known two years ago.

As he watched her, alarmed and angered by his body's instinctive reaction, she straightened in her chair, holding a fistful of file folders. When she met his eyes she stilled, her hand suspended over his desk in the act of giving him the files.

The moment seemed to stretch on forever. Neither of them unlocked their gaze, and the air in the room became taut and edgy. Finally Julia cleared her throat, laid the files carefully on the desk and looked away.

With a bitten-off oath, Luke jumped to his feet and shoved his chair back. It spun into the wall with a dull thud, and he whirled around and stood in front of the window, staring blindly at the busy street below him.

Julia Carleton was not a woman, he reminded himself. She was an investigator with the Internal Affairs section of the Chicago Police Force. And she was personally responsible for getting his butt thrown off the force. No matter how his body reacted to her, there was no way he was going to think of her as anything other than his enemy.

"Are you all right, Mr. McKinley?"

If he didn't know better, he could almost imagine that it was concern he heard in her voice.

"I'm fine." His voice was brusque. "I was up all night on a surveillance and I'm a little tired."

He forced himself to turn around and sit down, keeping his eyes on the stack of files on his desk. "Before I read this," he said, pausing as he picked up the top folder and finally looked up at her, "why don't you tell me what it's about?"

Julia took a deep breath, unclenched her hands, and settled back in her chair. She'd rehearsed this part so often that she could practically recite it in her sleep. She had to focus on why she was here, what was at stake, and not on the man watching her from the other side of the desk.

Lucas McKinley wasn't happy to see her. But then, she'd expected nothing less. If she'd had any other choice, she wouldn't be sitting in this office, steeling herself against his hostility. If she'd had any other choice, she wouldn't even have considered asking him for help.

But she'd run out of other options a couple of weeks ago. Even then, she'd refused to accept the inevitable, choosing instead to keep plugging doggedly ahead, looking for other evidence, trying to put together a case. When her boss told her yesterday to either come up with something or turn the case over to someone else, she'd known that she couldn't put it off any longer. It was time to go to Lucas McKinley.

And now that she was here, she had to persuade him to help her. Swallowing once, she shifted on the hard chair and forced herself to look directly at him. "I'm working on a case of corruption within the department."

From the flicker in his eyes, she knew she'd touched a nerve. People had said a lot of things about Lucas McKinley during his years on the police force, but no one had ever accused him of being less than completely honest. He was legendary for paying for every single cup of coffee and each doughnut he'd consumed. McKinley had held nothing but scorn for officers who'd bent the rules even a little.

"You don't need me for that." He tossed the folder over the desk in her direction and leaned back in his chair. "You have the unlimited resources of the Internal Affairs Department."

The bitterness in his voice made her flinch inside, but she didn't take her eyes off him. Taking a deep breath, she scooted forward on her chair. This was it. McKinley might resent her, he might hate her guts, but she had to have his help. If her next words couldn't convince him to help her, nothing would. And if he didn't help her... She wouldn't allow herself to think of that possibility. He *had* to help her. Too much was riding on this investigation.

"Internal Affairs is under a lot of pressure right now," she said carefully. "The head of the department has been mentioned as a candidate for a citywide job, and we've all been ordered to close our cases in order to...make him look good. No one is very disposed to help anyone else when their job could depend on finishing their own investigations."

McKinley stared at her with hard eyes, his mouth a tight line. "I hope you didn't come here expecting any sympathy from me."

"I came here to hire you. I need help with my investigation, and I need it now."

He eased his desk chair to the floor and leaned forward, his gaze skewering her in her place. "Let me see if I have this straight. You need help with one of your investigations, and you think I'm the person to help you. You want to pay me two hundred dollars a day to bail your butt out of trouble." His chair wobbled on two legs as he stood suddenly and towered over her. "What fantasyland are you living in, Ms. Carleton? Did you really think I would help you?" She heard the incredulity in his voice. "I wouldn't spit on you if you were on fire."

You expected this reaction, she reminded herself as she dug her nails into her palms. *Remember what's at stake. Ignore McKinley and think of Bobby.*

"I didn't expect you to jump for joy at the prospect of helping me," she said quietly. "But before you make any decisions, I think you ought to look at the file and the names of the officers I'm investigating."

He stared at her for a long time, challenge in his eyes. If she said another word, she suspected, he'd throw her out of his office and that would be it. So she just sat there, watching him, daring him to pick up the folder.

Slowly, still watching her, he reached across the desk and plucked the top folder from the pile. When his gaze dropped to the papers inside, she quietly let out the breath she'd been holding. Forcing herself to relax against the back of the chair, she watched his face as he read.

She saw him scan down the list of names. His face darkened and he threw the folder onto the desk. "What is Eddie Timmons's name doing on this list?" He glared at her, daring her to confirm what he'd seen.

"Detective Timmons's name is on the list because he's a suspect, like the rest of the officers on the list," she said evenly. "Now do you understand why I came to you?"

He rubbed at his face, and suddenly she saw the weariness in his unshaven jaw and gray skin. His blue eyes were shadowed with fatigue, and his clothes were rumpled and wrinkled. Apparently he *had* been up all night, just as he'd said. But it didn't surprise her—whatever McKinley did, he'd give it his all. He certainly had when he'd been a detective on the Chicago Police Force.

"What's going on?" he asked wearily. "Do you people at Internal Affairs have a vendetta against my old precinct? Or is it just detectives in general?"

"We don't make up the charges, Mr. McKinley, we just investigate them." She nodded at the folder lying in front of him. "Are you still sure you won't help me?"

"Look, I know I'm punchy because I didn't get any sleep last night, but do you seriously think I'd be interested in helping you nail my ex-partner to the wall?" His voice became tinged with scorn. "Even for two hundred dollars a day?"

"I thought you might look at it as an opportunity to prove that he's innocent, and get paid for it to boot." She scooted forward in her chair again. "I have to have some help on this, McKinley. You know as well as I do that no one who works with Timmons or any of the other people on that list will tell me anything. I have to hire someone from outside. That's why I came to you."

"You don't think I'll do everything I can to prove Eddie is innocent?"

"I'm counting on it. That way, if he does turn out to be guilty, no one can say he wasn't given the fairest shake possible."

He watched her for a long time, a brooding look in his eyes. "How do you know I won't make sure that Eddie is found innocent?" he asked finally.

"Because everyone knows that Lucas McKinley can't be bought and can't be corrupted. Whatever else you might have been, McKinley, you were honest. And I'm betting that you still are."

"A lot can change in two years." He watched her unwaveringly, as if gauging her reaction.

"Yes, it can." Her gaze flickered over the shabby office. "Let's just say I'm willing to gamble two hundred dollars a day that some things haven't changed."

He continued to stare at her for a moment, then looked down at the folder that lay open in front of him. Almost unwillingly, it seemed, he began to read.

She studied his bent head, her gaze drifting over his angular profile and the thick, slightly wavy black hair that lay against his neck. It was the same face that had so fascinated her two years ago, the face she'd seen in her dreams for months afterward. Except that two years ago, his eyes had been filled with a deep, searing grief that had muted the impact of his anger.

A part of her softened as she looked at him. Two years ago, she couldn't afford sympathy for him or for the horrible events that had precipitated her involvement. Worse, she couldn't afford to be attracted to the man she'd been investigating. Nothing she could have said or done would have changed the outcome, and she'd forced herself to keep an impersonal distance. But she wasn't investigating him now, and he was still the man who regularly haunted her dreams late at night.

She shouldn't have come here, she thought in a sudden panic. No matter how desperate, she shouldn't have sought out Lucas McKinley. Bobby might be in trouble, but she was afraid that if she spent too much time with McKinley she'd be in the worst trouble of her life.

"...enough," she heard him saying.

"I beg your pardon?"

"I said that two hundred dollars a day won't be enough. If I help you, you'll have to make Internal Affairs cough up more money. Call it an incentive for overcoming my distaste at the working conditions."

Something inside her stirred in anger. She opened her mouth to tell him where he could take his incentive, then slowly closed it when she saw the gleam in his eyes. He was trying to make her lose her cool, she realized. He was trying to rattle her, and he'd succeeded.

Clamping her lips together, she took a deep breath and managed to subdue her temper. "How much would you require?" She was amazed at how cool she sounded.

A quick look came and went that might have been admiration, if it were in any other man's eyes. In McKinley, it was probably just satisfaction at making her angry.

He tilted back in his chair, never taking his eyes off her. "Three hundred a day should cover it, plus expenses."

She shifted on the hard chair, thinking rapidly. If she was very careful about what she ate next month, she would just be able to cover the extra hundred dollars a day. Provided that they were able to find the evidence she needed in a week or less. She sat up and met his eyes again. "It's a deal. When can you start?"

He raised his eyebrows. "No time like the present." He gestured at the file in front of him. "This isn't all the evidence you have, is it? A few furtive tips from snitches who may or may not be wasted from drugs doesn't cut it in any court of law."

"No, that's not all the evidence I have." He wouldn't provoke her into losing her temper again. "I've spent the last couple of months studying the pattern of arrests of the suspects, their hours on duty, their partners, drug raids scheduled and completed, and about twenty-five other factors that could prove their innocence or guilt. I'm convinced they're guilty, but I haven't been able to come up with any concrete evidence. They've been as slippery as a pailful of eels."

"Have you considered the possibility that maybe you can't find any evidence because they're not guilty? That maybe whatever facts you've managed to assemble are nothing more than a pile of coincidences?"

"Of course I've considered that possibility! Do you think I *want* to find that seven police officers, seven decorated detectives, are guilty of accepting bribes to protect a group of slimy drug dealers?"

"I don't know. Isn't that your job at Internal Affairs?" He leaned back and waited for her answer. His eyes were faintly challenging, as if he'd figured he'd backed her into a corner.

She forced herself to meet his gaze. "It's our job to make sure the police don't lose their credibility with the citizens of Chicago. If that means uncovering crooked police officers, then yes, that's our job. That doesn't mean we like to do it." She leaned toward him. "How did you feel about dirty cops when you were on the force? Did you want them protected, or did you want us to get rid of them?"

His eyes darkened. "I feel the same way now as I did two years ago. Dirty cops are scum. I wouldn't tolerate them for a minute."

She settled back in the chair, beginning to enjoy the exchange. For the first time since she'd walked in the door, his anger was directed somewhere other than at her. And she felt vindicated. She'd somehow known he couldn't have changed that much, that his passion for doing what was right wouldn't have been eroded.

"That's why I came to you," she said softly. "I hoped you'd feel like that."

He slammed the folder shut. "Eddie Timmons was my partner. I know him. He wouldn't take a bribe. Hell, I *know* he never took a bribe in the three years I worked with him. He couldn't change that much in two years."

She took several more files out of her briefcase and pushed them across the desk. "One of the things I've learned is that you don't know nearly as much as you think you do, even about the people you're closest to." That was a lesson that had been burned into her soul. She wasn't likely to forget it.

Shutters dropped over his eyes and he stood abruptly and turned away. After a few moments, during which the tenseness of his back seemed to seep into the air around them, he slowly turned to face her, resting one hip against the edge of his desk.

"Supposing I assume, just for the sake of argument, that you're right. Where do you expect me to start looking?"

"*Just for the sake of argument,* I want you to look at all the indirect evidence I've collected. See if you can find any inconsistencies in it—make sure I haven't missed anything, even the slightest detail. When you've had a chance to go over everything, we can decide together on the next step."

"Together my rear end. I work alone. If you hire me, you let me do things my way."

"This is my case, Mr. McKinley," she said, sitting up straighter. "I'm responsible for the outcome. I'm not going to just hand it over to you and sit back and wait for you to tell me the answers. Either we work together or the deal's off."

She saw the struggle in his eyes. He wanted to tell her to go jump in the lake. But he also wanted to prove Eddie Timmons's innocence. She was counting on the need to exonerate his partner being the stronger one.

"All right, then I guess the deal's off." He spoke coolly, but anger swirled deep in the dark blue of his eyes.

Did she dare call his bluff, walk out the door and wait for him to call her back? She didn't have any choice. There was no way she was going to let McKinley loose on *this* case by himself.

"I'm sorry you feel that way, Mr. McKinley. If you change your mind, let me know."

She stood, reaching for the files that still lay piled on the edge of the desk. When she'd stashed all of them in her briefcase, she moved around to take the folder that lay in front of Lucas. He moved just as she reached for the folder, and his hand brushed her arm.

She went completely still, waiting for him to move his hand. His fingertips lingered on the skin inside her elbow. After what seemed like an eternity, he clenched his hand into a fist and dropped it to his side.

She couldn't seem to take her eyes away from the place his hand had touched. The skin there still burned. Slowly she raised her head to look at him. Something gleamed in his eyes, something she didn't want to identify.

Snatching up the folder as if something had bitten her, she stepped away and shoved it into her briefcase. Thank goodness he'd refused to work for her. The awareness that had just flared between them was something she hadn't foreseen. It was the one thing she hadn't planned about this case. She knew for a fact she couldn't handle it, even for her brother Bobby.

"Thank you for your time, Mr. McKinley." Turning, she clutched her briefcase tightly in her hand, conscious of his eyes on her back.

"Just a minute, Ms. Carleton."

She'd made it almost to the door before his voice stopped her. Slowly she turned around.

"Yes?"

"I've changed my mind," he said abruptly. "We'll be partners. Buddies. Just like in all the best cop movies." He gave her a bland smile. "Who knows? We might...enjoy it."

In spite of her determination to not let him get the upper hand, she felt temper curdle in her stomach again. "We don't have to enjoy it, Mr. McKinley. We just have to get the job done."

Walking back to him, she reached inside her briefcase and tossed the pile of folders onto his desk. "Give me a call when you've read through these." She then pulled out a business card, scribbling her home phone number on the back. Laying it gently on the pile of folders, she walked through the door and closed it quietly behind her.

She waited until she stood in the lobby of his building to lean shakily against the wall. She'd done it. She hadn't failed. "I hope you're grateful, Bobby," she whispered. McKinley was going to help her find the evidence that would put his ex-partner, Eddie Timmons, away where he belonged.

Remembering the flicker of pain in his eyes, she pushed herself away from the wall as she squashed the guilt that stirred deep inside her. Maybe McKinley was hurting, but she couldn't afford to think about that. Because whether McKinley believed it or not, Eddie was as guilty as sin. She knew it, deep in her soul. Just as she knew, deep in her soul, that working with McKinley was going to be the biggest mistake she'd ever made.

McKinley stood, staring at the door, long after her footsteps had faded away down the hall. What the hell had he gotten himself into? he wondered wearily, rubbing his hand over his unshaven face.

Eddie. He rolled his ex-partner's name around on his tongue, tasting the bitterness it left there. Even two years later, despite his partner's continued friendship, he couldn't quite forgive Eddie for testifying against him. He'd had no choice, Eddie had argued, and Luke knew it was true. There had been a slew of other witnesses. If it hadn't been Eddie, it would have been someone else. Someone else who might not have been on Luke's side. And Eddie had only been telling the truth, after all.

The final result had been the same. In the end, it hadn't mattered what Eddie had said. Julia Carleton and Internal Affairs had made sure of it. He'd been convicted even before he'd walked into the hearing room.

She'd done her homework, he had to give her that. She'd been unflappable that hot July morning, calmly stating the findings of her investigation, just as calmly calling witness after damning witness.

And now she was applying that same relentless will to an investigation of his partner, Eddie Timmons, an investigation she'd sucked him into. Well, if Eddie was innocent, he'd make damn sure she realized it. He owed his ex-partner that, if for no other reason than all the nights Eddie had come by to drag him out to dinner in the last two years.

He moved to the window, looking down on the crowds starting to hurry along the street. Business started early in this working-class part of Chicago. People who earned their living by the sweat of their brow couldn't afford to keep banker's hours.

He wasn't looking for a slim figure in a dark blue suit, he told himself. He'd be seeing enough of Julia Carleton in the next few days without deliberately looking for her. Still, his body reacted when he spotted her dark red head weaving through the people on the sidewalk. In spite of himself, he watched as she unlocked the door of a flashy red sports car.

Another little piece of the puzzle that didn't quite fit. She was the kind of woman who should have driven a small, foreign economy car. As he watched her fold herself into the driver's seat, a small movement on the edge of his vision caught his attention.

A figure dressed in dark jeans and a white T-shirt edged out of the alley behind her and slipped into a nondescript black sedan parked two cars behind her low-slung red one. The windows of the sedan were too heavily tinted for him to see the driver's face, but he really didn't need to.

Before he'd taken another breath he was out the door and running down the stairs. By the time he got to the street, the little red sports car was turning the corner, the black sedan right behind it like a big cat toying with its prey before it pounced. He watched helplessly as the two cars disappeared from view.

Chapter 2

Luke stood on the sidewalk for a long time after the two cars disappeared, battling the sick feeling in his stomach. It didn't necessarily mean what he thought, he tried to tell himself. For all he knew, Julia Carleton might have a bodyguard from the Internal Affairs Department because of the explosive nature of the case she was investigating. She might know all about the slimy character in the car behind her.

But he didn't think so. The punk who had been hiding in the alley looked too furtive, too sleazy to belong to the police. He'd been too careful not to let Julia see him. And as Luke stared down the street at the place where the two cars had disappeared, the hairs on the back of his neck were still standing straight up.

At least he was able to get the first three letters of the guy's license plate. Bounding back up the stairs to his office, he dialed his connection at the motor vehicle division.

"Hi, Babs, it's Luke," he said into the phone a few minutes later. "Can you look up a plate for me? Yeah, I know you're not supposed to do this. But hey, what are friends for?"

In spite of his anxiety, he grinned at the familiar exchange. "Yeah, I've got the bail money right here. And if they don't throw you in the pokey, we'll use it for dinner some night instead."

Leaning against his desk, he laughed softly at her answer. Babs Dugan had worked in the motor vehicle division forever, outlasting several police chiefs and a handful of mayors. She'd been outspoken about his dismissal from the police force, and had promised that if she could ever help him, she'd be glad to do it. He counted Babs among his closest friends.

"I don't know what kind of car, and I only got part of the plate. Yeah, the first three letters are *SRG.* The rest were numbers, three of them, and the car was a black sedan. That's all I can tell you."

He shifted on the desk while he waited for Babs to run through the computer listing, and picked up one of the files Julia Carleton had left on his desk. Before he could read any of the information, though, Babs came back on the line.

"There are ninety-two cars that fit that description," she reported. "Kind of tough to narrow it down."

"I'm pretty sure it was an American car," he answered. "Does that help?"

He listened to her type. A few moments later she said, "That brings it down to sixty-three. Want me to print them out and send them over?"

"Thanks, Babs. I'd appreciate that. And I meant it about dinner. Maybe next week, okay?"

He hung up, his smile lingering for a moment. Then he looked down at the files in front of him and the smile disappeared. He'd felt the tug of attraction toward Julia two years ago, even through the haze of grief and guilt that enveloped him. And it had only intensified his guilt and self-loathing. Now, in spite of himself, an image of Julia's slender body floated in front of his eyes. He could still see her creamy skin, touched with a hint of rose when he'd stared at her. He could almost feel the pulse in the crook of her elbow, pounding madly when he'd accidentally touched her there.

He didn't want to think about some thug on her trail. Worse, he didn't want to think about what could happen if that thug decided to do more than just follow her. Tossing the files back on the desk, he walked over to the window and shoved his hands into his pockets.

He was just protecting his paycheck, he told himself, watching the people on the street below him. His unwanted reaction to Julia Carleton had nothing to do with it. Three hundred bucks a day would pay a lot of bills. And if something happened to Julia, he could kiss that money goodbye.

It only made sense to protect his gold mine. It was just good business. The fact that his body reacted like he was sixteen again every time he thought about Julia Carleton didn't make any difference. She could be the last woman on earth and he wouldn't be interested in her.

A black sedan cruising by on Milwaukee Avenue caught his eye, and he leaned forward in the deep window. Was it his imagination or did the car slow down, just a bit, as it passed beneath his windows? He watched with narrowed eyes as it blended with the flow of traffic and turned a corner. There were a lot of black sedans on the road. This one might have nothing to do with Julia Carleton or the detectives she was investigating.

On the other hand, he was paid to be suspicious. Reaching into the top drawer of his desk, he pulled out his car keys. Stuffing the stack of files under his arm, he locked the door to his office and hurried down the stairs.

Police headquarters hadn't changed in the past two years. It still smelled like old coffee and stale air, and the walls were still painted the same dull gray. It was still full of suits, too, hurrying around as if they had someplace important to go. He stood inside the door and watched the activity for a moment, feeling the old excitement begin to drum through his veins.

He'd loved police work from his first day as a raw recruit at the police academy. Nothing else could ever provide quite the same high, the same rush of adrenaline, as stepping into a dark alley and coming out victorious. And nothing else provided the same sense of satisfaction as knowing you were one of the good guys, that you did make a difference in the world.

Julia Carleton had taken this away from him, he reminded himself, pushing away from the wall. The next time he was tempted to let his gaze linger on her face or her body, he'd do well to remember that.

He didn't have to look at the directory on the wall next to him to know where to find her office. The numbers on her door were burned into his memory. Heading for the elevator, he paused just before stepping into it and turned for the stairs instead. He'd never spent much time in this building until that summer two years ago, and he hadn't been thinking about architectural details back then. It wouldn't do any harm to become familiar with the layout.

When he emerged onto the sixth floor he headed straight for Julia's office. He'd seen enough of the building, and what he'd seen made him real nervous. The place was a maze of corridors and dead ends. Julia's door was open a crack, and just as he raised his hand to knock he heard her voice.

"I am not being nosy, I simply asked a civil question. I didn't think your whereabouts last night was a state secret."

In the silence that followed her words, he heard a faint tapping sound that made him wonder if she was bouncing a pen on her desktop.

She sighed. "Sorry, Bobby, I'm a little testy, too."

When he realized she was on the phone he lowered his hand. Faintly ashamed of himself for eavesdropping, he still couldn't force himself to move away. Telling himself he needed to get as much information about Julia Carleton as possible couldn't stop the hot licks of an emotion he didn't want to name from sweeping over him as he listened to her.

"I know," she continued. He thought she sounded weary. "I love you, too, Bobby. I'll see you tonight."

He slowly curled his hand into a fist and eased it into his pocket. *So what?* he asked himself. *You're not interested in her, anyway.* You couldn't be jealous because of a woman you dislike.

Scowling, he raised his hand after a few moments had elapsed and knocked softly on her door.

"Come in," she called, and he pushed the door open.

Surprise flickered across her face as he closed the door behind him. It only took a moment, though, for her to compose her features into the cool mask that so irritated him.

"Hello, Mr. McKinley," she murmured. "Have you read all the files already? I didn't realize you were such a quick study."

Not taking his eyes off her, he lowered himself into the chair that sat next to her desk. "I'm fast at some things. Other things—" he paused and watched her for a moment from heavy-lidded eyes "—I'm not."

"Which is the reason for your visit today?" She folded her hands on her desk and stared back at him.

He sat up slowly, fighting a smile. She was good, he had to give her that. She'd earned her reputation for being unshakable.

"First of all, the name's Luke. If we're going to be working together, it's going to be damned annoying to be so formal."

"You're right. Please call me Julia."

"Fine... Julia." He didn't like the way her name felt on his tongue. Smooth and soft, it felt too much like a caress.

"I haven't looked at the files yet," he said abruptly. "I came to ask you one question. Has Internal Affairs provided you with a bodyguard?"

She looked at him with astonishment. "Of course not! Why would they do that?"

"This is a pretty big case," he answered softly. "Seven detectives accused of accepting bribes from drug dealers isn't just a run-of-the-mill investigation. If it turns out to be true, even if only a couple of the detectives are guilty, it's going to make the papers big-time. Isn't the department concerned about your safety?"

Her gaze dropped to her desk. "They don't really know the extent of the investigation. It started out with just a suspicion of one or two guys. The more I looked at it, though, the bigger it got."

"You mean your boss doesn't even know what you're doing?" he asked, incredulous.

"He has a general idea," she said, finally looking up at him. "But like I told you at your office, everyone these days is looking out for themselves. 'Get the cases closed' is the word that's come down the pike, and everyone is scrambling to get their own work finished."

"So no one here at Internal Affairs knows exactly what you're up to," he said, watching her.

She looked him in the eye and said directly, "It seemed the best way to handle it. It's been hard enough to get the evidence I need. I didn't need any political pressure on top of everything else."

Once again, he had to admire her guts. "I guess it was the smart thing to do in terms of the investigation," he said reluctantly. "But it was damn stupid from the standpoint of your own safety."

Her eyebrows rose. "Aren't you exaggerating just a little?"

"I don't think so." He leaned forward, his elbows resting on her desk, until she unconsciously backed up. "There was a punk in a black car following you this morning. Did you know that?"

"Don't be ridiculous, Mr.... Luke. Why would anyone be following me?"

"You don't think that maybe you've annoyed someone with this investigation of yours?"

"The only people I've annoyed are the clerks at the precinct. I've been there a lot, having them pull records and arrest sheets. But I really don't think any of the clerks would be following me around in mysterious black cars."

His hand slashed through the air. "This isn't a joke, Julia. Who else knows what you're doing?"

He saw her grip her pen more tightly, then consciously relax her fingers. "I suppose any of the men I've asked about could have found out, if the clerks happened to say something," she said reluctantly. "If they are guilty, and I think they are, they would know immediately that we were on to them as soon as Internal Affairs was mentioned."

"Well, someone knows," he said grimly. "After you left my office, I saw someone come out of an alley near where you'd parked your car, get in his own car and follow you. I came down here to find out if there was any chance he was put there by your own department."

Slowly she shook her head. "No." Licking her lips, she said, "We're responsible for ourselves."

He stared at her for a moment, then slouched back in his chair. "And now I'm responsible for you," he added grimly.

"I hired you to help me investigate," she retorted. "Not to act as my personal bodyguard."

"But if I want to collect a paycheck I have to make sure you're around to write it out."

"Don't worry, McKinley," she said, a trace of scorn in her voice. "You do your job and I'll do mine. As long as you help me get the evidence I need, you'll get your paycheck."

He sat watching her for a moment, then stood. "I don't think so. Until I figure out who it is that's on to you, I'm sticking closer to you than a flea on a dog." He stretched and rubbed his suddenly burning eyes. "Do you have any coffee around here? It's a poor substitute for a few hours' sleep, but it'll have to do."

She stared at him for a moment, then leaned back and shook her head. "I don't need a nursemaid. Go home. Read the files, go to sleep, do whatever you want to do. But you're not going to hang around in my office all day."

"I thought that was what you wanted. Remember? This is your case and we're going to work together. You don't want me going off half-cocked on my own."

"I hardly think that going home and getting some sleep is going off half-cocked," she snapped. "Once you read the files and are ready to start nosing around and asking questions, then we can work out a strategy together."

"I've already worked out my strategy. Until I find out who's on your tail, you're stuck with me. You don't have to get the coffee for me," he added, turning toward the door. "Just tell me where it is and I'll get it myself."

She was watching him, that intriguing anger simmering just below the surface. Were all her emotions, all her passions so well controlled? Did she always keep such a tight rein on herself?

Interesting questions, but he wouldn't be exploring either of them. There was no way this would ever be more than a business relationship.

"Sit down," she said abruptly. "I'll get your coffee. How do you take it?"

"Hot, strong and naked." He lowered himself into the chair and leaned lazily back. "The same way I like my women."

Amazingly, he thought her lips twitched. "Not a bad line. You get points for originality," she said as she stood at the door. Now definitely fighting a grin, she added, "You'll have to work on delivery, though. Your leer was off just a little."

He sat up, watching in astonishment as she slipped out the door. Who would have thought that Miss Cool and Composed had a sense of humor? What's more, he realized with grudging admiration, she'd managed to turn the tables on him very neatly. By laughing at his crude remark she'd made him feel faintly ashamed of himself. He stared at the door where she'd disappeared. It could be an interesting couple of weeks.

A few minutes later he heard her heels tapping on the floor as she walked back to the office. As he wondered briefly why he was so certain that it was Julia and not some other woman walking down the hall, he heard her footsteps slow down.

"How're you doing, babe?" a male voice asked.

"I'm fine, Fred. And you?" she answered politely.

"I'm hangin'. You still haven't answered me, you know. When're you going to go out to dinner with me, Julia? We could have a real good time together."

"Don't worry, Fred. If I ever lower my standards that far, you'll be the first one I call."

Luke smothered a laugh as her heels resumed their tapping down the hall. If he wasn't careful, he could find himself actually liking Julia Carleton. But he was always careful nowadays, he reminded himself, his smile slowly fading. And where Julia Carleton was concerned, he'd be especially careful.

She walked into the room carrying a chipped mug that she set down on the desk in front of him. It bore a picture of a stick figure in a cowboy hat using a six-gun to blast away at some very nasty-looking bugs. Underneath the picture was an indecipherable word that was at least six syllables long.

Noticing him staring at the mug, she smiled slightly. "It was a gift from one of my brothers. He's a sales rep for one of the big drug companies and it's advertising for their latest miracle cure."

He raised his eyebrows as he took a sip of the coffee. It was just as bad as the stuff he used to drink in the station house. "You have a big family?"

For some reason she looked away. "I have three brothers. How about you?"

Setting the coffee cup on her desk, he shrugged. "One sister. She lives on the West Coast and I don't see her very often."

He settled back in the uncomfortable wooden chair and wondered briefly why she'd looked away when she mentioned her brothers. The question was forgotten, though, as he shifted again on the hard chair and thought longingly of the couch in his office. Even the high-octane coffee he'd been drinking was having a hard time cutting through the fatigue. "So tell me who you think could be following you."

"I already told you, I think it's ludicrous that any of the men I'm investigating could be following me."

"I never said it was one of them. I would have recognized any of the names on that list. This was some young punk. The kind of muscle that you'd hire if you didn't want to do a dirty job yourself."

She looked up from some papers she was sorting. "Are you trying to scare me, McKinley? Because it's not going to work."

"Damn straight I'm trying to scare you. If you're scared, maybe you'll pay attention to what I'm saying."

She dropped the papers onto the desk, flattened her hands on its surface and stared at him defiantly. "Don't you think I would have noticed if someone had been following me around? I would know if someone was watching me. And I haven't seen a thing."

"The whole point of following someone," he retorted, feeling himself start to get angry, "is not to let them know they're being followed. What good would it do them if you know they're watching you?"

She looked down at the papers she'd dropped on her desk, but not before he saw the flash of uneasiness, quickly hidden, in her eyes. "Even if someone is watching me, what difference would it make?" she said in a low voice. "It's not as if I'm going to give up."

"If you are being followed, then we figure out who it is and why they're following you." He scowled. That brief glimpse of vulnerability she'd tried to hide sent his protective impulses into overdrive, and he didn't like the feeling one damn bit. Julia Carleton was nothing more than his employer. "Once we do that, we know which direction we need to go with this case."

Looking back up at him, she gave him an unflinching look. "So if it's true, then it's a break for us, right?"

"Right," he muttered, wrapping his hand around the hot coffee mug and staring into it while taking a gulp. No, he didn't care for this feeling at all. Julia Carleton was his enemy, the woman who had ruined what was left of his life after that rainy evening two years ago. He did *not* want to admire anything about her.

When he realized she was still watching him, he shifted in the chair. "Go ahead and do whatever you were doing when I got here." He remembered her phone conversation with "Bobby" and her "I love you," and scowled again. "Don't let me stop you."

Julia leaned back in her desk chair and watched McKinley as he slouched in the supremely uncomfortable chair in front of her. How on earth did he think she was going to be able to concentrate with him stretched out like that in front of her?

"If I promise you that I'm not going anywhere until I leave this evening, will you go home?" she asked almost desperately.

"You wouldn't be putting the shuck on me, now, would you, Julia?" he asked, watching her unnervingly from under half-closed eyelids. "Because if I found out you were just trying to ditch me, I wouldn't be very happy."

"Why would I want to ditch you?" she asked, exasperated. "I'm paying you a fortune to help me with this case. Don't you think I'm going to listen to your advice?"

He sat up then stood in one smooth, liquid motion. After a moment she realized she was staring and looked hastily away.

"I don't know. I've never known what makes you tick," he answered quietly. "All I know right now is that I'm not letting you wander around Chicago by yourself until I figure out who's on your tail." He paused, his eyes hardening. "Like I said, you're the one who's paying my bills. Whether you like it or not, we're attached at the hip."

"Fine," she snapped, trying to hide the stab of pain at being referred to as his meal ticket. After all, she reminded herself, that defined their relationship exactly. "You can leave and reattach yourself tonight at seven o'clock. Right now I have some work to do, and I don't want to walk around you every time I need a file."

He stood by the door, watching her with that unwavering gaze of his. "I'll be one unhappy camper if I find out you've left this building, Julia." His voice was low and almost menacing. "I'll be back at seven o'clock tonight, and I expect to find you right here. Do we understand each other?"

"Perfectly," she answered coolly, forcing herself to meet his gaze without looking away. "Get some sleep, and I'll see you tonight."

He gave her one last, long look, then slipped out the door and was gone. Taking a deep breath, she slumped back in her chair and let out a long breath. What had she unleashed?

Even when she'd been investigating him after the accident two years ago, Lucas McKinley had had an unsettling effect on her. Now, when they were more or less on an equal footing, he was almost overwhelming. It would take all the strength she possessed to maintain her professional persona in front of him. If he ever suspected the effect he had on her, he'd be ruthless in using it to his advantage.

He should be out of the building by now, on his way back to his office or his home. She refused to think about the dark circles under his eyes, or whether or not he was going to get any sleep. That was none of her business, and she couldn't care less. There were plenty of things to worry about right here in the office.

Grabbing the stack of papers in front of her, she began to shuffle through them until the image of Lucas McKinley receded, replaced by questions about the seven detectives she was investigating. She had breathed, eaten and slept this case for the past two months, and it never really disappeared from her mind. It was always there, hovering on the edge of her consciousness, haunting every part of her life. Scanning the computer printouts, she again said a prayer of thankfulness that she had been assigned to this case. She couldn't begin to imagine the ramifications if someone else had gotten hold of it.

She was so engrossed in studying the charts in front of her that she almost didn't hear the soft knock on her door. When it came again, she looked up with a start to see Luke standing in the door. Her heart began to pound as she said, "Come in."

"I forgot to ask you the make and license number of your car," he said abruptly.

She gave it to him, watching as he wrote it down. "What's that for?" she demanded.

He gave her a humorless smile. "I thought I'd check and see if anyone's been inquiring about your car down at Motor Vehicles. It might be enlightening for you."

Another knock sounded at the door, and without waiting for an invitation a tall, slender man with dark blond hair slipped into the room and flopped into the chair next to Julia's desk. "How're you doing, Skinny?"

Julia licked her lips and struggled to look at her brother and not at Luke. She was afraid he would see the sudden fear in her eyes. "Hi, Bobby." She took a deep breath. "Do you know Luke McKinley?" She nodded in his direction. "Luke, this is my brother, Bobby."

"Only through department legend," Bobby answered easily as he turned around to look at Luke. "How're you doing?"

Luke took the hand Bobby had extended. Julia thought his gaze sharpened as he looked at her brother. "You a member of the force?"

Bobby gave him a charming smile. "Your old precinct. Is that coincidence or what?"

"Yeah."

Instead of leaving, Luke settled back against the wall and watched Julia with hooded eyes. Forcing herself to look away, she turned back to her brother.

"What are you doing here, Bobby?"

"Is that any way to greet your baby brother?" Bobby pulled his features into a mock frown. "A guy would think he wasn't welcome. Or was I interrupting something?"

She felt herself blush as she glared over at Luke. "Of course you weren't interrupting. Mr. McKinley was just leaving. I'm surprised you're here, that's all. I didn't expect to see you until this evening."

"Actually, that's why I stopped by." He looked away from her briefly, with the guilty expression she'd known since childhood. "Something's come up, and I can't make it tonight. Rain check?"

"Of course," she forced herself to say with a smile. "Did you get a hot date with that woman you met in the bar?"

"I wouldn't stand you up for another woman!" He sounded truly shocked that she would even suggest such a thing. "You should know better than that, sis. This is work related." He looked away again. "I have to work a little overtime." Staring down at his shoes, he said, "Can we make it another time?"

"Sure," she forced herself to say. Gripping the arms of her chair, she tried to ask in a casual voice, "Is something big going on in the department?" She didn't dare look at McKinley. Her stomach began to roll as she waited for Bobby to answer.

"Nah. Just a couple of guys out sick with that flu that's been going around." He looked back at her, his gaze clear and sincere. "I didn't want one of the guys with a wife and kids to have to do a double shift, so I volunteered."

"That was nice of you, Bobby," she murmured. Watching him for a moment, she forced herself to smile and said, "Give me a call when you have another free night, and I'll let you make it up to me. We haven't had a chance to get together for too long."

"Yeah, I know." He stood up quickly. "Thanks for being so understanding, sis. I'm sorry I had to cancel at the last minute like this, but I figured you'd understand."

"I understand," she murmured. "Take it easy tonight, Bobby. And be careful."

At that he gave her his normal cocky grin. "I'm always careful, Skinny. That's my middle name, remember?" He bent over and gave her a kiss, then strolled out the door.

"Don't I wish," she muttered at the place where her brother had disappeared. Reckless would be closer to the truth. And lately, she'd sensed a hint of desperation in his recklessness.

Feeling the noose growing tighter around her heart, she told herself for perhaps the hundredth time that there was no way Bobby could be involved in the case she was investigating. No way. Unwillingly her gaze dropped to the sheaf of papers in front of her. He couldn't be accepting bribes from drug dealers, betraying everything his badge stood for.

Luke slowly pushed himself away from the wall, his eyes hooded and impossible to read. "You didn't tell me you had a brother working in my old precinct."

"It doesn't affect the case, so why should I have?" She gripped her hands together in her lap, keeping them out of his sight. "He's just a rookie, so he probably won't stay there, anyway."

"Still, it's kind of a coincidence, isn't it? Cases with a lot of coincidences are always more interesting."

She stared at him, speechless, as he strolled out the door.

"I'll see you later, Julia."

Oh, God. Why did Bobby have to walk in the office right then? Why couldn't he have waited another five minutes? Why did Luke have to find out her brother worked in the precinct?

It didn't matter, she told herself, staring at the door as she listened to Luke's footsteps fade away down the stairs. Bobby wasn't involved in the case. There was no evidence linking him to Eddie Timmons and the rest of the crooked cops.

It was just a coincidence that he was busy tonight, she tried to assure herself. He was almost certainly telling the truth about the officers out with the flu. She'd heard there was a lot of it going around.

And now Luke knew she had a brother who was a cop in the precinct. Taking another deep breath, she waited for her stomach to settle down. He wouldn't find any connection between Bobby and the detectives she was investigating, because there wasn't any connection. There couldn't be.

Chapter 3

Leaden gray clouds hid the sun and darkened the early evening sky as Luke swung his battered navy blue sedan into a parking spot near police headquarters. He sat in the car for a few minutes, waiting to see if anyone behind him pulled abruptly into the curb. His gaze drifted over the other parked cars, looking for anyone lingering in his car. Spotting no watchers, he got out of the car and stretched his legs.

He strode toward the imposing and formidable structure that housed police headquarters, trying to concentrate on the case instead of Julia Carleton. She was his client, and he was picking her up to ensure her safety. Thinking any other way could be dangerous. To both of them.

As he walked through the lobby, he heard someone call his name. Turning around, he saw his ex-partner, Eddie Timmons, waving to him as he hurried across the scuffed marble floor.

"Hey, Luke, what are you doing here?" Eddie greeted him.

"Unfinished business." His answer was deliberately vague as he waited for the other man to reach him. Eddie was bound to find out he was involved in the case sooner or later, but Luke preferred to make it later. There was much to be said for the element of surprise.

"This is the last place I expected to see you," Eddie continued as he shook his hand.

"You do what you have to do," Luke replied, taking in his ex-partner's expensive suit and Italian shoes. "You look good, Eddie. You going undercover as a slick broker type?"

"Like you said, you do what you have to do." Eddie flicked an imaginary speck of dust off the lapel of his jacket.

"What're you doing in this neck of the woods anyway?" Luke asked casually. "Last time I heard, you weren't a big fan of IAD." He watched the other man carefully as he spoke.

If he hadn't been Eddie's partner, he probably wouldn't have noticed the slight hardening of the other man's eyes. "The same as you, Luke. Taking care of business."

"I won't keep you, then," McKinley said, taking a step toward the elevators. "We'll have to get together sometime."

"Yeah, I'll fill you in on all the latest gossip from the precinct. Take it easy."

Eddie clapped him on the back and headed for the door as Luke watched him go. Eddie Timmons could have a million reasons to be at police headquarters, none of them having anything to do with the case Luke was now working on. Except that Luke had seen the look in Eddie's eyes when he'd mentioned Internal Affairs.

As Eddie disappeared from view, Luke shook his head. A man wasn't tried and convicted for being in a busy building. But he'd still ask Julia to check on why Eddie might have been at headquarters today.

He chose another staircase to get to the sixth floor this time. It didn't hurt to know all the ways in and out of a building. You never knew when that kind of information could be important.

As he approached Julia's office, a swirl of anticipation swept over him. It was just the rush of starting a new case, he told himself. A case that was going to pay off a lot of his bills. Julia Carleton had nothing to do with it.

He stood outside her door, waiting for the hammering in his chest to subside. Shoving one hand in the pocket of his jeans, he took a deep breath and knocked on the door.

Julia sat at her desk, reviewing yet another set of statistics on Timmons and the other suspects in the case. She didn't believe in coincidence, especially in her line of work. And there was just too damn much of it in this case.

Timmons and the others were good detectives, as long as they weren't going after the gang that controlled the drug trade in their precinct. When it came to that gang, they were curiously inept. Busted raids and suspects walking for lack of sufficient evidence were the norm instead of the exception. When they did manage to make an arrest, it was inevitably just a kid caught dealing. It had to be more than coincidence, and somewhere in these printouts was the hard evidence that would convict them. She was sure of it.

"You look busy, investigator."

She jumped and looked up to see McKinley lounging against the door to her office. "Didn't your mother teach you to knock?"

"I did knock," he drawled lazily, one hip holding up the doorframe. "You just didn't hear me."

As her eyes met his, Julia thought that some women would consider Lucas McKinley a very attractive man. Wide shoulders and narrow hips emphasized his long, rangy body. His hard face complemented the reckless, I-don't-give-a-damn look in his eyes. The aura of sexuality that hovered around him was only more potent because he didn't seem aware of it.

She was staring at him, she realized suddenly. Hastily she looked down at the papers on her desk. "Let me get these together and I'll be right with you."

He moved away from the door and settled himself in the chair next to her desk. Too aware of how close he was, she wished fervently she hadn't placed that chair so close to hers.

"Any hot news flashes for me about the case?"

Her lips tightened as she shook her head. "No. I haven't found anything new. If you've had a chance to look at the files I gave you, maybe you have some suggestions."

"My first suggestion is to get out of here before we do any talking. I don't know who else in IAD is interested in this case, but I saw Eddie Timmons in the lobby a few minutes ago."

She paused in the act of putting the printouts into her briefcase to glance up at him. "Eddie was here? What for?"

"He didn't say," Luke answered dryly. "Just like I didn't tell him why I was here. And as far as I'm concerned, he's not guilty until you prove it to me beyond a shadow of a doubt. But given the fact that you're investigating him and he probably knows it, I thought it was very interesting."

She shoved the papers into her briefcase and stood up. "Tomorrow morning I'll do a little sniffing around and see if I can find out who he was here to see. As far as I know, there isn't any reason for Timmons to be in this building."

"There are other departments here besides Internal Affairs." McKinley spoke lazily as he looked up at her from the chair.

"I hardly think he'd be visiting with the superintendent or his staff," she answered tartly. "And detectives rarely need to see anyone in Communications or Identification or any of the other departments here. Any problems he'd have could be handled at the district level." She paused, trying to rein in her temper. After all, she had hired McKinley knowing he'd be adamant in believing Timmons innocent. "Tell me, how many times did you visit police headquarters while you were a member of the department?"

"Quite a few," he drawled, standing up and towering over her. "In fact, you probably know exactly how many times I visited this building. I'm sure it's all written down in your notes on my case."

She shifted her briefcase to her other hand. "Besides that, I mean." Her voice was tight.

He shrugged. "Who knows? Not often, I'll grant you that. But I did have to come down here occasionally."

"A few minutes ago you implied that Eddie was here for guilty reasons. Now you're trying to convince me that he wasn't. You can't have it both ways, McKinley. Which is it going to be?" She pushed her hair away from her face and stared at him with frustration.

He smiled blandly and moved to open the door for her. "Just playing devil's advocate. I know you're convinced that Eddie's guilty, but in order to investigate him objectively you have to be able to accept the fact that he may actually be innocent. It always pays to be able to look at both sides, Julia. Remember that."

Looking into his eyes, she saw the shadows of old pain lurking in the dark blue depths. Pain he tried to hide. He wasn't talking about Eddie Timmons at all, she realized. He was talking about his case, the one she'd investigated two years ago.

She lowered her eyes and walked past him into the hallway. "I always try to look at both sides."

"Do you?" he murmured. "I'm glad to hear that."

Holding her briefcase more tightly, she headed for the elevator. When he touched her arm she froze, feeling a surge of heat even through her suit jacket.

"We're going to take the stairs."

Shifting subtly to move away from his touch, she swallowed hard and said, "How come? And don't try to tell me that assassins lurk in the police department elevators."

He raised one eyebrow. "We don't know why Eddie was here. And we don't know who's going to get on that elevator with us. Are you sure you want to advertise our... association?"

"You're right," she muttered. "I wasn't thinking." *And it was your fault,* she added silently. From now on she'd stay as far away from Lucas McKinley as possible. She didn't need any more accidental touches distracting her from her purpose. His effect on her was far too disturbing. From now on, she'd make sure there was at least three feet between them.

He held open the door to the stairwell and she brushed carefully past him. She'd started down the stairs when he touched her shoulder lightly. Spinning around, she backed down a couple of steps and faced him.

"What are you so jumpy for?" His whisper echoed harshly off the cinder block walls.

"I'm not jumpy," she denied quickly. "And why did you stop me? I thought the idea was to get out of the building as quickly as possible."

"I want to go first. You were running down the stairs like the demons of hell were after you."

The description was close enough. No demon from hell could make her feel any more threatened than Luke did when he touched her. Plastering herself against the railing, she waited until he was several steps ahead of her before following him down.

When they reached the lobby they paused in the doorway for a moment, then Luke touched her elbow and started forward. Damning herself for her unwanted reaction and damning Luke for causing it, she followed him out the door of the building and headed for the parking lot where her car waited.

He was at her side in a moment. "Where do you think you're going?"

"To my car, of course. Where else would I be going?" Her voice was sharper than necessary, and she told herself to calm down. It wouldn't do any good if McKinley suspected the effect he had on her.

"I'll drive you home in my car." He turned so he stood in front of her, blocking her access to the parking lot. "If someone is following you, we'll look like a damned silly parade heading north and they'll know we're on to them. I can come back and get your car later."

"Don't you think you're being a little paranoid? And what are 'they' going to think if they see me in your car? Aren't they going to be suspicious then?"

"They'll think we're dating and that I picked you up from work. They'll think, 'How romantic.'" He took a step toward her and she backed up until she felt the chain-link fence against her spine. "They'll think we're so wrapped up in each other that we won't notice them, and then maybe they'll get careless."

Licking her lips, she stared at him. He was so close that she could see the deeper violet flecks in the iris blue of his eyes. "I don't think we ever discussed using a dating situation as cover. I'm not sure it's necessary."

He leaned closer. "You've hired me to get a job done, Ms. Carleton. I'll use whatever I think is necessary."

"Like trying to intimidate me in public like this?" She tried to step away but he put his arms on either side of her, trapping her only inches away from him.

"Do you think that's what I'm trying to do, intimidate you?" He smiled, a curving of his lips that was completely without humor. "If I was trying to intimidate you, it wouldn't be like this." Without moving his head, he scanned the area around them with his eyes.

"Where do you think they are, Julia? The people who are watching us, I mean. Maybe they're two cars down the block from us. Maybe they're across the street." He shifted, bringing his mouth close to her ear. "Maybe they're hidden somewhere so we can't see them. But they're here. Don't ever think otherwise."

His breath stirred the hairs next to her ear and made her shiver. She wasn't cold, though. Far from it. Her body pulsed with heat. She had to get away from him, but if she moved at all it would be into his arms. So she stood perfectly still and waited for him to back up.

"Haven't we stood here long enough to convince them?" she asked, trying to disguise the breathlessness in her voice. "I'll go in your car with you—just move away from me."

He pulled back slowly, watching her with an odd, shuttered expression on his face. "You're right, they've had enough of a show. Let's go."

She had to practically run to keep up with him as he strode down the street. When he finally stopped beside an old, dented blue sedan, she took a couple of deep breaths as she waited for him to unlock the door. At least he drove a big car. She could sit right next to the door and she wouldn't have to worry that he would accidentally brush against her while he was turning the wheel.

He slammed the door just a bit harder than he needed to and got in on the other side. Starting the engine, he gunned the motor and pulled out into traffic without any warning.

"How many safe driving certificates do you have?" she murmured under her breath.

Apparently he heard her. Without taking his eyes off the rearview mirror, he said, "When you think someone's tailing you, a few sudden moves can tell you a lot. For instance, when that black car peeled out of the parking lot where you left your car, I definitely took an interest in it."

Instinctively she swiveled around to look out the back window, but he put his hand on her cheek and gently pushed her face forward again. "Loving looks at me are okay, but don't look for our friends in back of us. I don't want them to know I've made them."

Jerking her head away from his hand, she eased closer to the door. "Why don't we just talk about the case?"

"Fine with me. Shoot."

"Did you have a chance to read the material I gave you?"

"Most of it. It doesn't prove squat."

"I know it doesn't," she answered impatiently. "But didn't it raise some questions in your mind?"

She saw his knuckles whiten on the steering wheel as he stared straight ahead. Finally, his lips compressed into a tight line, he said, "You're assuming they're guilty, but I'm assuming they're innocent. What I saw in those files was a lot of innuendo and supposition. There was no proof in the material you gave me. But there's a funny thing about suspicion and innuendo. Throw enough of it around, and some of it is bound to stick. Pretty soon it doesn't matter if there's proof or not."

She felt her temper begin to simmer. "Are you implying that everything in those files is a product of my imagination?"

"Of course not." He glanced over at her, and she saw equal parts anger and wariness in his gaze. "I'm sure that every single innuendo is well documented." His gaze softened slightly. "I think that you're too rigid, Julia. You see things one way, and when something doesn't fit your view you make it fit."

Her anger flared and burst into flames. "You know nothing about me, McKinley. Nothing at all. You have no right to sit there and tell me what I'm about. I didn't hire you to psychoanalyze me, I hired you to help me solve a case. And until you know me, I'll thank you to keep your personal comments to yourself."

"Touched a nerve, did I?" he said softly. Looking past her out the window, he suddenly spun the steering wheel to the right and pulled in next to the curb.

Turning to her in the semidarkness of the twilight, he said in a low voice, "You're right, I don't know you at all. I guess I'll have to remedy that."

Before she could react, he reached down the length of the bench seat and unbuckled her seat belt. Curling one hand around her shoulders, he pulled her slowly toward him.

One part of her mind yelled out a warning, told her to scramble out of the car now. The other part, the part that was in control, trembled with anticipation. She'd been fascinated with this man for two years, had fantasized about him just as long. She knew he was all wrong for her, knew it was dangerous to get involved with him, but she couldn't stop. Just once, she wanted to see if her fantasies matched the reality.

His mouth descended slowly, almost unwillingly. When he touched her lips with his, she felt him tense and strain away from her. It was almost as if she could read his mind. He wanted to tear his mouth away from hers, thrust her away from him. Suddenly, with a groan, he wrapped his arms around her and took her mouth in a frenzy of hunger.

Fire leapt through her veins and engulfed her as if she was dry tinder. Never before had she felt such instant desire, such immediate passion. The case, her brother Bobby, the things that had happened between them in the past were all forgotten. All that mattered was the man she held so tightly.

Luke closed his eyes and felt her lips against his, returning his kiss with a passion. His arms tightened around her, pulling her slim body closer to his hard and throbbing one. This was madness, he told himself as he slanted his mouth over hers and felt her lips softening and opening to him. This was the woman he had hated for the last two years, the woman who had shattered what little was left of his life after the accident.

He couldn't want her with this savage desire that threatened to engulf him. She moved her hand and touched his neck with a tentative, fluttering touch, and he felt his body tighten into one hard mass of trembling, wanting flesh. Never before had one kiss so completely overwhelmed him.

He had to stop now, he told himself frantically. He hadn't lost control like this, not ever. Not even as a hormone-crazed teenager in the back seat of a car. Drawing his mouth away from hers, he slowly untangled his arms from her. As he drew away, a subtle scent of herbs and flowers drifted up to him. He'd been so hot for her he hadn't even noticed it until now.

She seemed to come to her senses at the same time as he did. As she backed away, appalled, he watched as her face bleached of color. Touching her lips as if they still tingled, she looked at him with huge eyes in her pale face. In the rapidly falling darkness, they stared at each other for a long minute, neither of them speaking.

He forced himself to look away first and turned the key in the ignition. There was no sign of the black car in his rearview mirror, but then he didn't think whoever was following them would be stupid enough to park where he could easily be seen. He risked a glance over at Julia. She still stared at him with the same appalled look on her face. He felt his anger stir and deliberately fanned the flames. Anger was better than the bitter hurt he would otherwise feel at her reaction to his kiss.

"I guess we know each other a little better, Investigator. Is it all right for me to make personal comments now?"

She didn't answer, and he glanced at her again. Her back was turned to him and she stared out the window. She held herself stiffly, and for just a moment he wondered if she was crying. He looked back at the road and silently shook his head. Julia Carleton was one tough cookie. He'd bet she never cried.

He stopped at a red light, and in the silence he heard her draw a ragged breath. His anger faded as quickly as it had arisen, only a weary futility remaining.

"I'm sorry, Julia. I had no right to say that. I had no right to kiss you, either, for that matter."

"Forget it," she said, her voice low. He had to strain to hear her. "It's all part of the show for whoever's following us, right?"

"Right." They could pretend it was all make-believe, that the incredible passion that had flared between them for a brief instant never existed. They could pretend a lot of things, but he wasn't sure he'd be able to force his body to believe them late in the night.

As he drove north, he tried to block the disturbing images of her from his mind by keeping track of the black car. It had reappeared soon after he restarted the car and was carefully staying a few cars behind them. He reached the turnoff for her street and hesitated. They had to know where Julia lived, but suddenly he didn't want to abandon her there, knowing someone was stalking her.

"I don't want to drop you off just yet and leave you by yourself. How about coming back to my office with me for a while? I have a client coming in soon, and after I see her I can take you home."

"I'm perfectly content staying by myself, Mr. McKinley," she answered, her voice brittle. "I told you once before I didn't hire you to be my bodyguard."

He rolled to a stop at another red light and looked over at her, unable to suppress the hot desire that licked through him at her words. His hands ached with the need to touch her again. "No, by God, you didn't, did you?"

The air in the car tensed as they stared at each other. Emotions swirled around them, shifting and changing in the charged atmosphere of the car. Finally an impatient driver behind them honked and Luke jerked his gaze away from her and gunned the engine.

After a few more blocks he said quietly, "I don't want to leave you alone in your apartment until I can check it out and see what the goons behind us are going to do. If it makes you feel better, it's strictly business. Now will you come to my office with me? I don't want to keep Mrs. Bernowski waiting."

"Fine," she muttered.

Twenty minutes later they pulled up in front of the building that housed Luke's office. Julia looked at the building that towered over them. In the daylight, it was just another shabby office that had seen its best days a long time ago. At night, it looked a lot more sinister.

Parking by the curb, he opened the door for her and ushered her into the building. The hall was dim and gloomy, all the tenants long since gone home for the night. The low-wattage light bulbs in the overhead fixtures cast bizarre shadows on the walls as they climbed the stairs, and their footsteps echoed hollowly on the scuffed linoleum as they approached his office.

"Do you see many clients at night?" She forced herself to speak in what she thought was a normal tone of voice as she reined in her imagination.

He cast her an amused glance. "Spooky place, isn't it? And yes, I do see a lot of my clients at night." He turned the key in the door and flicked on a light, waiting for her to precede him into the room. "For a lot of different reasons."

Walking past her, he flopped in his desk chair. "Mrs. Bernowski works all day. This is the only time she can get over here to see me."

Eyeing the red leather couch dubiously, she finally lowered herself cautiously onto the worn cushion. When it didn't sway or shift, she settled back against it and watched McKinley pull a file out of an open drawer.

He had surprised her tonight. She hadn't expected him to kiss her, and she certainly hadn't expected the response she'd sensed in him. It had been almost as surprising as her own response to him.

She squirmed on the sofa as she remembered the abandoned way she'd thrown herself into his arms and pressed against his hard body, the way she'd kissed him back with a passion she hadn't believed possible.

Thank goodness he'd seemed as shaken and surprised by the whole business as she had been. There were too many reasons, all of them obvious, why she could never get involved with a man like Lucas McKinley. And right now, she had an even better one—her brother Bobby. Protecting Bobby was the reason she'd come to Luke in the first place. She'd better not forget that when her hormones began to stir.

She heard footsteps coming slowly up the stairs and swiveled around to face the door. Had the people in the black car behind them decided to take advantage of the deserted building and pay them a visit?

Luke looked up and listened to the footsteps, then stood and opened the door to the corridor. "Mrs. Bernowski," she heard him say. "How are you doing tonight?"

A middle-aged woman walked into the office, dressed in a plain dark blue dress and black sweater. Her head was covered by a scarf, and she walked heavily over to the chair next to Luke's desk.

"Have you found out about my Piotyr?" Her voice was heavily accented, and she leaned toward Luke anxiously. "He is not in trouble, no?"

McKinley leaned forward and took the old woman's hand. "Not now he's not, but I'm afraid he's going to get in trouble soon if he doesn't stay away from the boys he's spending time with. They aren't good boys, Mrs. Bernowski. They do bad things, and they'll eventually make your Piotyr do bad things."

Even from across the room Julia could see the older woman squeezing Luke's hand. "What do I do, Mr. McKinley?" she whispered.

Luke covered her hand with his other one. "I'll see what I can do. When a boy is seventeen, he doesn't want to listen to his mother. Maybe he'll listen to me."

"Thank you," Mrs. Bernowski said brokenly. "My Piotyr, he's all I have left. I don't know what I'd do if anything happened to him." She pulled her hand away from Luke's and fumbled in her purse. Julia assumed she was reaching for tissues, but instead she pulled out a roll of money.

"I can pay you this much today, Mr. McKinley. You tell me how much more I owe you."

Luke closed her hand around the money and gently pushed it back into her purse. "There will be plenty of time for paying when Piotyr has been straightened out. Right now we're going to concentrate on him, not on how much money is owed."

Suddenly Julia realized why Luke's office was so shabby. He probably didn't take money from half his clients if the way he treated Mrs. Bernowski was any indication. She could tell by the look on his face he had no intention of accepting money from her, now or later. She watched as he helped the old woman from the chair and escorted her toward the door. In spite of herself, her heart softened as she saw the solicitous way he held the woman's arm.

The woman stopped when she saw Julia sitting on the couch, and looked up at Luke uncertainly. "This woman is here about my Piotyr?"

Luke glanced over at her. "This is Julia Carleton, another one of my clients. She doesn't have anything to do with Piotyr."

Reassured, Mrs. Bernowski smiled at Julia. "You have chosen well. If anyone can help you, it is Mr. McKinley."

Julia smiled slightly in response. "I hope so."

Julia saw the old woman's eyes sharpen as she looked at her. "I have seen you before." She stared at Julia, and her eyes narrowed. "You were in the newspapers when Mr. McKinley had his troubles. I know, because I checked on him before I hired him." She turned away from Luke's supporting arm and faced Julia accusingly. "You are the policewoman who removed him from his job."

"I was the one who investigated him, yes," Julia answered in a low voice. "But I didn't remove him from the police force. He did that himself when he beat that drunken driver almost to death."

Chapter 4

Mrs. Bernowski studied her for what seemed like a long time, and Julia found herself wanting to look away. Instead she lifted her chin and returned the old woman's stare, ignoring the guilt that tried to surface. Finally Mrs. Bernowski shook her head and turned back to Luke.

"That one, she has no pity in her, no softness. She doesn't deserve your help."

"You're a good friend, Mrs. B." Julia almost didn't recognize the gentle murmur as McKinley's voice. "Don't you worry about me. You take care of Piotyr and let me worry about Ms. Carleton."

Their voices mixed and the words became indistinguishable as McKinley walked the other woman down the stairs. Julia heard the building door open and close. After what seemed like forever, Luke's footsteps started back up the stairs.

He shut the door behind him and walked slowly over to his desk chair. Lowering himself into it, he gazed down at his hands for a long time. Finally he said, "I wouldn't have done anything differently, you know." When he looked up at her, his eyes were flat and hard.

"So you said." She felt the treacherous sympathy stirring, the same emotion she'd been forced to suppress two years ago. She'd done her job then because she'd had no choice. "That's why we were forced to dismiss you. If you had come to the hearing and expressed remorse, said you had done it in the heat of the moment, we might have been able to suspend you for a while, then reinstate you. But you gave us no choice." She dropped her eyes, knowing that what she said wasn't true and not wanting him to see the shame in her eyes.

"Are you telling me I should have lied? Should I have said I regretted what I'd done, that I was sorry?" Unwillingly she looked up, and thought she'd never seen such bitterness on a man's face before, such hardness in a man's eyes. "That bastard was already out of the hospital by the time you had my hearing. My wife and son were dead and in the ground. No, I wasn't sorry I beat him nearly to death. I was only sorry I didn't have a chance to finish the job."

"You know the rules about the handling of suspects as well as I do. You beat the man senseless in front of a dozen witnesses, for God's sake. What did you expect us to do?" She recognized the pleading tone in her voice and clamped her mouth shut.

He shuttered his gaze and the eyes that stared over at her were cold and lifeless. "I expected you to do exactly what you did. I was guilty of police brutality. I beat a man until his skull fractured and his ribs and arm broke. And the fact that he was an alderman's son was just a bonus."

"We were all sorry that he killed your wife and unborn child," she said desperately. She'd had no choice, dammit. Orders had come down from the highest level and she'd had to follow them. The alderman had had a lot of political clout. Luke had beat the man almost to death and been entirely remorseless. "It was a horrible tragedy and the man deserved to be punished. And he is being punished. He's spending the next five years in prison."

"And in five years he'll get out of prison and be free to get drunk and kill someone else. In five years my son would have been seven years old. Starting second grade. Playing baseball. Playing with the brothers and sisters my wife and I will never have." He rose abruptly and turned to look out the window.

She looked at his rigid back and wished, just for a moment, that she had the right to comfort him. "I'm sorry you had to be the first one at the scene of the accident. I'm sorry that it had to be you who found her." *I'm sorry I had to be the one to fire you,* she thought silently.

"I'm not." His voice hardened. "I'm glad I was there. I want that bastard to remember my face every time he opens his eyes in the darkness. I want him to remember what he did. Every time he takes a drink, I want him to think about what my wife looked like when they cut her out of that car."

"Don't," she said in a low voice. "Why are you torturing yourself like this? What do you gain by dredging up all the details? It's over and done, Luke. There's nothing you can change now."

"Don't tell me what to do, Julia. You don't know anything about it." He spoke without turning around. His words slashed between them, erecting a barrier as effective as any brick wall.

And she had no intention of trying to break that barrier down. What had happened between them in his car earlier was nothing more than physiology, a normal reaction between two people of the opposite sex. There was no deeper significance, she told herself, clamping her mouth shut on the words that wanted to come tumbling out. She imagined Lucas McKinley had gotten plenty of sympathy in the days after his wife and unborn son had died and he'd been fired from the police force for brutality. He didn't need any more sympathy from her. And apparently he wouldn't welcome it, anyway.

After watching him for a minute, she stood up and smoothed her skirt, then reached for her purse. "Are you finished here?"

He turned around slowly and wiped all expression off his face. But not before she'd seen the anger, and the agony. In spite of her warnings, she wanted to offer him some comfort. But she remained silent, knowing he wouldn't accept anything from her right now.

"Yeah. I'll take you home."

The car ride from the northwest side of Chicago to her apartment in Lincoln Park seemed endless. They both watched the scenery blur, neither of them speaking. There was no sign of the black car that had been following them. When she glanced in Luke's direction, the brief flashes of illumination from the streetlights revealed a face that could have been carved from stone.

Desperate for some way to ease the tension, she finally blurted out, "Tell me about Piotyr Bernowski."

He glanced over at her, apparently surprised. "Pete?" His face became guarded again as he watched her. "Why do you want to know about him?"

She shrugged, trying to act casual about her request. She didn't want him to know that the way he'd interacted with Mrs. Bernowski had intrigued her, and disturbed her on some deep level. He no longer fit quite so neatly into the pigeonhole she'd labeled Lucas McKinley.

"His mother seemed so concerned about him. Not too many mothers would hire a private investigator to check up on a teenage son they were worried about."

His face softened as he concentrated on the street in front of him. "There aren't many mothers like Mrs. B." After a moment, he said, "Pete's a typical teenage boy, trying to rip the apron strings out of his mother's hands. Unfortunately, the form of rebellion he chose could get him into real trouble." He glanced over at her. "He's running with one of the local gangs. If he doesn't stop, he's going to get himself in too deep to get out."

"What can you do about that?" she asked as they pulled to the curb a block from her apartment.

He turned to face her in the darkened car, and suddenly something thick and heavy enveloped them. Remembering the last time he'd pulled over to the curb, she edged closer to the door and found the handle. If he made one move in her direction, she'd be out of the car. She didn't think she could cope with two encounters like that in one evening.

The corners of his mouth flickered upward for a moment, as if he could read her mind and her thoughts amused him. Settling himself back against his own door, a safe distance away from her, he crossed his arms in front of him and said, "What can I do about Piotyr? Well, there are several options. I could go to him and explain that his mother is worried about him, and that his new friends are bad boys. Or I could threaten him, tell him to quit hanging with the gang or I'll kick his butt. Or maybe I'll find him a job at a fast-food place, give him something else to think about."

He quirked an eyebrow at her. "Which option do you think I should choose?"

"I think you're too smart to use any of them," she retorted. "What are you really going to do?"

"I don't know. I guess we'll just have to see how it plays out, won't we?"

In one smooth motion he swung out of the car and closed the door. By the time he reached her door, she'd gathered her purse and her briefcase and was scrambling out of the car herself. Silently he took her elbow and steadied her while he closed the door.

She couldn't move away from him, even though she told herself she had to. The slight touch of his hand brought back the flood of desire he'd unleashed earlier when he'd kissed her. She stood in the street, the yellow light from the streetlamp pooling around her, and began to tremble.

Dropping her elbow as if he'd been burned, Luke rested his hand lightly in the small of her back as they began to walk toward her apartment. He told himself that the contact was necessary. If she spotted someone lurking in the shadows before he did, the tensing of her body would tell him instantly.

He wouldn't think about the way her spine curved gently under his fingers, or wonder if the rest of her skin was as soft as her mouth. He couldn't afford to remember the explosion of passion earlier.

His hand formed a fist on her back, then dropped away. He couldn't think about his job while he was touching her. Seeing the doorway to her apartment just ahead, he took a deep breath and lengthened his stride. She had to practically run to keep up, he noticed, but he refused to slow down. Once they were inside, he wouldn't have to stay so damned close to her.

He swung open the heavy glass door and almost pushed her into the brightly lit lobby. "Do you have your key ready?" he asked, nodding toward the security door.

Fumbling in her purse, she finally pulled out a key ring that looked as if it could double as a weapon in a bar fight. The D-shaped piece of brass would curve to go over her hand and was as thick as two of his fingers.

Taking it from her, he looked at her incredulously. "Do you have a permit to carry this thing?"

"I work a lot of late nights, Mr. McKinley, and I have to park on the street. Since I prefer not to carry a gun, it seemed like a sensible idea." Her voice sounded just a shade defensive.

"Hell, yes, it's a sensible idea." He turned the weapon over in his hand and shook his head. "I just hope you never mistake me for a mugger."

"As long as you don't lurk in dark alleys, you should be perfectly safe," she answered in a cool voice as she turned and unlocked the door.

He followed her up to the third floor and silently took her key ring from her. Unlocking the door to her apartment, he motioned her to stay behind him.

He flung the door wide, sending it crashing into the wall. When it rebounded slowly into the room, he reached in and flicked on the light.

His first impression of the room was that it was alive with color and light. A vibrant floral print covered her couch, and area rugs in matching bright colors covered the hardwood floor. The prints she'd chosen for her walls were scenes frantic with activity and color. Every corner of the room held greenery, lush and luxuriant.

It took only a glance to see that nobody hid in the living room. He crossed to the tiny kitchen, peering in the minuscule pantry and checking the lock carefully on the back door. The small bathroom was equally secure, and finally, with a feeling of acute discomfort, he entered her bedroom.

The colors in here were muted pastels, cool and soothing. He tried not to look at the bed that dominated the room, tried not to notice the pillows piled high or the down comforter that beckoned with softness. Hastily looking in her closets and under the bed, he ignored the whiff of her scent that floated to him as he lowered the comforter back into place and stood up.

The windows in the bedroom were tightly locked, too, and he quickly escaped back to the living room. She stood in the center of the floor, watching him with huge eyes that were more gray now than green.

"No bad guys hiding under the bed?" she asked lightly, but he could see the tenseness that shadowed her eyes.

"Not a one," he answered just as lightly, beating down the surge of admiration. Julia Carleton wasn't going to fall apart on him. He'd bet a million bucks she would rather die than show him any weakness.

"What time do we have to be out of here in the morning?" he asked, looking around the room.

Her eyes narrowed as she looked at him. "*We* aren't going to be out of here, period. *I* usually leave at seven-thirty or so."

"Don't get your shorts in a knot," he said mildly, although her quick assumption that he meant to stay the night had his blood heating. "I just wanted to know what time to pick you up."

"Oh." She turned away with a jerky movement. "I'm sorry, McKinley. I...it's been a long day. I don't usually jump to stupid conclusions like that."

"It's okay," he answered easily, thinking about all the conclusions he'd like to jump to with her. "But I thought we'd gotten past the 'McKinley' bit, Julia. My name is Luke."

She turned around to face him. "I'm sorry. I know you asked me to call you Luke. It's just...it reminds me of two years ago, and now...you just don't seem like a Luke to me. Your name is Lucas, isn't it?"

He scowled. "Nobody ever calls me that."

"How come?"

He shrugged. "I've been Luke for as long as I can remember."

As she watched him, he could tell she was framing her next question. Finally she asked, "Why don't you like being called Lucas?"

He knew it would be dangerous for Julia Carleton to start calling him Lucas. His name on her tongue sounded too intimate, too personal. And he had to keep it impersonal with her. "It's not that I don't like it, but nobody's called me that for a long time."

She waited, looking at him, and finally he sighed. "My grandmother used to call me Lucas. Nobody else has since she died." He refused to tell her about his grandmother, the woman who'd held a special place in his heart the whole time he was growing up.

"It's a beautiful name," she said softly.

"Yeah, well, I answer to Luke." He didn't want her to know how much he liked the sound of his name on her lips. There were a lot of things he didn't want Julia Carleton to know, it seemed.

"I'll pick you up here tomorrow at seven-thirty. Don't leave before I get here. Understand?"

Her eyes darkened, but she nodded. "I'll wait for you."

"See that you do." He paused with his hands on the door. "Sweet dreams, Julia."

Closing the door gently behind him, he mentally kicked himself. Now why did he say that? He didn't give a damn if her dreams were pleasant or not. He waited outside her door until he heard the dead bolt slide home, then ran lightly down the stairs.

Walking back to his car, he scanned the streets carefully. It was a lot easier to concentrate without Julia next to him, distracting him with her subtle scent and warm skin.

There was no sign of the black sedan, or anyone else watching him, for that matter. It wasn't that late, but the streets in Julia's quiet neighborhood were virtually deserted. He got in his car and drove around the block, just to be sure no one sat in a car watching her apartment. Maybe they figured she was safely settled for the night with her lover, he thought cynically, remembering their kiss in the car earlier.

His body tightened and he pressed his foot on the accelerator. If he spent a few hours at his office, looking over the files she'd given him earlier, he'd forget about his incendiary reaction to her. Not bloody likely, he thought savagely as he sped through a yellow light. But at least it would tire him out enough so he'd be able to fall asleep.

When he reached his office he parked just down the street. Unlike other parts of the city that stayed up all night, his blue-collar neighborhood went to bed early. He was always the only one in his office building this late at night.

Locking and slamming the car door, he shoved his keys into his pocket and headed for his office. He had his hand on the door to his building and had just begun to open it when an orange ball of flame burst through his office window with a dull roar, right above his head. He was looking up, amazed, when he slammed into something hard and slid to the ground and the world slowly spun away into a black void.

Julia lay in bed, wide-awake. The red numbers of the clock on the nightstand said it was 3:24 in the morning, but it felt as if she'd been lying in this bed, rigid and sleepless, for at least several days.

Rolling over onto her other side, she punched her pillow into place with a vengeance and closed her eyes, willing herself to sleep. It didn't make any difference. The same pictures still rolled through her head—Luke at his office, soothing Mrs. Bernowski's fears. The haunted, agonized look in his eyes as he talked about the accident that had killed his wife and unborn son and banished him from the police force. And the memory that heated her blood and set her nerves on edge, the kiss they'd shared in his car.

It was no use. She rolled over again and stared up at the ceiling. She might as well get up and do something useful, for nothing was going to banish his image from her mind tonight. For two years she'd been able to dismiss her fantasies about him, telling herself that no matter how attractive, he was a former cop and part of her job. She wasn't interested in getting involved with a cop ever again. And especially not one who hated her.

But pictures of him still swirled through her mind. Maybe there was more to Lucas McKinley than she'd thought at first.

It didn't matter, she told herself firmly. No matter what or who he was, there was no way she was going to get involved with him. They were doing business together, business that involved her brother Bobby. She couldn't afford to be distracted by any man right now, but especially not by the man who was doing the investigating.

She slid out of bed, thinking that maybe a cup of tea would help her sleep. As she walked into her living room, the darkness was shattered by the harsh ringing of her buzzer. Feeling her heart pound, she stared at the front door as if it could somehow tell her who stood in the lobby, demanding entrance.

Wrapping her robe around her with shaking hands, she moved to the door on stiff legs and pushed the intercom. "Who's there?" she asked, praying that the static would disguise her shaking voice.

"It's Luke McKinley, Julia. Let me in."

His voice sounded strained and urgent, and she pushed the lock button without thinking twice. In just a few seconds she heard him coming up the stairs, moving slowly and heavily. She waited until he knocked on the door, then looked through her peephole to make sure it was Luke before opening it.

She drew in a sharp breath when she saw him. His face was covered with fine red lines, and she realized with horror that they were dried blood. Glancing down, she saw that the backs of his hands were smeared with the same red, and that his clothes were covered with dirt.

"My God, what happened to you?" she cried, taking his hand and pulling him into her apartment.

For a moment he clung to her hand, then he let go and headed for her kitchen. "Do you have a gas stove?" he asked, opening the oven door and peering inside.

"No, it's electric." She stared at him, wondering if he'd lost his mind. "Do you often show up at people's houses at three-thirty in the morning, covered with blood, to ask what kind of stove they have?"

He walked out of the kitchen and stood in front of her bookcases, scanning the titles. "Come over here and tell me if any of these books don't belong to you. And do it quickly."

The fear that had been curdling in her stomach ever since he'd rung her buzzer now moved to her chest, threatening to suffocate her. Her legs felt frozen and stiff as she moved slowly over to stand next to him. "Why do I . . . ?"

"Don't waste time asking questions. Just do it now." He answered without looking at her, occasionally pulling out a book and leafing through it quickly. "Hurry, Julia."

She looked dutifully at the books, checking each title as she scanned down the shelves. When she got to the bottom, she said, "They're all mine."

He looked at her sharply. "Are you sure?"

"Yes, I'm sure. Now will you please tell me what this is all about?"

"In a minute." He examined her stereo, television and VCR, then disappeared into her bedroom as she watched numbly, unable to move.

When he reappeared a few minutes later, some of the tension was gone from his face. He started to ease down on the couch, then caught himself. Kneeling on the floor, he looked under the couch and all the other furniture, then removed the cushions and slid his hands into the cracks.

Finally he slid down onto the couch and looked at her. "Come sit down," he said in the gentle voice she'd heard him use with Mrs. Bernowski. "It's all right, I think."

Forcing herself to move, she sank down on the couch next to him. "What do you mean it's all right? You don't look 'all right' to me. What happened to you?"

He closed his eyes and eased himself upright on the couch. His slow, careful movements made her realize he was in pain, and she scooted over next to him. "Tell me," she insisted, taking his hand.

He stared down at their joined fingers as if the sight was completely unexpected. Then he turned his hand so their palms were touching and entwined their fingers.

"My office exploded tonight," he said in a flat voice. "It was completely destroyed. Another minute and I would have been in the building when it happened. I was just going inside when I heard a boom. I looked up and saw a fireball come out my window, and that's the last thing I remember until the paramedics woke me up."

"Your office exploded?" she repeated, fear driving into her chest with stunning force. "Was it an accident?"

"I'm afraid the only thing accidental about it was that I wasn't in there when it happened," he answered grimly. "The Bomb and Arson Squad found the remains of a fairly sophisticated little explosive device in what was left of my desk." He looked at her and quirked one eyebrow. "It looks like someone isn't too happy with us."

"It can't have anything to do with my case," she whispered, shocked. "You haven't done anything yet. I just hired you yesterday."

"Apparently these guys are fast workers." He looked at her impatiently. "Do you honestly think this isn't connected with your case? Can you sit there and tell me that someone like Mrs. Bernowski is responsible for bombing my office? Because that's who the rest of my clients are, people just like her."

"I'm sorry," she murmured as she looked at him, horrified. "I could have gotten you killed."

"But I wasn't killed." His voice was gruff. "And now I've got to admit there's a lot more reason to believe your story. It may not be Eddie, but someone doesn't like the fact that I'm working for you."

"But who could know? It's not like you've been asking any questions yet."

"I was at headquarters twice today, and more than one person saw me each time. Someone saw us together in my car. Anyone who knew what case you're working on could put two and two together."

She looked at him, seeing the weariness and pain beneath the dried blood on his face. "Why didn't the hospital clean you up? It was the least they could have done."

"I didn't go to the hospital." He closed his eyes and leaned back on the couch.

"But you said the paramedics woke you up."

"At the scene." He opened his eyes to look at her. "I couldn't afford to take the time to go to the hospital. Have you ever gone to an emergency room? You sit there half the night, and when they finally look at you you're either dead or healed."

"Why couldn't you afford the time?"

"I had to get over here, of course," he said impatiently. "I was afraid they might have tried to bomb your apartment, too. Gas stoves are handy for that kind of thing. So are electronic devices."

She still held his hand, she realized suddenly, and she gripped it harder. "You didn't go to the hospital so you could come over here and make sure I was all right?" she said in a soft voice.

As he watched her face, she thought she saw a momentary softening in his eyes. Then he abruptly dropped her hand and pushed himself to his feet. "I have to protect my source of income," he said as he moved toward her small bathroom.

She banished the disappointment that lanced through her at his words and told herself he was right. This was nothing more than a business relationship. Standing up, she moved to the bathroom door and watched him. He stood at the sink, trying to wash away the blood on his face with hands that were suddenly shaking.

"Here, let me," she said, pushing past him to take the washcloth out of his hands. "Sit down." She eased him gently onto the edge of the bathtub and began to clean his face.

He closed his eyes and clenched his hands at his sides. Was she hurting him? Her hands faltered and dropped away uncertainly.

Opening his eyes, he said in a deep voice, "Why did you stop?"

"I don't want to hurt you."

"You're not." His voice was harsh, and for just a second something that wasn't pain or weariness filled his eyes. She took an involuntary step backward. "You're not hurting me," he said more gently. "I'm just not used to having someone take care of me."

She didn't move until he closed his eyes again, then she dabbed as gently as she could. Once all the dried blood was wiped away she could see that his face was covered with a crisscross pattern of cuts and scratches.

"How did you get these?"

He shrugged. "Probably from the glass in my window. I was standing right underneath it when it blew." He looked down at his hands critically. "Looks like glass cuts."

She filled the sink with warm water and, taking one of his hands in hers, began to clean it, being careful to look for pieces of glass. She tried to ignore the shape of his hands, long and slender and strong. As much to distract herself from the feel of his hand as anything else, she said, "You said the explosion knocked you out. How did that happen?"

He shifted so he could put his other hand in the water, and his hip bumped up against hers. He didn't seem to notice, she thought as her leg tingled. "The paramedics found me slumped against a car. The force of the explosion probably threw me into it and knocked me out."

Dropping his hand, she swung around to look into his eyes. "Are you sure you don't have a concussion?"

"Positive." Taking his hand out of the water, he looked around and reached for a towel. "The paramedics told me I was okay. They wouldn't have let me go otherwise."

She stepped back and watched him dry himself off. Without the dried blood, she could see his wounds were all superficial. But he moved with a stiffness that told her he would be uncomfortable tomorrow.

"What are you going to do now?"

"Go home and get some sleep, I guess."

She couldn't stand the idea of his going home alone and waking up tomorrow stiff and sore with no one to help him. It was only because it was her fault his office had been blown up, she tried to tell herself. He moved toward the front door, and she found herself saying, "Why don't you stay here tonight?"

He paused and turned around slowly. "I beg your pardon?"

"I don't think you should be alone tonight," she answered hastily. "What if the paramedics were wrong and you did get a concussion? What if you wake up and need help?"

He looked at the couch. "Thanks, but I'll take my chances at home. I'm going to be sore enough tomorrow without sleeping on that thing to boot."

"You can have my bed," she said, her voice gruff.

He raised one eyebrow at her, but she could see what an effort it was. "Any other time and I'd take you up on that offer."

"I'll sleep on the couch," she snapped, but her voice softened when she saw he was swaying on his feet. "Come on, you're not going home tonight." She steered him toward the bedroom, but he stopped dead when he saw her rumpled bed.

"I didn't have a chance to make it when you rang my buzzer," she began, suddenly uncomfortable.

He turned to her, and even in the dim light that reflected from the living room there was no mistaking the look in his eyes. "The fact that the bed isn't made isn't the problem, Julia. The fact that you're not in it with me is." He reached out for her, and his hands were as hard as steel. Setting her away from him, he let his hands drop to his sides. "Close the door behind you."

Backing out of the room, she stared at the door for a long time before she stumbled to the couch. Wrapping her afghan tightly around herself, she made sure the front door was locked again and turned off the light. She lay on the couch, shivering in spite of the blanket wrapped around her; all she could see was his eyes, glittering at her in the darkness of her bedroom.

Chapter 5

Luke stirred as a warm breeze drifted over him, enveloping him in an unfamiliar scent. He seemed to be sleeping in a garden, he thought drowsily, a garden that reminded him of Julia. The smell of flowers and a more subtle, spicier scent wafted up to him as he rolled over and stretched.

His muscles screamed in pain and he froze, the events of the previous night flooding back into his memory. Opening his eyes slowly, he looked around Julia's bedroom.

If possible, it was even more inviting in the daylight. Soft and feminine, it seemed like the complete antithesis of the woman he'd thought of as hard and unfeeling.

He'd thought of her that way until yesterday, anyway. He'd found out that parts of her were very soft and definitely felt good. Fighting against the flood of desire that swept over him, he told himself he wasn't responding to Julia personally. He'd just gone too long without a woman. He couldn't have been that wrong about Julia Carleton, could he?

Remembering her gentle bathing of his cuts the night before, and her insistence that he stay in her apartment so he wouldn't be alone, he swung his legs over the side of her bed and stared at the closed door uneasily. Maybe there was more to Julia than he'd thought.

It didn't matter, he told himself. She was as off-limits to him as every other woman in the world. Oh, he'd enjoy a quick roll in the hay with her, he acknowledged, or maybe even a not so quick one, but that was all it would ever be. He'd had a relationship once, a marriage, and he didn't care to repeat that mistake.

Slowly and painfully he pulled on the dusty, blood-spattered jeans and sweater that he'd tossed onto the floor the night before. Moving stiffly to the bedroom door, he opened it and looked out into the living room.

Julia lay on her side on the couch, a multicolored blanket wrapped around her and her hands tucked under her cheeks. In the morning sunlight she looked remarkably young and very innocent. Her dark red hair gleamed like the glossy leaves of oak trees in the fall, and her eyelashes lay thick and dark against her cheeks.

His body tightened as he watched her, and he wanted nothing more than to scoop her up in his arms and carry her back to the bed in the other room. As he looked down at her, he imagined how it would feel to lie with her in the sunlight, her scent surrounding them, her long legs sliding around his.

Get real, he told himself harshly as he forced himself to move into the kitchen. *Not only does she think you're some kind of brute animal, you're working for her.* If ever there were two people who were absolutely wrong for each other, it was Luke McKinley and Julia Carleton. Hell, she didn't even like his name, he reminded himself, remembering their discussion the previous evening.

He yanked open the refrigerator door and stared blindly inside. When he heard her stirring in the living room behind him he tensed, reaching to grab the first thing he saw. By the time he sensed her standing in the doorway behind him, he was peering intently at the label on the jar.

"There's only so much you can do with coffee," she said dryly behind him. "Let me make it."

She brushed past him to take the jar out of his hands and moved to fill the coffeemaker with water. The multicolored blanket was draped over her shoulders and wrapped around her completely. It hid every bit of her body, but perversely it only made him ache more. He wondered if the blanket felt as soft as it looked, and what she was wearing underneath it.

Her back was ramrod straight as she measured out coffee carefully. He wondered if it was his imagination or if her hand was really shaking. Before he could move closer to find out, she said, "How do you feel this morning?"

"About the way you'd expect after getting caught in an explosion. I hurt like hell."

At that she looked over her shoulder, sympathy in her eyes. "Do you want to take a shower? It might help get some of the kinks out."

"Thanks," he said gruffly, "but I'd rather wait and shower at home. Then I can get some clean clothes." He didn't think he'd be able to bear doing something as intimate as showering here in her apartment. Sleeping in her bed was bad enough.

Water gurgled through the coffeemaker and hissed as it hit the heating element. Slowly, almost reluctantly, she turned around to face him. Pushing her tousled hair out of her face, she clutched the blanket tightly in her other hand. Her eyes looked bright green in the light, shadowed by the faint purple smudges beneath them.

As they faced each other something seemed to stretch between them, gripping both of them and pulling tight. Her hand desperately held on to the blanket until her knuckles turned white. He told himself to move, to back out of the kitchen, do something to defuse the tension. He was rooted to the ground.

Slowly he reached out and touched her face, his fingertips sliding over the warm satin of her skin. She blinked but didn't move away. "Thank you for taking me in last night," he said softly.

"I'm glad you came here," she whispered. "I'm glad you stayed."

"Why, Julia? Why are you glad I came here and stayed?"

Her gaze slid away from his and focused on his wounded hands. "You needed someone to take care of you, someone to be there if you needed help."

His stomach clenched in fear as he watched the tenderness slowly fill her eyes. He stepped back until he bumped into the counter and turned around blindly, opening the glass door of her cabinet and fumbling around until he found two mugs. "I didn't need help." His voice was harsh. "I just wanted to make sure you were all right."

After a long pause, she said stiffly, "I appreciate that. Would you like some coffee now?"

As he turned to hand her the mugs, she averted her face and let her hair swing down to cover it. He watched her for a moment, astonishment gradually replacing his fear. She had actually looked hurt at his words.

Julia had never seemed the kind of woman who would be hurt by what anyone said to her. She seemed so self-contained, so aloof, that he imagined nothing could wound her. Maybe he'd been wrong.

"Julia, I'm..." What? Sorry he'd come here? He couldn't be. He'd had to know that she was all right. He swallowed. "I guess I'm a little grouchy in the morning. I'm sorry I said I didn't need help. Thank you for all you did."

"You're welcome. Here's your coffee." Her voice was back to the cool, detached tone that made him want to throttle her, the tone she'd use with a total stranger who was out of line.

She set his mug on the little table in the kitchen then sat down without looking at him. Staring down into the black coffee, desperate for something to say that would ease the tension in the room, he said, "You remembered how I like it."

She looked up at him then and gave him a brief, impersonal smile, one completely lacking in warmth. "I have a very good memory."

Whatever barriers Julia felt were necessary to protect herself from the world were back in place. For a while last night and this morning, she had lowered them enough to let him in. Now he sat at the table, only inches away from her, but he might as well have been in the next state. Wrapping his hands around the coffee mug, he found that not even its heat could banish the chill he felt.

A half hour later they stood on the sidewalk in front of her apartment in the early spring sunshine. "What's the plan for today?" she asked in a voice a total stranger would use.

Irritated by her calm remoteness, and angry at himself for letting it bother him, he snarled, "First, we make sure we don't get killed."

"I kind of took that as a given," she answered calmly. "I meant after that."

He wanted to shake her. Or maybe he wanted to kiss her. Clenching his teeth, he took her elbow and steered her toward his car. He was being perverse, he knew it, but he couldn't seem to help himself. A little while ago he'd snapped her head off because she'd been concerned about him. Now he ached to do something that would bring the life back to her face.

He hated the impersonal mask she'd assumed this morning, hated knowing he'd put it there. Busy trying to figure out how to get her to lower her barriers again, it took him a few moments to realize her arm was trembling where he held it.

Slowing his steps, he glanced down at her in surprise. Her head was bent and she was apparently absorbed in the cracks in the sidewalk. He relaxed his hold and eased in front of her, forcing her to stop.

"It would help if you paid attention too," he said, more gently than he'd intended. "Two pairs of eyes are better than one for spotting something out of place."

At that she looked up and tried to pull her arm out of his grasp. "I didn't think anything would happen in the daylight. These guys seem to prefer to work at night." Her voice was weak and a little breathless.

"That's what they'd like you to think."

He didn't miss how quickly she stepped backward when he released her elbow, and he felt a surge of visceral satisfaction. She wasn't as unaffected by him as she'd like him to think. He moved toward his car again, this time not touching her as she walked along next to him, and he felt his temper draining away. She could pretend all she wanted, but he'd felt her trembling.

When they reached his car he looked around one more time, but didn't see anything suspicious. She reached for the handle on the passenger door, but before she could open it he grabbed her arm and pulled her back.

"Just a minute, I need to check something."

Very carefully, he leaned across the seat and pulled the hood release. Easing the hood open, he examined all the engine parts until he was sure there wasn't anything extra mixed in. Before he lowered the hood, he got to his knees and peered under the car. It, too, was clean. After he looked in the trunk and through the back seat, he finally closed the hood of the car and allowed Julia to get in.

"Aren't you being a bit melodramatic? Surely they wouldn't take a chance and put a bomb in your car in such a public place," she said as she buckled her seat belt.

Turning on the car, he snapped his own seat belt shut and looked over at her. "Who knows what they would do? It looks like they're getting desperate, and these guys seem to like bombs," he answered in a flat voice. "I didn't think about it last night when I drove over here, but by now whoever set that bomb in my office has to know it didn't do its job. I don't want to take any chances." The engine sputtered as he pulled out into the street. "You can't be too careful with a finely tuned machine like this one."

"I can see you wouldn't want anything disturbing its delicate balance," she agreed gravely, surprising him with a flicker of a smile. After a minute, she asked, "What about my car?"

"A very good question. We're leaving it right where it's at for now. You won't need it, anyway. From now on, we're inseparable." He didn't like the emotion that surged through his body at his words.

Julia glanced over at his profile and felt panic stir in her chest. Last night was bad enough. He'd stirred up feelings in her she'd banished from her life long ago, feelings she had no intention of succumbing to. The only thing that had reassured her last night was that in the morning it would be over. He'd go his way, she'd go hers, and they'd meet occasionally to discuss the case. She was horribly afraid to ask about his definition of inseparable.

She'd handle it one small bit at a time, she thought. "Where are we going now?"

"I thought we'd go to your office so you can pick up the rest of your files on the case. I don't think it would be wise to stay there, though. Right now I don't know who we can trust, so we don't trust anyone."

"We don't have to go back to the office. I keep everything about the case with me." She glanced at the briefcase at her feet and added, "I haven't left anything there from the beginning. This is too sensitive a case."

The look he gave her was one of respect. "I'm glad," he said softly. "You never know who your enemies might be."

"Does this mean you believe me about Timmons and the others?"

"I told you that I need some solid proof, especially about who specifically is involved. I still can't believe that Eddie could be involved in something so dirty, but I can't deny that something's going on. That bomb at my office last night was sure as hell real."

She noticed that they were heading toward the northwest. "Where are we going?"

"I want to stop by my office, see if the Bomb and Arson Squad has found anything. It might also be interesting to see who else is hanging around there."

His voice was hard and implacable. He was talking about stalking the men who'd tried to kill him, and his voice was completely matter-of-fact. Lucas McKinley would make a formidable enemy.

He pulled into a parking space down the block from his office, and as she got out of the car she could see the blue police barricades in front of his building. Something glittered on the sidewalk, and as they got closer she saw that it was broken glass.

She stared, appalled at the destruction, as they stopped next to the barricades. It was a miracle that he hadn't received more than a few superficial cuts. Anyone standing at the door to the building at the moment of the explosion would have been showered with jagged fragments of the windows above.

Luke approached one of the fire fighters coming out of the building. "I'm the tenant in that office. Have you found anything yet?"

The fire fighter shook his head wearily. "Everything in the room was reduced to matchsticks. It's a miracle they found anything at all. You can call headquarters later, but I doubt if they'll find anything more. It was a pretty professional job."

"Yeah, that's what I was afraid of." Luke shoved his hands in his pockets and Julia followed his gaze up to the windows above them. The tiny bits of glass remaining looked like sharp teeth waiting to devour anyone who ventured too close. She'd seen bomb sites before, but the thought of those points of glass ripping into Luke made her shudder. She instinctively moved closer to him.

Even though he stood inches away from her, she felt his body tighten. Following his line of sight, she saw a teenage boy leaning up against the building across the street. Grabbing her hand, Luke slipped through the crowd of people that still milled around in front of the office and darted across the street.

When the boy turned around and saw Luke, his face paled. He didn't have a chance to run, although she could see that he wanted to. As he backed away from them down the sidewalk, Luke said casually, "Good to see you, Piotyr." He paused, then said deliberately, "I saw your mother last night. What are you doing out here this morning?"

The boy licked his lips as his gaze darted between Luke and the bombed-out building. Julia thought she saw guilt flicker deep in his eyes before he answered.

"Just looking. Nothing wrong with that, is there?" he said defensively. His accent was much less noticeable than his mother's, and if she didn't know who he was she would have assumed he was just another kid, hanging out on the streets.

"There's nothing wrong with looking," Luke agreed. "But I think your school might have something to say about doing it now. Why aren't you in class?"

"They got nothing to teach me," Piotyr said with false bravado. "I'm thinking about dropping out."

"Oh, yeah?" Luke's voice was soft. "What kind of job are you going to get, Pete? You don't make a lot of money working as a bag boy at a grocery store."

"I'll get a job where I can make plenty of money," the boy boasted. "I don't need to go to school for that. Why do you think I'm here...?" He clamped his lips together and looked at them with fear in his eyes. "I've gotta go." He scooted around them and disappeared down a side street.

Luke watched him go, then turned to her with a thoughtful look on his face. "It looks like Piotyr is in deeper than I'd thought. Damn." He looked back for a moment to where the boy had disappeared, then shook his head. "Come on, let's get out of here. I've seen all I need to see."

She had to trot to keep up with him as he strode back to the car. Once they were inside, he started the engine and pressed the accelerator to the floor. Watching the rearview mirror, he frowned and slowed down.

"Are we being followed again?" She gripped the armrest on the door and resisted the urge to look behind her.

"There's no one behind me."

"Why is that wrong?" She looked over at him, bewildered.

"Because if they're not following us, they must have a reason. And none of the reasons I can think of are real appealing to me."

They cruised slowly up Milwaukee Avenue, but Julia could tell by the dark expression on his face that no one was behind them. When they got to Devon, he made a sharp right and sped up.

"Where are we going now?"

"To my house. There are a few things that I need."

After driving through a forest preserve that seemed out of place in the city, he turned down a side street and stopped in front of a small Cape Cod-style house. It was painted white with black shutters on the windows, but there were no flowers planted in the boxes that hung under the windows. The grass was just a little too long, and the shrubs were overgrown and gangly. The house had a depressed, dispirited look about it.

"I want you to wait in the car for me," he instructed as he got out. "I'll only be a minute."

She was surprised at the pang she felt at his words. He'd spent the night at her apartment, but he wouldn't even let her in the door of his house.

He must have noticed the expression on her face, because he opened the door on her side of the car and squatted next to her. "I don't want you to come in because I'm afraid there may be a bomb waiting for me here. There's no reason for both of us to get hurt."

As he pushed himself up from the ground and turned to the house, she jumped out of the car and grabbed his arm, ignoring the sudden tensing of his muscles. "If you think there may be a bomb in there, why go in at all? Call the Bomb Squad and have them check."

He turned around slowly. "This is a big case we're working on, Julia. You have no idea who may be involved. It may be only some of the men on your list, or it may be a lot bigger than that. Until we have more information, we don't trust anyone. There are a few things in that house I need, and I'm going to get them. Whoever set that bomb in my office knew what they were doing. It would be damn stupid to set another one in my home so soon afterward, and I don't think we're dealing with stupid people."

"In that case, why can't I come in with you?"

He stopped and turned around. "Because I'm not willing to gamble their stupidity against your life."

With that he disappeared into the house. Julia stood on the lawn and stared at the door, willing him to reappear quickly. The minutes seemed to stretch on forever as she waited, her muscles tensed against the explosion she was sure was coming any second.

He finally slipped out the door with a duffel bag in his hand. Locking the door carefully behind him, he said, "Nothing was disturbed, as far as I could tell. Let's get out of here."

He tossed his bag into the back seat and started the engine. She longed to ask him what was in the bag that was worth risking his life for, but instead she asked, "Where to now?"

He swung the car back onto a busy street and seemed to relax. Nodding toward her briefcase, he said, "Read me the names of the informants you've talked to."

It was back to business, back to something she had some control over, and she took a deep breath of relief. Standing in front of Luke's house, worrying about him and wondering when the explosion was coming that would blow him to tiny bits, she'd felt too naked and exposed. She'd felt some of her control slipping away, and it terrified her. It was way past time to get this relationship back on the business track, where it belonged.

Riffling through the papers in one folder, she pulled out a list and read him the names. When he looked over at her, she saw surprised respect in his eyes.

"You found a lot of the snitches the guys in my precinct use. How did you do it?"

"I did my homework." She shrugged. "If you're patient, you can find out almost anything."

"You did a good job."

The praise from Luke made her feel ridiculously proud. Her cheeks warm, she murmured, "Thank you."

"You missed one, though." He looked over at her and actually grinned, pleased, she was sure, to have one up on her. "My own personal snitch. He doesn't talk to anyone but me."

"Is that where we're going now?"

"You got it."

He accelerated and headed southeast, toward the inner city and downtown. In what seemed like a very short time they were in Humboldt Park, one of the neighborhoods in Luke's old precinct. As he parked the car on a side street, she looked at the dilapidated two- and three-story buildings and felt the depression of the neighborhood press in on her.

"Where are we going?"

"I told you, to talk to an old friend of mine." He eased out of the car and came around to open her door. "You'll find Raul very interesting. He knows a lot of people in this neighborhood."

"Why doesn't that impress me?" she muttered under her breath. Looking around, she couldn't help but notice the stillness. It was midday in the city, but there were no children playing in the front yards of the houses, no women walking down the street. It looked like an urban ghost town, only the occasional sound of music coming from an open window telling them there were people around.

She squared her shoulders as they walked down the silent streets. Luke didn't seem to notice her. His head moved constantly, looking at the buildings and the cars, but he moved with confidence, as if he belonged in this neighborhood.

"When we find Raul, keep your ears open and your mouth shut. He'll be wary enough as it is. I haven't talked to him in a long time."

I haven't had to talk to him much since I was dismissed from the police force. He didn't say the words out loud, but he didn't have to. Guilt rose in her and she pushed it furiously away. She had done the only thing she could have done, dammit. She hadn't had any choice.

Luke turned abruptly down another street, and she had to swerve to keep up with him. He walked down two blocks, still warily checking everything, before he slowed and turned into an alley. Briefly she wished she carried a gun. Alleys were notoriously dangerous, even in broad daylight. She prayed that Luke knew what he was doing.

He stopped in front of a garage that was just as neglected as all the other garages in the alley. The paint was peeling and the door hung in its frame at an odd angle. Several shingles were missing from the roof, and the windows were so encrusted with dirt and grime it was impossible to see through them.

Luke rapped sharply at the door with two knuckles. It was a code of some sort, she realized as he repeated the knock. In a few seconds the door opened and Luke pulled her through, shutting the door behind them.

The inside of the garage was as tidy and clean as the outside was dirty. In one corner stood a bed and a dresser, close to a hot plate and a tiny refrigerator. The majority of the space in the garage seemed to be used as a workroom.

Blocks of wood stood piled against the wall and on a workbench that dominated the room. Tools that looked like chisels were scattered on the surface of the workbench, and other oddly shaped instruments were attached to a Peg Board above the bench. Julia looked around the room, speechless, as Luke stepped to one side and she saw the man standing in front of them.

Slight and wiry, he wasn't much taller than she was. His black hair was pulled back into a low ponytail and a gold hoop glittered in one ear. His olive skin proclaimed that he was Latino, as were most of the other residents of the Humboldt Park neighborhood.

"I've missed you, Raul. How've you been?" Luke's voice was low, but Julia realized with surprise that he meant it.

"I'm okay." The other man's eyes were fixed on Julia. "Who's this?"

"Her name is Julia Carleton," Luke said easily, reaching for her hand. His palm slid over hers, warm and comforting. She curled her fingers around his and clung. "We're working together."

Raul's eyes narrowed. "You've always worked alone since you went out on your own."

"Things change and you do what you have to do." He stared at Raul. "You ought to know about that."

The smaller man flushed slightly. "If you vouch for her, I guess she's okay."

"I vouch for her." Luke's hand tightened on hers. "How's the carving going?" He nodded toward the workbench.

Raul smiled and his face softened as he walked over to the table and picked something up. Handing it to Luke, he said, "You tell me."

Luke let go of her hand and cradled the object in both of his. "It's beautiful, Raul."

Luke held a duck in his hands. The colors shimmered in the dim light by the door, and she would have sworn the duck was alive. It looked poised to dive under the water, every feather on its body quivering with anticipation.

"This is wonderful, Raul." She looked up from the carving to find Raul's eyes on hers. "It looks so real."

Raul's face relaxed into a proud smile, and he reached out and took the duck from Luke and placed it gently on the table. Luke ran his hand over it one more time, then looked at Raul.

"Have you enrolled in the Art Institute yet?"

The smile faded from Raul's eyes and he silently shook his head. "This isn't art, man. This is just wood carving."

"That's as beautiful as any sculpture I've seen at the Art Institute," Julia heard herself say.

Raul looked at her and he finally smiled again. "Thank you," he said softly. Then he looked at Luke and the smile slowly faded. "But I don't think you came here to admire my carvings."

"No, we didn't." Luke paused and looked at Raul, and Julia felt something unspoken swirl in the air for an instant.

Raul nodded. "I knew you would come here sooner or later." He glanced over at Julia. "She has been talking to a lot of people."

Startled, Julia opened her mouth. Luke's hand tightened on hers until she glanced over at him. The message in his eyes was plain. *Let me do the talking.*

"What do you know, Raul?" Luke asked.

Raul stared at him for a while, troubled, then turned and picked up one of his chisels. "There are a lot of rumors. The

Demons are boasting about certain things." Anger swept over his face. "Not only are they arrogant, it appears they are stupid, too. I have heard that some of the detectives from your old precinct have been cut into the action. The Demons are selling their drugs quite openly these days, and the only ones they arrest are the children who do the selling."

Julia felt the tension building in Luke. It sizzled through the hand she held like an electric current. "Have you heard any names?"

Raul shook his head. "Unfortunately, they aren't that stupid. But it is more than one. That I do know."

"Have you seen any of the detectives?"

He shrugged. "I don't know. The Demons are aware of my feelings and they stay away from me. It's possible I might have seen one or more of the detectives in the neighborhood, in places they shouldn't have been, and didn't realize it."

Julia knew how the gangs operated. If you weren't one of them, you were the enemy. She couldn't contain her curiosity about how Raul managed to live in this neighborhood and be openly scornful of the Demons.

"How do you manage to do it?" she asked. "Live here on your own terms, I mean."

Luke frowned, but Raul looked at her and smiled slightly. "I am a wood-carver. I have many talents with a knife."

She stared at the knives lying casually on the worktable as Luke pulled her toward the door. "Thank you, Raul. Your information has been valuable, as usual." He paused at the door before opening it. "You really should check with the Art Institute, you know. You're every damn bit as good as any other student there."

Two dull spots of color burned in Raul's cheeks. "Thank you, my friend. I will keep your words in mind."

Luke nodded then slipped out the door, pulling Julia with him. As they walked down the alley he didn't let go of her hand. She was ridiculously grateful as she eyed the decrepit garages that seemed to press in on them.

"He has an amazing talent," she said tentatively.

"Raul? Yeah, he's something, isn't he? I wonder why he won't apply to study at the Art Institute? He ought to know how good he is."

"I'm sure he does," she said dryly. "Didn't you see? He can't afford to go to school at the Art Institute and he knows it."

He stopped in his tracks and looked at her, amazement on his face. "Why do you think that?"

"It's pretty obvious, isn't it? Does he ever display his birds at craft shows or art fairs?"

"Not that I know of. He'd have no way to get to one."

"Do you think he lives in a garage by choice?"

"What's that supposed to mean?"

"It means that he doesn't have any money and he's too proud to admit it," she said impatiently. "Honestly, Luke, you're supposed to know him. Why haven't you figured that out yet?"

He looked at her, dumbstruck, and she almost laughed at his expression. She'd known immediately what the look in Raul's eyes meant. "You mean he's hiding in that garage because he doesn't want to ask anyone for the money to go to school?" he asked slowly.

"I'm sure he is." Her voice was gentle. "He's too proud to ask for that kind of help."

Luke stared at her for a moment, then his lips curled up in a smile. His grip shifted on her hand and he started down the alley again. "If you're right, I know just the cure for Raul's kind of stubbornness." They turned onto the side street again and headed for the block where they'd left their car. He smiled again and got a faraway look in his eyes.

A strange warmth flooded through her as she watched him. Just as she opened her mouth to ask him what he was going to do, he jerked to a stop and let go of her hand. Slowly she turned her head to find a group of five youths in orange-and-green jackets blocking their way.

Chapter 6

One of the boys flicked open a switchblade knife and began to clean his fingernails. All of the others crowded closer to him, forming an impenetrable wall on the sidewalk.

Julia felt Luke tense beside her as she beat down the panic that wanted to bubble up to the surface. *Think,* she ordered herself fiercely. They wouldn't win this fight if they relied on brute strength or her badge or even the gun she'd glimpsed under Luke's jacket. They were outnumbered, and the punks in front of them stood too close and watched too carefully.

"Thank goodness," she gushed, looking at the group in front of them. Her hand clamped on Luke's, willing him to be quiet. "You don't have any idea how glad we are to see you."

The gang members watched her, an excited, predatory expression stirring in their eyes. "Yeah, well, that's good to hear. Because we're real glad to see you, too."

It was the one with the switchblade who spoke. Apparently he was the leader. She addressed her next remark to him, ignoring the way he was testing the blade of the knife against his thumb. "Oh, good, you must have been looking for us." She reached inside her briefcase and pulled out a piece of paper at random, proud of the fact that her hand barely shook. "Is Sylvia Mendenez related to one of you?"

She looked from one face to another expectantly. The excited expression slowly faded from their eyes and they simply looked wary now. "You said you were glad to see us. I assumed one of you must be related to Sylvia." She let her voice take on a petulant tone as she watched them. "Well? Which one of you is it?"

The five boys looked at one another, bewildered. Finally the leader took control again, stepping closer. "We don't know anyone named Sylvia." His voice was low and menacing.

"Well, then, maybe you can tell us how to get to her house. Her address is 2612 Evergreen Street." She paused and looked at them expectantly.

"We don't give a damn about Sylvia Mendenez." The knife glittered and the leader took another step toward them. "There's only one thing we're interested in." His eyes raked over her, lingering at her breasts. "Maybe two."

Julia prepared to swing her briefcase as she felt Luke gathering himself. She let her hand slide from his hand up his arm in what she hoped looked like a casual gesture. She gripped his sleeve and held on tightly, hoping he understood. "If you don't care about Sylvia, you should care about your own relatives." She took a step forward, pointing her briefcase at the leader. "Do you have a sister? Or a girlfriend?"

He frowned, and the knife was briefly still. "What do they have to do with anything?"

Julia nodded at Luke. "We're visiting nurses. It's our job to make sure that the people in your neighborhood have good medical care." She paused and glowered at him. "If it was your sister I was visiting, I'm sure you'd want to help. And if you can tell us where 2612 Evergreen Street is, we would appreciate it. Sylvia is expecting us, and we're already late."

Luke must have figured out what she was doing, because he gently disengaged his hand and rested it lightly on his hip.

His relaxed appearance didn't fool her at all. She knew he would spring into action if the gang leader took another step forward, and as she waited she held her breath, praying she'd done the right thing.

"Remember when one of them visited Yolanda last year?" It was one of the boys who stood behind the leader, a child who couldn't have been older than fourteen. "The nurse took real good care of her."

The leader turned around slowly. "Are you saying you want to let them go?"

Julia heard the menace in his voice and prayed silently. She didn't dare look at Luke.

"Tell her where this Sylvia lives and leave them alone. My mama hasn't been feeling too good lately. Maybe they'll come back and help her." It was another of the boys who spoke, and Julia slowly let out the breath she'd been holding.

The leader turned back to them. He watched them for a long time, then suddenly flicked the knife blade back into its case with a fluid motion. "Since you are here to help our families, we will help you." He gave them directions to the fictitious address on the street Julia had remembered seeing, then stood aside so they could pass. All the other boys fell into place behind him.

Julia inclined her head. "Thank you for your assistance. Perhaps we'll meet again if anyone in your family ever needs help."

Luke nodded curtly to the gang as they walked past them. The hairs on the back of Julia's neck stood straight up as they walked away. Every muscle in her body tensed, expecting to be grabbed from behind at any moment. When they had put a half block between them and the gang, she started to walk faster. Luke took her elbow and made her slow down, muttering, "Don't blow it now. If it looks like you're panicking, they'll be on us in an instant."

When they turned the corner onto the block where they'd left his car and were out of sight of the gang, she took a deep shuddering breath and let her shoulders sag. Luke looked down at her, then put his arm around her.

"It's just a few more feet to the car. Come on, Julia. Don't fall apart on me now." His voice was low and soothing, and she wanted nothing more than to close her eyes and lose herself in its comfort.

"I am not falling apart. It's just a reaction to the adrenaline." Gritting her teeth, she fixed her eyes on his car and forced herself to put one foot in front of the other.

When they got to the car, Luke yanked open the door and practically pushed her into it. In another moment he was behind the wheel, pulling away from the curb and heading for the nearest busy street. Neither of them said a word until he pulled up at a small park in the Lincoln Park neighborhood.

Luke turned and looked at Julia. She sat rigid on the seat, staring out the window. When he reached over and touched her hand, it was ice-cold.

Unbuckling his seat belt, he slid across the bench seat and curled his arm around her shoulders. She went into his embrace willingly, burying her face in his shoulder.

"It's all right, Julia," he murmured into her hair. Her subtle scent drifted up to him and he tightened his hold on her. "We're okay. We got away and nothing happened."

She leaned back and looked at him. He felt the tremor that ran through her. "I've seen some horrible things in my years with Internal Affairs," she whispered. "But do you know what got to me? Their eyes." She shuddered. "Did you see their eyes? They were only children, and their eyes were dead. They would have killed us, Luke, and not thought anything of it."

They wouldn't have been killed, he thought grimly, pulling her close once more. But he wasn't sure Julia needed to know what it was they had in mind. Thinking about the way the leader of the gang had looked at Julia's breasts brought the fury bubbling up in Luke all over again. He still wasn't sure how he had managed to restrain himself.

"They didn't do anything to us," he said again. "And it was because of the way you handled them." *No thanks to you, McKinley.* He eased her away from him and looked down at her, his face grim. "It's a good thing one of us was awake."

She shrugged and looked away. "I knew it wouldn't be a fair fight with five of them against two of us. It was the first thing I thought of."

She obviously had dismissed the gun tucked into the small of his back, and rightly so. A hell of a lot of good it had done since he'd let those punks get too close to take a chance on pulling it out. If he hadn't been so preoccupied with her and Raul, he would have noticed that group of hoodlums earlier and been ready to handle them.

That's what happened when you let yourself be distracted on the job. One small slip could have big repercussions. If it hadn't been for Julia's quick thinking, it could have gotten very messy. The last thing he'd wanted to do was advertise their presence in that neighborhood today.

His hand curled around Julia, pulling her close for the space of a heartbeat, then he set her away from him. Forcing himself to move away from her, when all he wanted to do was pull her back into his arms and hold her there, he said, "Why don't we go for a little walk?"

Before she could answer he was out of the car and around to her door. When he opened it, she looked up at him and got out without a word. Shoving her hands into the pockets of her blazer, she headed toward the playground, where several children ran and played on the elaborate equipment.

"Thank you," he said as he caught up with her. "You saved my neck back there, and I know it." He bit the words off one by one.

She slanted him a look and kept going, her toe kicking up small bits of gravel as she walked. "You don't sound real happy about it," she murmured.

"Of course I'm not happy about it," he snapped. "If I'd been doing my job, it wouldn't have been necessary for you to play out that little charade."

She turned to him, a flare of anger in her eyes. That was good, he told himself as he looked away. If she was angry enough, there wouldn't be room for her fear.

"Your way would have left bleeding bodies behind. Is that what's necessary for you to feel you've done your job?"

He met her gaze and held it, thankful for the anger that now swept through him. It was better than the guilt. "That's certainly been the case in the past, hasn't it? The drunken driver who killed my wife would attest to that."

As he watched, her anger drained away, replaced by a softness in her eyes that he didn't want to see. Turning away from her, he marched toward the center of the park, not bothering to see if she was following.

Picking out a bench that stood in the early spring sunshine, he lowered himself down and looked at the children playing. Women sat in small groups on the other benches, keeping a watchful eye on the children climbing on the playground equipment.

She slid onto the bench next to him. Watching the children for a while, she finally murmured, "You're not a comic book hero, you know. You can't always save everyone."

He wondered if she was talking about what had just happened, or about the accident that had killed his wife. It didn't matter, he thought bleakly. Nothing could ever change what had happened that night, or the responsibility he felt for it.

"I didn't have to be a hero of any kind to see the problem with that gang coming," he retorted. "I just needed to be paying attention." He turned to look at her then. "That's a dangerous neighborhood, Julia. There's no excuse for allowing something like that to happen."

"A lot of things happen that you can't control, Luke." Her voice was very gentle, and again he wondered if she was talking about that morning or a rainy night two years ago. "What matters is that we survived and handled it. Can we forget about it and go on?"

"Yeah," he muttered. "It's not something I'm going to want to remember, anyway."

"At least you could give me some credit, instead of brooding about the fact that you weren't paying attention," she said with asperity.

He watched her indignant face and felt something loosen inside of him. She was right. Instead of brooding about his own failures, he should be giving her the credit she deserved. In spite of himself he smiled. "You did a hell of a job, Julia. It was a brilliant idea." His smile widened until he almost found himself laughing. "That gang leader didn't know what had hit him."

She grinned. "Apparently he'd never run into a determined woman before."

"Apparently not." Luke's smile faded as he looked at the woman beside him and thought about what might have happened to her today. Slowly he reached out and pulled her toward him. "Thank you, Julia," he whispered. "Thank you for saving both of us."

She didn't resist as he lowered his mouth to cover hers. Her lips were cold and tasted of the fresh spring air, and they trembled as he brushed his mouth over hers. Closing his eyes, he told himself to stop. This couldn't happen, not with this woman. But when he deepened the kiss and she opened her mouth without hesitation, he knew he was lost.

Her hands on his chest clenched into fists, but she didn't try to push him away. Instead she slowly uncurled her fingers and pressed them into his chest. His skin burned, even through the flannel shirt he wore. With an inarticulate murmur, he let go of her shoulders and pulled her into his arms.

As he held her close he felt her struggling against him. He immediately loosened his hold, but she pulled her arms free and wrapped them around his neck.

She leaned into him, uncapping a volcano of need inside him. He burned with it, his muscles tightening and his blood pounding until he could think of nothing but the need for her driving inside him. He wanted to bury himself inside her, sink into her softness and claim her as his.

He tore his mouth away from hers and trailed kisses down her neck. Her blazer was an intolerable barrier and he pulled it aside, crumpling the soft material in his fist. Vaguely he felt her hand in his hair, holding him tightly. As he dipped his tongue into the hollow of her collarbone she whimpered once, into his ear. Blindly he began to unfasten the tiny buttons on her blouse, until she pulled back and looked at him with startled eyes.

Her eyes were as full of passion and desire as he knew his own had to be. Letting go of her with one hand, he brushed the hair back from her face, noticing that his hand shook. "I'm sorry," he whispered. "I forgot where we were."

He watched as desire fought with common sense in her eyes. It seemed like a long time before the common sense finally won, and he groaned and pulled her back to him. She resisted stiffly, and he bent down to her ear.

"It's okay. I just want to hold you for a minute." He slipped one hand under her wool jacket and stroked down her back. The silk of her blouse was hot, heated by her skin. His hand hovered near her waist, and when he felt the shiver she tried to hide it took all his strength not to pull her close again.

Finally he pulled away from her. When he looked at her, he found her watching him with equal parts desire and fear in her eyes. Her emotions so closely matched his own that he closed his eyes and with a supreme effort of will forced the shuddering need into a box and slammed down the lid. He tucked it away in a dark corner of his soul where it could stay untouched. He couldn't allow himself to want anyone this way, especially not Julia Carleton.

"Reaction makes you do funny things, doesn't it?" Her voice was too bright, and her cheeks were a dull red as she plucked at the material of her skirt and refused to meet his eyes. "Release of tension and all that, I guess."

"Right." He stared at her averted head and felt a perverse kick of anger. "God knows it would be completely unthinkable that you could actually want me."

At that she raised her head to look at him. "Just like you would rather die than want me," she agreed. Her cheeks still flamed, but she met his eyes squarely.

"I'm glad we have that straight." He stood up abruptly. "We've given these women here enough of a show. Are you ready to go?"

"Yes." She stood up and brushed her hands down her skirt. "Where are we going?"

He ran his fingers through his hair and thought for a minute. There wasn't actually any place where he was sure they'd be safe. "I'm not sure," he answered reluctantly. "But since we're in your neighborhood, we might as well go back to your apartment for a while. It's probably safer than my house right now."

She nodded wordlessly and began to walk back to his car. She'd managed to draw that mantle of cool disdain around herself again, and he swore under his breath as he looked at the aloof expression on her face. Dammit, he didn't like the ice princess persona of Julia Carleton.

But the ice princess was much safer than the vulnerable woman. At least for him.

From now on he'd damn well keep his hands to himself. He watched her walk around to the other side of the car until he realized that his hand hurt. Looking down, he saw that his fist was closed over his keys and they were cutting into his palm.

As he forced his fingers to loosen, he looked at her again and reminded himself of all the reasons why he couldn't want her. Having to keep a cool head and an objective eye on this case was just the first one. If he forgot what had happened two years ago, he would be doomed to repeat his mistakes again. And he knew he'd never survive a second time in hell.

Julia looked around her apartment and wondered why it looked like a stranger's home. It had only been a few short hours ago that she'd left it, but it didn't seem the same somehow. Shaking herself, she began to walk toward the kitchen. She'd never been so fanciful before.

"Would you like some coffee?" she asked over her shoulder.

"Sounds good."

Luke's voice was muffled, and she stopped and watched him for a moment, curious. He had the door to her entertainment center open and he seemed to be fiddling with something in the back of her television. When he backed out and went to stand in front of her bookcase, she shrugged and turned back to the kitchen.

She'd just poured the water into the coffeemaker and was about to turn the switch when his hand reached out and circled her wrist. She turned around with a start to find him standing too close, his face grim.

"What is it?" She searched his face. "What's wrong, Luke?"

"Don't turn that on. Don't touch anything in here, in fact." He tugged on her wrist and led her out of the kitchen. "Someone's been in your apartment since we left this morning. And in light of what happened in my office, I don't think we can take any chances."

"Someone's been in here?" she whispered, looking around, feeling sudden fear tighten around her like a vise.

"Yes. Someone involved with this case is playing hardball. I didn't think they'd go after you, but I don't want to play the odds on that. I think the safest thing for both of us is to assume that this apartment is wired and get the hell out of here."

"What do you mean, wired?" she said dumbly. Her brain was frozen. She heard Luke's words, but they didn't register. She knew she looked like an idiot, standing there and repeating everything he said, but she couldn't help herself. The fact that someone had been in her apartment was all that registered. She shivered and wrapped her arms around herself. Someone had violated her home and her privacy.

Instead of the impatient disgust she expected to see in his face, his eyes suddenly softened and a rueful smile flitted across his mouth. "Your usual Internal Affairs cases aren't like this, are they?"

She could only stare at him, amazed by the transformation.

Misunderstanding her silence, he said softly, "Julia, someone searched your apartment while we were gone. That's probably all they did, but I don't want to take any chances. I'm afraid they might have stashed a bomb in here."

When she continued to stare, he shook his head. "You're a damn good investigator, Julia, but obviously you've never been a part of this kind of case before. There's a lot at stake here for everyone involved. They've demonstrated once that they don't object to a little violence, and I don't want you to be the next victim of it."

Finally she shook her head. She couldn't tell him the reason she was speechless was the concern in his voice. And even if she could, she told herself, he wouldn't want to hear it. "I'm just surprised, that's all," she finally said. "I didn't think they were that desperate. After all, I don't have any real evidence yet."

"But they don't know that," he replied. "All they know is that you're investigating this, and they've obviously figured out that you've hired me to help you." His mouth thinned. "I told you yesterday that you were going to have to prove to me that you had a case, but someone is doing a damn good job of proving it for you."

He looked around the room again then headed for her bedroom. "Come on, Julia. Grab some clothes and let's get out of here."

She didn't need to be told again. Hurrying into her bedroom, she opened her closet and stared at the rows of suits, trying to decide which ones to take. Behind her, she could hear Luke rummaging in her drawers.

"Don't bother with those monkey suits," he said impatiently behind her. "You're not going into the office for a while, anyway. Here." He handed her a stack of jeans and sweaters. "This is the kind of stuff you need."

She accepted the clothes and stood staring at him while he turned back to her dresser. He went through her drawers, pulling out her clothes and inspecting each article before handing it to her. Something stirred inside her and a faint throbbing began, deep in her belly. Never before had a man performed such an intimate task for her. As she watched him, a faint whisper of the desire she'd felt in the park echoed through her.

"Here you go." He turned around and handed her another pile of sweatshirts and sweatpants. "You're going to have to get your own underwear. I draw the line at—"

He stopped abruptly as his eyes met hers. Desire that answered hers bloomed in his eyes, and she took a step backward. She didn't want this. She *couldn't* want this, she told herself desperately. She knew only too well what happened when you mixed business with pleasure. That lesson had been burned into her. Luke was working on this case with her and she had to keep her wits about her when she was with him. She couldn't afford to forget what was at stake.

And every time he'd touched her she'd done just that. Thoughts of Bobby and what she was risking came flooding over her, and she took another step backward and spun around, fumbling on the top shelf of her closet.

Pulling down a suitcase, she turned around with a bright smile plastered to her face. "This should hold everything."

Luke watched her for a moment, then turned on his heel and walked out of the room. "Get everything packed and do it fast." His voice was flat and carefully controlled. "I want to get out of here now."

Her hands trembled as she folded her clothes into the suitcase. Was it because she was afraid to be in the apartment, or was it because she was afraid of the feelings Luke aroused in her? a small voice in her mind asked. Ignoring it, she grabbed a handful of the silk-and-lace underwear she wore and stuffed it all into the suitcase, then slammed the lid shut.

Walking into the living room, she said, "I'm ready to go."

She looked around again as Luke led the way to the door, wondering if there really was a bomb in her home. Would she ever see her belongings again? Impulsively she stopped in front of the bookcase and reached for her photo albums. She couldn't bear it if twenty-eight years of family memories were to disappear in a flash of smoke and flame.

As she bent to pick up her suitcase the blinking red light of her telephone answering machine caught her eye. "Just a moment, Luke," she called. "There's a message on my answering machine."

"Forget it." He reached for the doorknob.

"What do you mean, forget it? It could be something related to this case."

He strode over and grabbed her hand just as she was about to push the button. "I mean don't touch it. That's one of the newer ways of detonating bombs. Who can resist a message on the answering machine? You see the light flashing, you push the button, and bam, next thing you know you're wearing wings and playing a harp."

Her hand froze in midair. Luke's fingers were warm on her suddenly cold flesh. This was real, she thought numbly. She had been one second away from pushing that button and possibly killing both herself and Luke. Her hand dropped nervelessly to her side and she backed toward the door, never taking her eyes off the telephone answering machine. Instead of the harmless piece of plastic and wires that stood on the shelf, she saw a living, breathing monster, just waiting for the opportunity to devour both of them.

Luke closed the door behind them and locked it with a quiet click. Then, setting her suitcase carefully on the floor, he touched her shoulder. "I'm sorry, Julia. I'm sorry I had to scare you. But there's no getting around the fact that someone has been in your apartment. Maybe they just wanted a look at those files that you carry around with you. Maybe they planted a bug so they could hear what we were talking about."

He paused, and she wondered if he knew how much his eyes revealed. There was concern in their dark blue depths, and real fear. Fear for her, she realized slowly, feeling some of the warmth return to her skin.

"Maybe there wasn't a bomb in there at all. But I didn't want to take that chance." He smiled slightly. "At least not until you've paid me."

He was making a joke so she'd forget about her fear, she tried to tell herself. But it didn't work. Memories came flooding back of the time in the past when she'd made the mistake of thinking someone cared for her, only to find it was her job he cared about. It was the same thing now, except that this time it was her money. That's all she was to

Luke, a paycheck, and she'd better not forget it. Perhaps he thought the paycheck had a nice body, but that was as far as it went. He'd made that clear enough.

"Don't worry," she said in a cool voice. "I've left a note in my files regarding your employment. You'll get paid, regardless of what happens."

The smile faded from his face. "Dammit, Julia, that's not what I meant and you know it. It was a joke, for crying out loud."

"Was it?" She gave him a frosty look. "It sounded like the simple truth to me."

They'd reached the bottom of the stairs, and he yanked open the security door and stormed through it. Just as he was about to bolt through the outer door of the apartment building, he stopped so abruptly that she bumped into him. She jumped backward as if she'd accidentally stepped onto a live wire, and watched as he looked out the door.

"Is there a back door to this building?" he asked in a low voice.

Her anger and hurt dissolved instantly, replaced by the fear she'd thought she'd left upstairs. "There's a door from the laundry room into the alley." She began moving toward the door half-hidden under the stairs as she spoke.

"Is it locked?"

She wondered at the tenseness in his voice as she nodded. He handed her the keys without a word, and she fumbled for a moment until she found the right one. Her hand shaking, she unlocked the door and reached for the light switch.

He stopped her just before her hand touched the switch on the wall. "There's enough light from the window. We don't need to advertise that we're here."

She nodded again, jerkily, and began to lead the way through the narrow room. The building maintenance man left most of his tools propped against the wall, and in the semidarkness the odd shapes took on a menacing appearance. She kept her eyes firmly on the light from the door at the back of the room and steadily made her way toward it.

When she reached the door she stopped. There was nothing to see through the dirty window except the tiny square of grass that constituted the backyard of the building, and the tall fence that surrounded it. Luke unlocked the door and eased out into the yard, signaling for her to follow him.

There was no one in the alley when they slipped out the gate in the fence. She gulped in fresh air as they walked toward the street. This alley was suddenly as sinister as the one in Humboldt Park where they'd visited Raul earlier that morning. The narrow walkways next to each garage made perfect hiding places for an ambush. Their footsteps seemed to echo as loudly as gunshots, and each piece of gravel they kicked down the concrete sounded like the click of a safety being drawn off a gun.

By the time they reached the end of the alley, sweat had run in rivulets down her back and sides. Her heart was pounding so loudly in her ears that when Luke spoke, she had trouble hearing him.

"What did you say?" she asked in a harsh whisper.

"I said it was a good thing we parked around the corner from your apartment." His voice was matter-of-fact. "Our friend in the black sedan was sitting right in front of your building, waiting for us to come out."

Or waiting for the sound of an explosion. Luke didn't say the words, but she could see them in his eyes. "What do we do now?" she said through stiff lips.

"We get in the car and leave. If they follow us, I can lose them."

He began walking toward his car, and she hurried to keep up with him. She felt numb inside. In the space of a morning, she'd been threatened by a gang, warned that her apartment might be rigged with a bomb, and now told that someone waited for them at the entrance to her building, not even concerned about keeping himself hidden. What had happened since yesterday that had set her world on its end?

She looked at the man next to her. Lucas McKinley had begun to disrupt her carefully constructed world from the moment she'd walked into his office the day before. But then, she'd known all along that he would, hadn't she?

Chapter 7

Julia turned around in her seat again and peered out the rear window. "It's kind of strange, isn't it?" she asked Luke.

"What is?" He didn't look over at her as he continued to drive, his eyes moving almost constantly to the rearview mirror.

"That we were able to get away this easily. Shouldn't they have had someone following us?"

He scowled, never taking his eyes off the road. "Yeah. Which is why I'm worried. Either I'm a genius or they're the dumbest bunch of dirtbags to ever come down the pike. And I know I'm no Einstein."

"Maybe they really are that stupid."

He shot her a quick glance then looked back at the street again. "Never underestimate your enemy, Julia. It could be a fatal mistake."

She studied him for a moment, his hands gripping the steering wheel and his eyes watching everything, then glanced around. They were on Lincoln Avenue, on the north side of Chicago. She was a Chicago native, but she'd never been in this part of the city before. The street was lined with motels, one after another for blocks. All of them looked identical—seedy and run-down, with a furtive air about them that made her want to look over her shoulder.

"Is this where we're going to stay?" she asked as Luke pulled into one of the motel parking lots. The blinds were tightly drawn on all the tiny windows of the three-story building. Quiet and almost deserted, it looked like the kind of place that hugged its secrets to itself.

"It looked as good as any of the others." He tore his gaze away from the street to glance over at her. "It won't be luxury accommodations, but these places don't ask many questions."

"Why are there all these motels in the middle of nowhere, anyway?" she asked, glancing over at him. "It's not like they're close to downtown or any of the typical tourist attractions."

He shrugged. "Who knows why they were built here originally? Now, I suspect, they serve a clientele that demand discretion." He slanted a look in her direction. "You have heard of no-tell motels, haven't you?"

She let her gaze drift over the string of motels once more. They did look like the kind of places that would cater to the long-lunch-hour crowd, she reluctantly conceded. Her eyes shifted to the man sitting next to her and she shivered. She was going to be staying here with Lucas McKinley.

Refusing to let her mind diverge in that direction, she looked instead at the highway in front of them. After a while she began to feel dizzy, watching one car after another zip by. Just as she turned to Luke to ask him how long they had to sit here and watch, he turned the key in the ignition and pulled around to the back of the motel.

"I'm going to go in and register. You wait in the car."

Without waiting for an answer, he got out of the car and strode away. As she watched his long-limbed, flowing walk, she realized there was no trace of the stiffness she'd noticed earlier this morning. He must heal quickly, she thought, letting her gaze linger on his lean, tough frame. That toughness was deceptive, she thought. For a man of his size, he'd been surprisingly gentle when he'd held her that morning.

She closed her eyes to block out the memory of the kiss they'd shared. They were both just reacting to stress, she told herself. That's all there was to it. When she opened her eyes again, Luke was the first thing she saw. He stood at the door to the hotel, adjusting his jacket. When he moved, she saw the flash of metal at the small of his back.

She stared at the spot until he'd disappeared into the office. She'd known the gun was there, had seen it earlier, but it still repelled her. It was an ugly symbol of everything they were hiding from.

It seemed like only a minute before he came striding out the door and toward the car. The wind picked up his long dark hair and blew it around his face, and he hunched his shoulders against its force. When Julia found herself watching the way he moved, she swung around in her seat and fished for her bag in the back seat. She was tugging the bulky bag onto her lap when Luke got into the car.

"We're all set." He reached into the back seat for his own bag, then slid out the door. "We're on the third floor, in the back. If anyone asks, you're Sally Smith."

Her heart boomed as she wondered whether he'd thought to ask for two beds in their room. "And I suppose you're John Smith?" she asked waspishly.

He looked wounded. "I'm more original than that. I'm John Jones."

Some of the tension eased, and she forced herself to smile. "I beg your pardon, Mr. Jones. Lead the way."

They walked up the stairs and through the dimly lit corridors of the third floor until he stopped in front of a room. When he unlocked the door and stepped inside she followed him, trying to see the layout of the room in the darkness.

He flipped a switch on the wall, and bright light flooded the room. There was one king-size bed that seemed to take up the whole room, and she felt color flood her face as she stared at it. Surely he didn't expect her to sleep in that bed with him. It looked enormous from here, but she knew it would feel minuscule if they were both lying in it.

"It seems okay," he said with a critical glance around the room. She had no idea what the rest of the room looked like. The only thing she saw was the bed. When she realized she wasn't sure if she was appalled or secretly thrilled at the idea of sharing it with him, her face flamed even hotter.

"My room is the next one. That door connects them."

When she realized what he was saying she tore her gaze away from the bed and looked at the door in the wall right next to it. He wasn't sharing this room with her. He had his own room, right next door. Willing the color to recede from her cheeks, she mumbled, "Okay."

"You're blushing." He sounded thunderstruck. "You didn't think we were sharing a room, did you?"

He was standing much too close and studying her too carefully. "I had no idea. But you can be sure I'm relieved that we're not." Snapping her mouth shut, she refused to look at him.

"You're not the only one," she thought she heard him mutter as he turned to pick up his bag. "Open the connecting door," he instructed. "And keep the chain on the door to the hall."

He closed the door gently behind him. After a moment, she heard him moving around in the next room and she unlocked the connecting door. When she heard him push it open a few minutes later, she was kneeling in front of the lopsided dresser unpacking her suitcase.

"Like I said, the accommodations aren't luxurious, but they're nice and anonymous."

She turned around to find him leaning against the doorframe, watching her with expressionless eyes. He looked relaxed, but tension seemed to pour off him and the muscles in his arms looked tight and hard.

"No black sedans in the parking lot?" she asked, trying to make her voice sound light.

"Not a one," he drawled. His eyes left her and drifted over the pile of clothes she'd placed on the bed. Following his gaze, she realized that the underwear that he hadn't wanted to see back at her apartment was spread over the rest of her clothes, out in plain view. She snatched it up and stuffed it into a drawer without looking at him.

"I hope you brought something to do." His voice was remote, and when she looked at him, she saw he was looking at a spot over her head. "We're going to be here for a while."

"It'll be the perfect chance to go over my notes again." Putting the last of her clothes away, she stood up and faced him. Taking a deep breath, she added, "Maybe this time I'll find something."

"Maybe you will." He brought his gaze to hers and added, "Why don't I look at some of them? In all the excitement, I've never had a chance to look at all your notes."

"That's a good idea." Maybe if they were working on this case she could ignore the charged atmosphere in the room. Maybe if they were both looking at her notes, she wouldn't feel as if she'd been burned every time he looked at her.

As she took the pile of file folders out of her briefcase, she remembered the blinking red light on her telephone answering machine. "Would it be all right if I called my answering machine?" she asked. "There was a message on it, remember? It might be from someone connected with this case."

He shook his head. "I'm going to get the Bomb Squad in there first. If they don't find anything you can get your messages."

An hour later, Luke got an all-clear, so she called her phone number and punched in the security code for her answering machine. After listening to her own voice asking the caller to leave a message, she heard a click and then her brother Bobby's voice, startlingly loud.

"Hey, Skinny, how're you doing? I thought I'd make good on that rain check I owe you tonight, if that's okay with you. Meet me at the usual place at eight o'clock. If you can't make it, give me a call. Otherwise, I'll see you there."

The machine clicked off, and Julia stood staring down at the telephone that stood on the night table. Bobby's words had sounded light and jovial, but underneath his voice was strained. Beneath the casual, teasing words was a desperation that was barely concealed.

Oh, Bobby, what's going on? she cried silently. *What's wrong?*

Slowly she replaced the receiver in its cradle and looked up at Luke. His eyes had sharpened, as if he'd heard Bobby's words.

"There was a message from my brother Bobby." It took every bit of effort she could manage to make her voice sound casual. "He wants to go to dinner tonight."

Luke watched her for a long moment. He'd shuttered his eyes, so she had no idea what he was thinking. Finally he said, "That sounds like a good idea."

Julia stopped twenty feet away from the door to the restaurant and turned to Luke. "All right, you can come into the restaurant with me. But you can't sit with us. You sit at a table by the door and I'll sit with my brother."

He shook his head. "No way, Julia. Either I'm with you or we're going back to the motel. I've already told you, this isn't negotiable. If you want to have dinner with your brother, that's fine. But I'm going to be there."

She looked at him, frustration and desperation burning a hole in her stomach. When he'd told her to have dinner with Bobby, she'd been surprised and pleased. Bobby obviously had something important to say to her, and she had to hear what it was. But when Luke had added that he'd be joining them for dinner, she'd panicked.

Whatever Bobby had to say wasn't for Luke's ears. She knew that with every instinct in her soul. The whole reason for hiring Luke was to protect Bobby. And now, when Bobby was apparently finally ready to tell her what was going on, Luke insisted on being there.

She stopped at the restaurant door. "Luke, Bobby is my brother," she pleaded. "Surely I can trust my own brother, can't I?"

"You'd think so," he said, pulling open the door. "But we don't want any nasty surprises, do we?"

She stared at him, speechless, as he stood waiting patiently for her to go inside. "What is that supposed to mean?" she finally demanded.

"I mean that until we know who's involved in this mess, we don't trust anyone. Not your brother, not your best friend, not even my mother. No one. That's how we stay alive to find out what's going on."

The smell of garlic and butter drifted out of the restaurant into the cool spring air, but Julia had completely lost her appetite. She wanted to turn around and run back the way they'd come, but she didn't dare. Luke would immediately wonder why she didn't want to meet with her brother in his presence. No, she'd have to bluff her way through this evening.

And so would Bobby. Her troubled gaze searched through the restaurant until she found her brother, lounging back against a booth and drinking a beer. If her suspicions were correct, bluffing was something Bobby had become very good at lately.

"Hey, Skinny," he began, standing up with a broad grin when he saw her approaching. "I was beginning to worry that—"

He stopped abruptly when he saw Luke behind her, and the grin faded. "I didn't know you were bringing someone."

"Luke wanted to get to know you better." Her eyes pleaded with her brother for understanding, and his nod was almost imperceptible.

"Any particular reason?" Bobby looked at Luke, challenge in his eyes, and Luke obligingly slipped an arm around her waist.

"The usual," he answered smoothly. Looking down at her with what she figured was supposed to be fondness, he added, "I want to know everything about Julia."

Julia wanted to gag. Stepping away from Luke, she said to Bobby brightly, "I hope you don't mind that I brought company. Luke just insisted on coming with me."

Her eyes warned her brother to be careful, and Bobby grinned at her reassuringly. Turning to Luke, he said, "Ain't young love grand?"

"You could say that." Pulling out a chair, Luke sat down at the table between Julia and her brother and smiled blandly. "How about a bottle of wine?"

An hour and a half later Luke leaned back in his chair and watched Julia talk to her brother. At first she'd been stiff and uncomfortable, and the conversation at the small table had been stilted. Even when she wasn't looking at him he felt the waves of anger and resentment that rolled off her.

But as the evening progressed there had been a gradual lessening of the tension that hovered over the group. Bobby Carleton had gone out of his way to be charming and sociable, telling stories about his precinct that had even Luke smiling. Luke had been very careful not to touch Julia again, and as he'd watched Julia he'd realized that she was gradually relaxing her guard.

Why she felt she needed to be on her guard in the first place was another question altogether. On the surface Bobby and Julia were a typical brother and sister, teasing each other and talking about their siblings and their parents. But Luke sensed a wariness about Julia, as if she were watching Bobby too closely. And Bobby was too glib and too charming, Luke thought. It made him wonder if Bobby had something to hide.

Glancing at her watch, Julia pushed away from the table. "I guess it's time to get going." She reached for the check, as did Luke, but Bobby snatched it away.

"This one's on me, guys," he said with a grin. Looking over at Luke, his eyes calculating, he added, "Think of it as a welcome to the family, McKinley."

"Knock it off, Bobby," Julia said, looking uncomfortable. "I've only known him for a few days."

"Love at first sight, huh?" Bobby raised his eyebrows. "How romantic."

"You got it." Luke rose from the table and reached for Julia's coat. "Thanks for the dinner, Carleton."

"Anytime," Bobby answered easily. "You're always welcome when Skinny and I get together. Right, Skinny?"

"Don't call me that, Bobby." Julia's voice was sharp, and Luke looked over at her, surprised.

Her eyes were stormy and the anger was back. But this time it was directed at her brother instead of him.

"Hey, sorry, Julia." Bobby held up his hands in mock surrender. "It's just a nickname."

Luke held her coat as she slipped her arms in, then slid his hand down to her waist. "But not a particularly apt one," he murmured. Her hip was soft and curved under his fingertips, and he let his hand linger there for a minute before he placed it in the small of her back. He wasn't sure if the heat was coming from him or her.

He felt her stiffen next to him, and she tried to move away. Smiling blandly at Bobby, Luke said, "Thanks for dinner. We'll be seeing you."

They stepped into the windy night and he had to fight the urge to wrap his arm around her and pull her close. Just to protect her from the cold, he told himself. In silence they walked the two blocks to where he'd parked the car.

When he'd started the car and pulled into traffic, Julia said suddenly, "I'm sorry."

Looking over at her in surprise, he asked, "For what?"

"For making a scene in the restaurant when Bobby called me Skinny."

His lips curved into a smile. "Honey, if you call that making a scene then you must live the life of a saint."

She smiled briefly in return, then looked down to play with the buttons on her coat.

"Does he always call you that?" he asked carefully after a while.

She sighed. "Yes, and I don't know why I got angry at him tonight. Maybe it's because he doesn't take anything seriously. Skinny is a stupid nickname that he used to call me when we were kids, and it reminded me of all the other things that Bobby does that sometimes irritate me." She turned to look out the window.

"Like what?"

Biting her lip, she shook her head. "Life in general, I guess." With an effort, she pulled herself together and turned to him. "So. Did you enjoy crashing our party tonight?"

"It was interesting." As well as informative, he said to himself. Bobby Carleton was only a rookie cop, but he seemed to know a lot about the workings of his old precinct. And Julia seemed awfully worried about him. Making a mental note to look into Bobby Carleton a little more closely, he drove back to the motel.

The third-floor corridor was dark and deserted. The only light came from low-wattage light bulbs in dirty fixtures that dotted the ceiling, and all the doors in the hallway were firmly closed. Not a sound came out of any of the rooms. Luke waited next to Julia as she fumbled in her purse for her room key.

"You should always have your key in your hand before you get to your door, you know." His voice was a low rumble, but it sounded shockingly loud in the quiet corridor.

She shot him a look that brimmed with resentment as she pulled the key out of her purse. "I know that. But since you insisted on coming along to 'protect' me, I assumed I wouldn't have to use my key as weapons tonight."

Taking the key from her hand, he gently pushed her against the wall and said, "Don't assume anything, Julia." Unlocking the door, he kicked it open and stood aside.

The sound of the door bouncing against the wall reverberated down the corridor and echoed in his ears. There was no sound coming from the room, so Luke reached in and turned on the light. A quick search showed everything in its place and nothing disturbed.

"Lock your door behind me," he instructed, pausing in the doorway to turn and look at her. That was a mistake. She stood next to the bed, looking lost and alone, and he grabbed the door handle to keep himself from going to her. Dammit, didn't she know that Julia Carleton was always supposed to be composed? She looked too vulnerable when she let her guard down. It made him want things that he had no right to and ache to do things he knew he would regret later.

She nodded, a brief jerky movement, and he swore to himself. He took a step forward before he was able to stop himself. "Keep the connecting door unlocked," he added in a harsh voice. "If there's trouble I want to be able to get to you quickly."

She nodded again and sat down on the bed. "All right." Looking around the room, avoiding his eyes, she said, "I'll probably try to get some work done tonight. I don't think I can sleep yet."

So who could? Luke thought to himself savagely. Out loud he said, "Fine. I'll see you in the morning."

Pulling the door shut, he waited until he heard the rasp of the chain sliding home. Then, opening his own door, he went through the same routine as he had in Julia's room. As he expected, there was no evidence that anyone had been in his room. They were safe so far.

Throwing himself onto the huge king-size bed, a twin to the one in Julia's room, he stared at the ceiling and tried to concentrate on the case and not on Julia. She'd been right, it *was* odd that no one had followed them here from her apartment. The black sedan had been sitting in front of her apartment, big as life, making no effort to hide. There should have been someone else lurking near his car, ready to follow them if the black sedan missed them.

Maybe there had been, he thought uneasily, and he just hadn't spotted them on the way here. Easing off the bed, he turned off the lights in his room and walked over to the window. Cracking the curtain just enough to see the parking lot, he scanned the cars that sat in the darkness.

None of them looked suspicious, and as far as he could tell they were all empty. Letting the curtain fall back into place, he flicked the lights back on and stared at the door that led to Julia's room.

He had to get this case solved and get away from her. Until the day she'd walked into his office he'd been content, his soul and heart numb and nothing able to touch him, and he wanted to stay that way. Dammit, he didn't want to lie awake at night and think about any woman, let alone Julia Carleton. For two years she'd been the one thing that could keep his anger alive and his guilt at bay. When he thought about her and her role in his firing, he could concentrate on the shaft job he'd gotten from the police department instead of his own culpability for his wife's death.

And now Julia was ripping the carefully sewn fabric of his life to shreds without even trying. Hell, it was obvious she didn't want to get involved with him. But the more he got to know her, the more he craved her.

It was only physical, he told himself. It had nothing to do with the kind of person she was. He pushed the picture of her standing up to the street gang out of his mind. So what if she had courage? So what if she had more guts than any two women he'd ever met?

He remembered the way she'd trembled in his arms afterward, and he wanted to punch something. Sitting there in the park, she'd looked at him as if she thought Luke McKinley was more than a brutal cop, more than a seedy, low-life private investigator. She'd looked at him as if she cared about *him*.

A hesitant knock at the connecting door interrupted his thoughts. Walking over to the spot that had been tempting him ever since he'd walked in the room, he yanked the door open and stepped aside. She'd managed to pull herself together since he'd left her, and she stood in front of him composed and calm.

"I needed a few files that I think you have," she said in a low voice.

"Come on in. They're all over on that table," he said, jerking his head in its direction.

He left the door open as she walked toward the table. The room would be too small if the door was closed. She flipped through the files quickly and pulled out a handful, then turned to go back to her room.

"I have to ask you something," he said suddenly. *Stop,* a voice inside his head warned, but he couldn't stop himself. He had to know, and the question was eating at his gut.

She inclined her head, waiting. She was the self-composed ice princess, and he had to smash that facade, make her open up to him. Just once, he had to know what was inside her.

"Why did you crucify me the way you did two years ago? Why did you insist I be dismissed from the force instead of just giving me a reprimand?"

He watched as she paled, then she seemed to stand straighter. "There were five of us on that panel, Luke," she said carefully. "I was the chief investigator, but I wasn't the only one making the decision. And we felt that you left us no choice."

"That's crap and you know it. You had a lot of other choices. You could have suspended me for ninety days and everyone would have been satisfied. So why did you do it?"

Her cheeks blanched even more as she stared at the pattern in the worn carpet. "The public has very little tolerance for police brutality. There had been too many incidents and we didn't think the department could afford the bad publicity." Her eyes refused to meet his.

"You're spouting the company line, Julia. What's the matter? Can't you think of a better argument?" He leaned forward, curling his hands into fists to keep himself from shaking her. "Did it have something to do with the fact that the bastard was the son of a politically powerful alderman? Was that more important than the lives of my wife and son?" he taunted. What was she hiding? he wondered. Why wouldn't she look him in the eye?

"I didn't need a better argument because you stood there and admitted it and said you'd do it again," she retorted. "You left me and the rest of the panel with no alternatives."

"That suspect also had just killed my wife and unborn child," he said softly. "I could argue that I wasn't responsible for my actions."

"Then why didn't you argue that at the time?" she cried, passion in her voice. Running her hand through her hair, she finally looked at him. "Why didn't you say that at the hearing? Maybe things would have turned out differently."

Beneath the anger in her eyes was anguish and guilt, a guilt that made no sense. Watching her, he promised himself he would find out why.

Clutching her folders more closely to her chest, she moved toward her room. "I don't particularly want to rehash this issue. I have work to do, so I'll see you in the morning."

As she walked past him a trace of her scent drifted up to him. Suddenly he wanted to stop her, to take back the harsh words he'd spoken. He wanted to feel her soften in his arms, to melt into him the way she had earlier.

As he raised his hand to stop her she turned to face him. "Can we forget what happened two years ago? Neither one of us can go back and change what we did. I think it would be best to put it out of our minds."

He let his hand drop to his side. "I wish like hell I could forget about it, Investigator. I wish I could."

Her knuckles whitened around the folders in her hands, and again he saw the guilt in her eyes. She opened her mouth and he tensed, waiting to hear what she would say. With the instinct that had saved his hide more than once, he knew what she said would be important. Then, without another word, she clamped her mouth shut and walked into her own room. The door closed quietly, and he knew he wouldn't see Julia again that evening.

He stood staring at the door for a long time, thinking about the guilt he'd seen in her eyes. He knew all about guilt, knew how it corroded the soul and ate away at the heart. But if she thought she was right, what did she have to feel guilty about?

The black despair threatened again, and with an effort he pushed it away. She was right. He shouldn't have asked her about her investigation two years ago. It was over and done with, and he should have left it alone.

But he couldn't leave it alone, he reminded himself. Not ever. Striding over to his bag, he pulled out the picture of his wife that he'd grabbed at his house earlier today. He stared down at her face, a face that had become that of a stranger even before she'd died. If he ever began to forget, there was always this to remind him.

* * *

The noise woke him instantly. It reverberated inside his skull and jarred him loose from the fitful dream that lingered on the edges of his consciousness. Pausing only to pull his gun from underneath his pillow, he pushed open the connecting door to Julia's room. As he did so his mind identified the sound.

It was the fire alarm. Apprehension tightened his gut as he realized she'd already gone out into the hall. Running across the room, heedless of the fact that he wore only a skimpy pair of briefs, he slammed the door open and looked down the hall. She stood in front of his door, pounding on it with her fist.

The relief he felt was staggering. Stifling an almost overwhelming urge to wrap his arms around her and hold her next to him until his heart stopped pounding, he strode down the hall and touched her arm.

She jumped and whirled to face him, slumping against the door when she realized it was him.

"Thank God. When you didn't answer the door, I got a little worried." She looked terrified. Her eyes were huge in her pale face and her mouth was trembling.

"Come on," he said, urging her toward the stairs. "Let's get out of here."

Doors were opening up and down the corridor and people dressed in their nightclothes were peering out into the hall. As they began to move to the staircase, a man in jeans and a sweater opened the door and stuck his head through.

"Sorry, folks, it's a false alarm." As if to underline his words, the alarm stopped abruptly. "Go on back to bed. Sorry for the interruption."

One by one the doors down the corridor closed, until they were the only ones in the hallway. Julia started to walk back to her room, but without looking at her Luke caught her arm and stopped her. He kept his attention on the door to the stairwell where the manager had disappeared.

"Come on, Luke," Julia whispered. "He said it was a false alarm."

"I know." He didn't take his eyes off the door. "And maybe it was just a clever way to get us out of our rooms and into the open."

He felt her shiver as she instinctively moved closer to him. "So we're just going to stand here and wait for them?"

"No, we're not." He walked over to the stairs and silently pushed the door open. The bulbs that lit the stairwell were even dimmer than those in the hall, and he waited for his eyes to adjust to the darkness. When he could see that no one lingered in the shadows, he strained to listen.

No sounds drifted up to him. He waited for a long time, knowing that if someone waited on the stairs, sooner or later they would make a noise. When it became apparent that the stairwell was deserted, he let the door shut and walked back to where Julia stood.

He watched her eyes flicker over him and realized that he was as good as naked. The low briefs that were all he wore didn't cover much, and if she kept looking at him like that it wouldn't be long before they'd cover even less. Taking her arm, he pulled her back into her room and bolted the door.

For the first time he noticed what she wore, and his mouth went dry. Her nightgown covered her from her neck to the floor. The delicate material was white with some kind of tiny flower on it, and the collar was edged with lace. It certainly wasn't the kind of gown that was meant to inhabit erotic dreams, but in Julia's case he'd make an exception.

As his gaze drifted down from her neck, his breath caught in his throat. The top three buttons of her gown were undone, and in the dim, shadowy light that filled the room the inside curve of her breast gleamed white in the darkness.

Chapter 8

Julia followed Luke's gaze and realized that the top of her nightgown had come unbuttoned. Instant heat washed over her face, and she reached up to pull the material together.

His hand captured hers on the way. "No, don't," he whispered. "I've never seen anything so beautiful."

Her skin seemed to tingle and she felt her breath quicken. Even in the darkness, Luke's eyes glittered. Licking her lips nervously, she tried to tug her hand away from him and back up.

He didn't let her go. Bending his head, he brushed his mouth over the curve of her breast, then pulled her into his arms. Her pulse stopped, then roared into life as he moved up and took her lips.

Her hands pressed against his chest and she felt his muscles quiver under them. An answering tremor rippled through her. His skin was hot and slick, covered with a fine sheen of perspiration even though it had been cool in the hallway and he was practically naked.

His muscles tensed and tightened as she moved her fingers, tangling them in the soft, curly hair on his chest. He groaned, the sound torn from his throat, and deepened their kiss. When his tongue caressed her lips, she opened her mouth without hesitation. The one tiny bit of her brain that could still think rationally screamed at her to stop. The rest of her, the part that had been fascinated by Lucas McKinley for the past two years and obsessed with him for the past two days, ignored it. She was falling headlong into an abyss that was hot and dark and filled with pleasure, and she went willingly.

Somewhere between the time she walked into his office yesterday and the moment he'd pulled her into his arms in this shabby motel room, she'd realized that there were depths to Luke that she hadn't even suspected two years ago. Depths that she wanted to explore.

Stepping closer to him, she struggled to free her hands from between their bodies. When his hold on her loosened, she slid her arms around his back. It was hard and smooth, the muscles bunching under her fingers.

One of his arms tightened around her. The other, she dimly realized, hung at his side. Pulling away slightly, she looked down at it. "What's wrong with your hand?" she asked. Could that breathless voice really belong to her?

Luke slowly looked down at his right hand. "Nothing," he said after a minute. "It's just attached to this." He raised his hand until she could see that there was a gun in it.

The piece of metal gleamed dully in the dim light. Stepping away from her, he set it gently on the night table next to the bed, then pulled her close again. "It was cramping my style anyway."

This time both his arms surrounded her and he pulled her close. His bare legs burned hers, even through the material of her nightgown. When he put one hand in the small of her back and pressed her against him, she could feel the heavy weight of his arousal throbbing against her abdomen.

"I can't stop thinking about you, Julia," he whispered. Brushing her hair away from her face, he stared at her in the semidarkness. "I see your face just before I fall asleep at night and as soon as I wake up in the morning. I shouldn't want you like this, but I can't seem to help myself."

She didn't answer, couldn't answer. She couldn't tell him that she'd thought about him, too, and not just for the last two days. All the air was trapped in her chest, making it feel as if it were going to burst. All she could do was open her mouth to his and lose herself in the sensations as his tongue stroked hers.

Every inch of her skin throbbed with the need to touch him. Sparks danced through her veins, igniting fires wherever he touched her. The case, Bobby, the reason she'd originally investigated Luke all fell away, disappearing into the rush of pleasure that surged inside her when his tongue swirled through her mouth.

She was falling, tumbling headlong into a place filled with heat and desire. Wrapping her arms around Luke, she held on tightly. When she felt herself actually moving, her eyes snapped open.

He had picked her up in his arms and was carrying her through the connecting door into his room. His room was dark, too, except for the sliver of moonlight that filtered through the edge of the curtain. The pale light silvered his chest and emphasized the lean muscles that rippled in his arms as he carried her.

Laying her down on the bed, he stood next to her for a moment, looking at her. His gaze was hot and fierce, full of desire and something more she was afraid to name. Finally he lowered himself to the bed, but instead of pulling her close he propped himself up on one elbow next to her.

"Julia," he whispered, smoothing her hair away from her face. "Why do you keep all this passion bottled up inside?" He bent and kissed the hollow below her ear. "Why do you pretend to be so icy and composed all the time?"

She tried to explain, to tell him how she'd been caught once and never would be again, but his hand was sweeping slowly down her neck and the words caught in her mouth. He lingered at the base of her throat to smooth through the hollow there, every small movement of his hand sending tremors rippling through her. As his fingers trailed away his mouth took their place, tasting and exploring as if he had all the time in the world.

When his fingers slipped down into the valley between her breasts and casually brushed against their sensitive inner curves, she moaned, deep in her throat, and turned blindly to him. His mouth met hers and danced over her lips before returning to her throat.

His fingers continued to do magical things, still moving lazily and never coming close to the nipples that were taut and swollen, begging for his touch. His bare leg moved slowly up and down hers, nudging her nightgown aside, to tangle with her bare legs. The throbbing that was centered in her lower body spread over her arms and legs in a slow-moving wave.

Reaching out for him, she tried to pull him closer. Gently taking her hands in one of his, he held them above her head as he nuzzled the unbuttoned flap of her nightgown aside. When she felt the hot moistness of his tongue trail lightly over the curve of her breast, she drew in her breath sharply and bucked beneath his leg.

"I should have known," he whispered, his breath hot against her skin. "Anyone as buttoned up as you seem has to be hiding something." His mouth dipped lower, pushing the nightgown aside ever farther, and she gasped again. "And now I know what you've been hiding."

Letting go of her hands, he tangled his fingers in her hair before cupping her breast through her nightgown. She arched helplessly up into him, completely consumed by desire. "Luke," she gasped, "you're driving me crazy."

Suddenly he loomed over her, his features hard and taut with his own desire. "You've been driving me crazy for the past two days," he murmured, brushing her nipple with the lightest of touches and watching her reaction. "Turnabout is fair play."

Sensations shuddered through her as he continued to tease her, touching her nipple lightly then brushing over the side of her breast. Finally he let his hand slide into the open neck of her nightgown and close over her swollen breast. When he gently squeezed her nipple between his thumb and forefinger, she cried out, "Luke!"

He shifted, moving off her and reaching for the jeans he'd draped over the chair next to the bed. When she turned to watch him, her gaze fell instead on the picture that stood on the night table.

She felt as if she'd been suddenly dipped in ice water. Luke stared back at her from the side of a pretty blond woman, and he had his arm wrapped around her in an intimate way. Even if she hadn't already known who the woman was, she would have realized that she was looking at a picture of Luke and his wife.

Slowly she sat up, clutching the open neck of her nightgown together with one hand. She wrapped the other arm around her stomach, as if she could somehow protect it from the blow she'd already received. After a moment, when she felt as if she could breathe again, she tried to slither off the bed and away from Luke.

He turned around then, a silver packet in his hand. She kept her gaze fixed on his face. Even now, the sight of his magnificent body made her feel weak-kneed. Pushing herself off the bed, she forced herself to stay and face him rather than run off to her own room and lock the connecting door.

He looked puzzled and surprised, sitting on the bed wearing only his briefs and holding the packet in his hand. When she allowed her gaze to drift down him, she felt her face fill with heat. The skimpy briefs he wore didn't hide much in his aroused condition.

"What's the matter, Julia?" His voice was low and husky with desire.

She clutched the collar of her nightgown more tightly. "I don't want to be a substitute for another woman," she said, swallowing hard to keep her voice from cracking. When her gaze drifted toward the picture of Luke and his wife, he followed the direction of her eyes. He let out an ugly curse, shocking in its violence, before he slammed the picture facedown on the table.

"You're not taking anyone's place. If you couldn't tell that I wanted you and not a replacement for Linda, then you're not as smart as I gave you credit for. But you were right to stop. I forgot a lot of things tonight, things that I have no business forgetting." Hurling the silver packet across the room, he stood up and turned to her. "And the first one is not to mix business and pleasure," he added grimly.

Tearing her gaze away from the place where the small square of foil had hit the wall and fallen to the carpet, she looked at Luke. In the pearly moonlight that managed to steal into the room he looked magnificent. His broad shoulders tapered to slim hips, and his legs were hard and lean. The bulge in the front of his briefs was mute witness to what had happened between them just minutes before.

What on earth had she been thinking of? He was absolutely right. She knew, none better, about the follies of mixing her private needs with those of her job. And the job that she'd hired Luke to do was one that required her full attention. She'd learned in the past two days that Luke was both smart and clever. She needed to have all her wits about her if she was going to steer him away from Bobby in this investigation. The last thing she needed to do was forget why she was here with him in the first place.

"You're right," she said quietly, trying to draw her dignity around her as she gathered the gaping neck of her nightgown. "I guess it was the stress of the day. I wasn't thinking."

"You're right, you weren't thinking. But I think I like that Julia Carleton a hell of a lot better than the one who has to plan every move three days in advance," he said harshly.

She headed for her own room, brushing against the wall to keep as far away from him as possible. Sexual desire still rolled off him in waves, trying to draw her closer, and one part of her ached to respond.

She paused in the doorway of her own room. "I'm sorry, but it's the second Julia that hired you, and that's the one you'll have to deal with. Good night, Luke."

Closing the door gently, she knew her last glimpse of him would be engraved on her mind for a long time. As she lay down on the big bed, desire still a faint throbbing in her abdomen, she closed her eyes and saw again the pain on his face and the bleak desolation in his eyes.

The first faint signs of daylight streamed through the window as Luke pulled the curtain aside and stared out at the parking lot. There were a few more cars in the lot than last night, but they were all empty. He dropped back onto the rumpled bed, not bothering to look at the clock on the table. It was damn early and he knew it.

He hadn't gotten much sleep last night, and now he just wanted it to be late enough to leave this stinking motel room and get this job over and done with. He needed to get away from Julia Carleton, to run as far as possible from her and never look back. The only way he could do that now was to solve this case for her, accept her check then walk away.

For a few precious minutes last night he had forgotten. He'd forgotten about his guilt, about the reasons he'd sworn to never get involved again. He'd forgotten about Linda and what he'd done to her. For a little while, it had seemed like anything was possible. He had forgotten everything except the way Julia felt in his arms, the sounds she made when he touched her and the way she touched him. He had almost believed that the impossible was happening.

Thank God she'd stopped him in time. Thank God he'd come to his senses before he could make a disastrous mistake. Now all he wanted was for this to be over.

Yanking on his pants, he left the top button undone as he pulled on his shirt and shoved the buttons through their holes. It was time to get out of here. This room had become a prison, with memories of him and Julia together surrounding him wherever he looked. Striding over to the connecting door, he raised his hand to knock.

He paused when he glanced outside into the brightening dawn. It was still so early that she was probably asleep, he thought, his anger dissolving. His hand dropped away from the door and he finished buttoning his shirt and jeans. He didn't want to wake her up. She'd gotten little enough sleep the night before when he'd turned up at her apartment, dazed and bedraggled from the explosion.

As he sat down on the bed to put on his shoes, he heard noises from Julia's room. She was moving around, he realized, and immediately he wondered if she'd had trouble sleeping last night, too.

She'd tell him no, he realized with a flash of insight. She tried hard to maintain her facade of composure and unflappability. But after last night, he knew better.

His body remembered just how uncomposed she'd been, and he felt the familiar tightening in his lower body again. Her image had taunted him all night, and not even a long, freezing-cold shower had been able to tune her out. It didn't matter, he told himself, standing up and going to the window again. He was in control of his body. Wanting her was a physical thing, that was all, and he wouldn't let it take control of his life. He wasn't sixteen years old anymore.

He stood at the window for a long time, staring blindly out at the cars in the parking lot. He heard the shower in the room next to his, heard the minute she walked out of the bathroom and began to dress. His senses were so attuned to her because they had to be, he told himself. Their lives could depend on it. But when he found himself thinking about what she'd look like fresh out of the shower, dripping wet and rosy from the heat, he slammed his fist against the wall and went to look for his gun.

It was still in her room, he remembered, and his gut tightened with fear. What was the matter with him? He *never* forgot about his gun, especially when it was as important as it was on this case. Striding over to the connecting door, he pounded on it with his fist.

She opened the door almost immediately, clutching a sweater in front of her chest. "What's the matter?"

"I left my gun in here last night." He tried to look at her face and not notice the lacy straps on her shoulders that weren't covered by the sweater she clutched to herself.

"I know. It's on the table there." She nodded toward the night table and he reached out and took his gun. "What's wrong?" she asked again.

"Nothing's wrong. But it was damned careless of me to leave it here." He checked the gun quickly and instinctively, then shoved it into the waistband of his jeans at the small of his back.

Looking back at Julia, he saw that her hair was still wet from her shower, and it hung to her shoulders in thick waves. Surprised, he frowned at her. "Why does your hair look so curly?"

She touched her head self-consciously. "Because it *is* curly."

"I've never seen you with curly hair." His voice was almost accusing.

Backing toward the bathroom, she said defensively, "Maybe we can discuss these personal grooming questions after I get dressed." When he continued to watch her, she snapped, "I dry it every day, all right? I don't like to walk around with curly hair."

"Why not, Julia? Doesn't it fit with your image? Would curly hair make you seem more human or something? Is it because you can't control curly hair?" He felt his voice rising and clamped his mouth shut. What the hell difference did it make to him what she did with her hair? She could cut it into a Mohawk for all he cared. If she wanted the world to think she was interested in nothing but business, that was fine with him.

Except that he knew otherwise. He'd seen her concern for her brother, even though he didn't know yet what she was worried about. He'd seen the way she treated Raul, how she'd known just what to say to him about his carvings.

His body tightened. He'd felt her melt in his arms last night, had heard every sigh and moan that had escaped her mouth. And he'd felt the ones that hadn't.

With a low curse he turned around and walked back into his room. Without turning around to look at her again, he said, "Let me know when you're ready. We need to get going this morning."

He closed the connecting door behind him, being very careful not to slam it. Then, going over to the window, he stared through the crack in the curtain into the parking lot, not seeing any of the cars parked there.

* * *

"Those things will kill you, you know."

Luke looked up from the jelly doughnut he was eating and raised his eyebrows. "Maybe, maybe not. But I'll die a happy man." He looked at her bran muffin and made a face. "I'm not about to go through life eating twigs and sawdust."

She gave him a strained smile as she raised her cup of coffee to take a drink. "You might be surprised. Don't knock it until you've tried it."

He scowled, thinking of other things he wouldn't mind trying. He didn't like to see her smile, or loosen up in any way. It made her too damn appealing. "You about done with that thing? We can take the coffee with us."

She looked around at the pink-and-orange decor of the doughnut shop where they'd stopped for breakfast, then glanced out the windows that lined the walls. "I'd think this would be the ideal place to sit and talk for a while. No one can hide in here."

Not even him. Tapping his foot against the metal leg of the table, he tried to think of a good reason to leave immediately, but had to admit she was right. They'd spent too much time in his car the last few days. He was getting as sick of it as she must be.

"All right, let's have another cup of coffee and talk. I suppose it's as good a place as any." He signaled the waitress and waited until both their cups were full. "I'm going to visit Eddie today," he said abruptly.

She paused in the act of taking a sip of coffee. "You are?"

He nodded. "I want to talk to him, see what he has to say."

Carefully she set her coffee cup on the table. "You're not going to ask him if he's done a deal with a gang of drug dealers, are you?"

"Of course not," he said impatiently. "Give me a little credit, will you? When I ran into him at headquarters, we talked vaguely about getting together sometime. I'll use that as an excuse, say that I realized it had been too long. I just want to talk to him."

She nodded slowly. "That sounds like a good idea. You were his partner for a long time. If anyone can read between the lines it'd be you."

He snapped his coffee cup onto the Formica table. He was beginning to assume that Eddie was guilty, and it bothered him. "It remains to be seen if there's anything between the lines to be read." Throwing a crumpled wad of dollar bills on the table, he stood up. "Let's get going."

A few minutes later he stood at a phone booth, watching Julia sitting in the car and waiting for someone to answer the phone at his old precinct. When he heard the desk sergeant's voice he asked for Eddie, and was told that he was off today. Replacing the receiver thoughtfully, he walked back to the car.

"That was a quick call," Julia said. He could hear the question in her voice.

"Eddie's off today." He started the engine and headed back to the motel. "But I think that's okay. Now I can surprise him at home."

"Where am I going to be during your little heart-to-heart?"

"You're going to be in that motel room with the door chained shut. There hasn't been any sign that they've found us, so I think you'll be safe there for a few hours. And don't go calling your office to tell them where you are. Don't even call them to tell them you won't be in."

"I'd already figured that out, Luke." She looked over at him with exasperation. "We have no idea who could be involved in this case."

"That's right." His voice was grim. "I don't want to find out the hard way that someone in Internal Affairs is feeding information to your suspects."

"Don't worry. I won't call anyone."

He glanced over at her. She was staring out the windshield, but he thought she looked a little pale. "Julia?"

When she turned to look at him, he realized she was scared. Her eyes were huge in her white face, and she had to bite her lip to keep it from trembling. "What?"

"Are you going to be okay by yourself for a little while?"

He saw her pull herself together, and could only guess at the effort it took. Julia Carleton had guts, he had to give her that. More guts than most people he knew, man or woman.

"I'll be fine. As you said, they have no idea where I am. And nobody's attacked me."

She didn't have to say *yet*. The word hung between them, vibrating in the air. "You'll be fine, Julia. Just think of it as your brief reprieve from my company."

"Time off for good behavior?" she asked, trying to smile.

"Yeah. But don't get too used to it, because I'll be back before you know it."

"I know you will, Luke."

She actually sounded as if she were looking forward to it, and he looked over at her again. She was intent on watching something out the window. Before he asked her what was bothering her, he glanced again into his rearview mirror.

And let out a string of curses.

She looked over at him with alarm. Without taking his eyes off the car behind him, he said grimly, "It looks as if they found us again."

He could feel the effort it took for her not to look behind her. "Are you sure?"

"Short of pulling over and asking the guy for an ID, I am. The same car's been behind us since we left the doughnut shop. I'm going to cut down a couple of side streets to make sure."

Several blocks later the car was still behind him. It was careful not to get too close, but it didn't fall back, either. It was a silent, menacing presence behind them, making him all too aware of the fact that he hadn't outsmarted them, after all. "It looks like there's been a slight change in plans. You're not going back to the motel by yourself now." He slanted a quick look over at her. "Where do your folks live?"

She glanced at him in surprise. "On the north side of the city. Why?"

"Would they be home now?"

"They should be. My dad's retired, and they're not away on a trip. Even if they have errands to do, it's pretty early."

"Okay. As soon as we lose this joker on our tail, tell me how to get to their house."

"Can I ask why we're going to my parents' house?"

"I can't think of anyplace else where you'd be safe. I'm not even sure you'll be safe there," he said bluntly, "but I don't have any other choice. I can't show up at Eddie's with you."

"I'm sure I'll be safe with my parents."

Her voice was firm but she sneaked a look over her shoulder. He could have told her that the car was sticking to them like a leech. The entrance to the Kennedy Expressway was approaching, and he veered onto it. Their shadow followed them down the ramp.

After driving for a while, he moved over to the left and signaled that he was entering the express lanes. He saw with grim satisfaction that the car behind him did the same. He waited until the last possible minute, until he was sure the car following him was boxed in and couldn't make a similar move, then cut in front of another car and barely made it out of the express lane.

When he looked back, he saw that the car behind him was trapped and had no choice but to continue in the express lanes. He wouldn't be exiting the expressway for another eight miles. Luke took the next exit that came up.

"That was one slick maneuver."

Julia's voice was genuinely admiring, and he looked over at her long enough to grin. "Stick with me, honey. I know all the moves."

"I noticed," she said wryly.

Fifteen minutes later he pulled up in front of a neat brick bungalow on a quiet, tree-lined street. When Julia would have opened the door and gotten out of the car, he put his hand on her arm. "Not yet. I want to make sure we don't have company."

She settled back into her seat as he scanned the street. A few children played in the crisp early spring sunshine, and an occasional car cruised down the street, but otherwise it was quiet and peaceful. After five minutes, he opened the door and got out.

By the time he got around to her side of the car she was standing on the sidewalk waiting for him. Resisting the urge to take her hand, he let her lead the way up to the front door of her parents' house.

Moments after she rang the bell an older man answered the door. Luke saw immediately where Julia got her looks. From his curly red hair to his determined chin, he was clearly her father.

"Hi, Dad." Julia's voice was breathless, and he wondered why. "This is Luke McKinley. He's working with me on a case, and I need to stay here with you for a little while. Do you and Mom have any plans for today?"

"No, we don't. Come on in, Mr. McKinley." Julia's father held the door open while Luke shook his head.

"Thanks, but I can't right now." He turned to Julia. "I'll be back in a couple of hours, maybe a little more. You stay in the house and away from the windows. Make sure your dad doesn't let anyone in that he doesn't know."

He could sense her father bristling in front of him and turned to the older man. "Sorry, Mr. Carleton, I don't have time to explain. Julia will tell you as much as she can." He looked back at Julia and gripped her arms. There was a shadow of fear in her eyes, and he leaned forward.

"You're going to be fine. I'll be back soon."

"I'm worried about you," she whispered.

He stared at her for a second, thunderstruck. She was worried about *him*. Something moved in his chest, something so tender it was almost painful. Giving in to an uncontrollable urge, he leaned forward and brushed her lips with his. "Don't worry about me. I'll be fine."

He wheeled and ran down the steps of her parents' house, getting in the car and driving away without looking back. If he had, he wasn't sure he could leave her there. Glancing at his watch, he headed in the direction of Eddie's house. In two hours he would be with her again.

Chapter 9

Eddie's house looked the same as it always had, the grass a little too long and the paint a little too faded. At least some things hadn't changed, Luke told himself as he rang the doorbell.

Eddie answered the door wearing sweatpants and a T-shirt that was blotched with sweat. When he saw who was standing there, surprise and wariness filled his eyes for a moment, then he smiled and opened the door.

"Luke, you son of a gun. What are you doing here?"

"After I saw you the other day I realized it'd been a long time," Luke answered easily. "When I called the precinct, they told me you were off today. I thought I'd stop by, see if you were interested in lunch."

Eddie glanced at his watch, a high-tech model full of buttons and gauges. "Kind of early for lunch, isn't it, buddy?"

Luke shrugged. "I wanted to catch you before you found something else to do today."

"Come on in." Eddie opened the door and Luke walked into the house. "I won't be able to make lunch, but we can catch up while I finish my workout."

As they walked through the house that used to be as familiar to Luke as his own, he couldn't help noticing the changes. "Looks like you finally got your act together in here," he commented, looking around at the new furniture and the expensive stereo and big-screen television.

"I was getting tired of listening to my sister and mother harp about my bachelor's existence," Eddie answered. He waved a hand dismissively at the expensive furnishings. "I figured that I could kill two birds with one stone and stop their complaints while I made myself comfortable."

"Seems like a lot of money to spend to keep your sister's mouth shut. Why didn't you just stop inviting her over?" Luke took one last look around as Eddie led him to the spare bedroom.

"Hey, I made some good investments and decided I might as well enjoy it now. Life is too short to be so tight. But then, you always were too conservative about money. I guess it was because you were an old married man, right, buddy?"

"I guess."

Luke kept his face poker straight, but Eddie realized he'd made a faux pas. He turned around, contrition on his face. "Hey, I'm sorry, Luke. I didn't mean to throw it in your face like that."

"Don't worry about it. And besides, you were right. I never was a swinging bachelor even when I was a swinging bachelor."

"And when was that? When you were twelve?"

"I met Linda when we were sixteen," he said, then added a shade defensively, "but we didn't get married until we were twenty."

"Yeah, a couple of senior citizens," Eddie scoffed, turning to his exercise equipment. The argument was a familiar one. Before Luke's wife was killed, Eddie was the only one he'd confided in about his dissatisfaction with his marriage. Eddie had always maintained that it was because they'd married so young. Luke knew there was more to it than that, but there were some things you didn't talk about, not even with your partner.

To change the subject, he looked around the room that had been turned into an exercise facility. A top-notch exercise facility, he noticed. The equipment Eddie had was as high-quality as that found in any health club. "Nice setup you have here, Eddie," he commented.

Eddie grinned at him and continued to lift weights with his legs. "Some of us are still interested in looking good," he panted. "And you know my motto has always been to buy the best."

"I remember." And he did. Eddie had always had champagne taste on a beer budget. Luke felt his stomach begin to roll. Had his ex-partner found a way to finance his big-budget life-style?

Luke watched as Eddie worked up a sweat on his expensive equipment, then asked a question about the precinct and some people they'd both worked with there. Eddie seemed relieved that the conversation had drifted into impersonal waters, and they talked for a while. When Eddie reached for his towel and began wiping his face, the signal that his workout was over, Luke stood up.

"I guess I'll get going. Give me a call sometime."

"I'll do that." Eddie flashed him a grin from behind the towel, a grin that told Luke more clearly than any words it would never happen.

He walked to the front door, managing to carry on an innocuous conversation, but once he was back outside and the door to Eddie's house was closed, he allowed himself to feel the pain. And underneath the pain, buried deep, the rage simmered.

Eddie had been his partner, his best friend. Their relationship had become strained when Eddie had testified against him, but as Eddie had pointed out, there were plenty of witnesses to the beating he'd given that drunken killer and better he have a friend in the inquiry room than an enemy or even a casual observer. And since Luke hadn't cared about anything in the months after his wife had been killed, he tried not to think about the fact that his best friend and partner had actually betrayed him.

But now he wondered if his best friend had not only betrayed him but had betrayed everything he stood for. Could Eddie really have become one of them, one of the pieces of garbage that infested the sewers of the community? Luke could think of only one explanation for Eddie's sudden wealth, and it left a foul taste in his mouth.

Getting back into his car, he stared at the house for a few minutes, wondering bitterly if Eddie was on the phone right now, calling his boss in the gang and telling him about Luke's visit. Turning the ignition key with a savage twist of his wrist, he gunned the engine and roared down the street without looking back.

In spite of Luke's warning Julia paced in her parents' living room, pausing every few seconds to peer out the front window. As far as she could tell, no cars had gone by the house more than once and no one sat parked along the curb, but she really didn't care. All she was looking for was one battered old blue sedan.

"Honey, what's wrong?" her mother asked for the tenth time.

Julia turned around and went to her, taking her hands. "This is an important case, Mom, and I need to get busy working on it." She needed to be sure Luke was safe, but she wasn't about to tell her mother that. Just as she wasn't about to tell her parents about the cars following them, or the fact that Luke's office had been blown up and her apartment searched. "I'm just anxious for Luke to get back."

"Will you bring your young man in this time so I can meet him, too?"

"He's not my young man, Mom," she answered, willing herself to look nonchalant. "He's just an...an associate on this case."

"That's not what your brother told us. He said you all had dinner together last night and that the two of you seemed quite cozy."

She'd forgotten how quickly news flew through the family grapevine. At least Bobby apparently hadn't told them about the love-at-first-sight remarks. She supposed she should be grateful for that. Sighing, she said, "All of you, Bobby included, are seeing things that aren't there."

"We worry about you, Julia, being alone. We just want you to have someone to take care of you."

"I can take care of myself just fine, Mom."

"But it's so much more fun when you don't have to," her mother murmured, and Julia looked at her sharply.

Before she could answer, the doorbell rang. Julia practically fell over her feet to get to the door, but remembering Luke's words of caution she looked through the peephole before wrenching the door open.

"Luke!" she said, too breathlessly. "Come in."

Something had happened. She recognized those grim lines around his mouth and that tension in his eyes. "What is it?" she asked in a low voice, grabbing his hand.

He looked down at their joined hands for a moment, as if puzzled by the contact, then turned his palm to hold hers with a grip that felt almost desperate. "Nothing," he answered just as softly. "As far as I know, no one followed me back here."

That wasn't what she'd meant and he knew it, but instead of pursuing it she turned to her mother. In spite of the fact that she knew her mother's gaze was riveted to her and Luke's joined hands, she couldn't break the contact.

"Mom, this is Lucas McKinley. Luke, this is my mother, Dolores Carleton."

Luke murmured pleasantries while he shook her mother's hand. He couldn't be unaware of the speculative looks her mother was giving him, but he met her eyes squarely and managed to carry on a normal conversation. After an edgy few minutes, Julia said brightly, "Are you ready to go, Luke? We've got a lot to do this afternoon."

He squeezed her hand then let it drop. She tried to ignore the feeling of loss, turning to pick up her coat and briefcase. After another few words to her mother, they were down the steps and into the front seat of Luke's car.

Luke looked around but apparently didn't see anyone suspicious. Turning the ignition key a little harder than necessary, he shot out of his parking spot and down the street. Out of the corner of her eye, Julia saw her mother standing in the front window of the house, waving goodbye the way she normally did.

But there had been nothing normal about her life for the past two days, Julia thought. Alice and the rabbit hole had nothing on her. In two days one man had managed to turn her world upside down, making her question almost every aspect of her life.

She turned to look at Luke. His face was grim as he stared out the windshield, hands tightly gripping the steering wheel. She wondered if he even saw the street in front of him.

"What happened?" she asked gently.

He tore his gaze away from the street long enough to glance over at her. "I saw Eddie."

As explanations went, it left a little to be desired. "And...?"

"And you may be right." His voice was hard and abrupt, but underneath she sensed the anguish.

"What happened to make you change your mind?"

The silence stretched so long that she didn't think he was going to answer. Finally he shrugged. "Nothing happened. But Eddie's...changed. Different."

She sat and watched him, waiting for him to elaborate. He glanced over at her again, and suddenly he rolled his shoulders and sighed.

"Eddie was always a big talker. He was going to get the biggest television they made, the best car, the nicest house. I never paid much attention to him. It was just the way he was. Big-time Eddie. It was a joke around the precinct."

He glanced over at her again, and she saw the sorrow in his eyes. "He lives in a little house on the northwest side that used to be furnished in typical bachelor style. A couple of cast-off chairs, a couch that should have been retired years ago, that sort of thing." He paused and his lips tightened. "Things have changed."

"Has he moved?"

He shook his head. "No, Eddie still lives in the same little dump. The only difference is that now it's filled with all those expensive things Eddie always talked about getting. The best stereo equipment, a television the size of a station wagon, and an exercise room that's nicer than the one at my old health club."

His knuckles whitened on the steering wheel. "Things that a cop's salary could never pay for."

"Maybe he used his credit cards to buy all that stuff." She didn't think so, but somehow she couldn't bear to point that out to Luke right now. Not when his pain at his ex-partner's betrayal was written so plainly on his face.

Luke gave her a look. "Not a chance. He told me he'd made some good investments." The sound that came from him could only be described as a snort. "Besides, with his credit history, he's lucky if he can buy lunch with a credit card."

Julia tried to marshal her thoughts. "Expensive possessions aren't proof of his guilt. We'll need more evidence than that."

This time when Luke looked at her he didn't try to hide the pain. "Oh, I think we'll be able to find it. It's just a matter of time."

After a long time had passed, she said softly, "I'm sorry."

He gave her a surprised look. "For what?"

"For Eddie. For you. I know you wanted to believe he hadn't turned, and I'm sorry that you had to find out otherwise."

"What I feel isn't important. The truth is important, and we still don't know what that is." He accelerated the car sharply and spun around a corner, then pulled into a parking lot and stopped abruptly. "But we're going to find out. And soon."

Julia realized they were back at the motel where they'd spent the night. Before she could ask why, Luke was out of the car and opening her door. "Let's get our stuff together and check out. Nobody followed us here from your parents' house, but I don't want to take any chances."

They hurried into the building and up to their rooms. It took only a minute for Luke to make sure no one had been in their rooms while they were gone, and just a little longer than that for Julia to pack all her belongings. She could hear Luke through the open connecting door, throwing things into his duffel bag. She wondered if the picture of his wife was the last thing he put in the bag.

"Ready to go?"

Julia looked up at Luke standing in the doorway between their two rooms. Levering herself off the bed, she gripped the handle of her small suitcase and nodded. "All set."

"I'm going to have you wait in the car while I check out. There's no reason for the clerk to get a look at both of us."

"Okay." She moved toward the door, but stopped instantly at the feel of his hand on her arm. Turning around slowly, she faced him as he snatched his hand away from her.

He studied her face for a long time. Finally he said, "You're a real trouper, Julia. Thank you."

"You sound surprised," she said, a shade defensively.

He shrugged and looked away from her. "I guess I am. I never gave it much thought before, but if I had I would have assumed you'd be a whiner."

"Why on earth would you assume that?" The hurt stabbed deeply, and she set her suitcase on the floor with a trembling hand.

Jamming his hands into his pockets, he glanced around the room, looking everywhere but at her. "I've hated you for two years, Julia," he said quietly. "There was only one thing I wanted or needed after my wife died, and you took it away from me." He held up his hand. "Yes, I know, I took it away from myself. But I already had enough guilt on my soul to last a lifetime. I wasn't ready to take the credit for losing my job, too."

He watched her for a moment, and she saw his face soften. "But you're not a whiner, Julia. You're not a lot of things I thought you were. And I'm glad you hired me to work on this case with you."

The pain in her heart eased just a little. Rubbing her hands on her jeans, she asked slowly, "Does that mean you don't hate me anymore?" It was just an academic question, she told herself. His answer didn't really matter to her.

"What do you think?" His eyes darkened and he leaned closer. "Last night, did it feel like I hated you?"

"Last night it felt like you wanted my body," she answered flatly. The pain stirred again, stabbing through her chest. She tried to tell herself that Lucas McKinley's opinion mattered less than nothing to her. This was just another case, after all. But some stubborn part of her insisted that Luke was more than just a case and had been for the past two years.

"Last night I made several mistakes, and the biggest one was forgetting that all we have is a business relationship. It won't happen again." He shuttered his eyes again as he stooped to pick up her suitcase, but not before she'd seen the longing he tried to hide. Shifting her hand on her briefcase, she followed him out the door.

Fifteen minutes later Luke pulled into a gas station and stopped at the public telephone. Parking his car, he gave Julia a reassuring smile as he slid out of his seat. "This should only take a minute." He quickly dialed a number from memory. After only two rings, he heard Raul's voice at the other end of the line.

"Raul, this is Luke. Could you meet me for lunch?"

There was dead silence. Finally Raul said, delicately, "You sound agitated, my friend."

"You're damn right I'm agitated. Can you get down to the Loop in—" he looked at his watch "—an hour?"

"I can be there," Raul promised. "At the usual place?"

"No. Too many people seem to know too much about me. Meet me at the Golden Coin," he said, giving Raul the address. It was a greasy spoon on the outskirts of the Loop that he'd never patronized before. Unless they were followed, and Luke would make damn sure they weren't, no one would look for him there.

"I'll be there," Raul answered, breaking the connection.

Luke hung up the phone and focused on the car, thinking. After a minute, he pulled out his wallet and fished out a card. It was creased and worn, the result of sitting in his wallet for the past few years. But just because the card was old didn't mean it wasn't useful. Taking a breath, he dialed the number and waited for a voice to answer. Turning away from the car, he licked his lips and started to speak.

He slid back into the car several minutes later. "We're all set. Raul is going to meet us in a little less than an hour. Maybe he'll know where the next meeting is going to be."

"If he knew that, wouldn't he have told us yesterday?"

She was sharp, he thought. "Yeah, you'd think so. But Raul knows me too well. He knew that yesterday I wasn't ready to listen to him. He knows how to play me like a violin. He gave me enough information to make me wonder about Eddie and the others. Today, I have more specific information I want from him."

"But if he's not a part of the gang, how would he know that?"

He shrugged, concentrating on the car next to them that was determined to cut over a lane. "I don't know how Raul gets his information and I don't want to know. He hates them as much as I do, and he manages to find out about them. That's all I care about."

"Is there a reason besides the obvious why he hates the gang so much?"

He looked over at her. She had one leg curled under her and was leaning against the door. Her dark red hair was smooth and tamed, framing her face neatly. He wondered again how it would look if she allowed it to curl freely. A car honked, and he jerked his attention back to the road. Just like he needed to keep his attention on this case, he told himself grimly.

"You mean besides the fact that they've infected his neighborhood and are doing their best to destroy it?" he asked, his voice sardonic. When he looked over at her and saw her wince, he immediately regretted his words. "They killed his sister," he added more gently. "A drive-by shooting. The gunman was never caught. I was the investigating officer, and Raul and I got to be friends." He shrugged again. "The rest, as they say, is history."

He maneuvered the car into a parking spot next to the curb and underneath the elevated train tracks on the western edge of the Loop. The business center of Chicago was only blocks away, but this part of the city had a seedy, neglected air about it that contrasted sharply with the gleaming skyscrapers that dotted the skyline.

"Come on," he said as they made their way to the Golden Coin. "We're early, but we can have a cup of coffee and make sure nobody is interested in us."

A half hour later Raul strolled through the door. Spotting them at a booth in the back of the restaurant, he slid in across from them.

"Hello, Ms. Carleton," he said to Julia, then looked at Luke. "What has happened, my friend?"

Luke quickly described everything that had happened since Julia had hired him, ending with his visit to Eddie's house. "Now I have to assume she's on to something. Eddie's getting money somewhere, and I want to know where that is. Can you find out when the gang is meeting again?"

Raul's gaze flickered between the two of them. "Assuming that I can find this out, what will you do?"

"We'll find a way to see what's going on, of course," Luke answered impatiently. "I've got to get this case sewn up. I don't want anyone hurting Julia."

Raul's dark eyes shifted to Julia, and he shook his head. "No. That cannot happen." Luke saw the pain in his eyes and knew he was thinking about his sister. "I will find out for you." His words were a statement of fact, and Luke knew that he would. "Where can I call you?"

"We're between motels right now. I thought it was best to move every night."

Raul nodded. "Very wise. They have a long reach."

"Aren't you two going overboard a little?" Julia spoke for the first time. "This is just a street gang. It's not as if they're omnipotent."

"In their own neighborhood, I'm afraid they are," Raul answered. "That is why you must be very careful."

"I have been," Luke answered.

Raul looked at him and nodded. "You will be safe, Ms. Carleton. Trust Luke."

She surprised him with the readiness of her answer. "I do trust him, Raul. And please call me Julia."

Raul smiled at her and began to slide out of the booth. "Perhaps all of us can have lunch together again, after you have solved your case."

"We'd like that, Raul. Maybe we'll have something to celebrate."

Raul looked at him questioningly, and Luke pushed a piece of paper across the table at him. "My friend Eleanor is on the board of directors of the school of the Art Institute. Give her a call. I think she'll be able to arrange a scholarship for you."

For a second, fierce hope flared in Raul's eyes, then it was carefully damped. "I am not interested in charity, Luke."

"Charity?" Luke snorted. "Hell, it's not charity. The woman was practically drooling when I described your work to her. I had to make her promise not to drive out to your house today. She said that if you're as good as I think you are that the school would take you in an instant."

Raul stared at the paper in front of him as if he were afraid it would vanish if he moved to pick it up. Why hadn't he ever realized that Raul needed a scholarship if he wanted to go to school at the Art Institute? Luke thought. He glanced over at Julia. He owed her a lot for pointing that out to him.

Finally Raul looked back up at them, excitement stirring in his eyes. Luke wanted to reach over and kiss Julia right now. He hadn't seen his friend this happy, ever.

"How do you know this Eleanor?" Raul asked softly. His hand had curled around the piece of paper as if he would never let it go.

Luke shrugged, suddenly uncomfortable. "I, ah, served on a couple of committees with her a few years ago. She's a straight shooter, Raul. She doesn't say anything she doesn't mean."

"And she has said there are scholarships available at the Art Institute school?"

"For qualified students." Luke grinned. "It's up to you to make sure she knows you're qualified."

"All she'll have to do is see your work to know you're qualified, Raul." Julia spoke quietly, but with unshakable conviction.

"She's right." Luke watched Raul as he looked reverently at the paper in his hand, then carefully folded it and placed it in his wallet. "You're a talented artist and you should be studying someplace where your work can get the exposure it deserves."

Raul looked up at them, his eyes luminous. "I won't forget that you did this for me, my friend. Thank you."

Uncomfortable, Luke looked away. "It wasn't any big deal. I just had to make a phone call."

"You're wrong, Luke," Raul corrected gently. "It is a very big deal."

"Yeah, well, let's take this mutual admiration society on the road. It's time to get out of here."

Raul slid out of the booth and stood up, nodding. "You're right. We need to go."

"We'll give you a ride back to your neighborhood, Raul," Julia said. She turned to him and grinned. "That way you can get to your phone more quickly."

Raul frowned. "I don't know if that is wise," he said slowly. "There are eyes everywhere."

"We can drop you off in that big mall close by. That should be anonymous enough," Luke answered.

They stopped in front of Luke's car. "Come on," Luke urged. "It'll save you almost an hour." His friend was practically vibrating with the need to get back to his house and make the phone call.

"All right," he finally agreed. "But no farther than the mall."

"You've got it." Luke waited for him to close his door then pulled into traffic. He turned back to grin at Raul. "Just remember, I'll expect a hell of a steak dinner when you make it big-time."

* * *

Luke sat next to Julia in the front seat of the car and watched Raul disappear into the mall. Instead of driving away again, he turned to her.

"I don't know how to thank you for opening my eyes to Raul. Why didn't I realize that he needed a scholarship to go to school at the Art Institute?"

She turned to look at him, her eyes shining. "Because he's your friend," she said gently. "You can't stand back and look at your friends objectively."

He couldn't look away from her. The tenderness in her eyes was drawing him in, pulling him under. He wanted to drown in it, to pretend just for a moment that it was for him and he had a right to reach out for it.

"How did you know the woman on the board of directors?" Her voice was soft, the tenderness still there. Was it possible it could be for him and not for Raul?

He wanted to look away, but couldn't. He felt as if she were staring straight into his soul. He couldn't tell her anything less than the truth. "Just like I told Raul. We were on a couple of committees together a while back."

"Committees for what?"

"You don't give up, do you?"

Something shifted in her eyes as she watched him. The tenderness deepened, if that was possible. "No, I don't, Luke. You should know that by now."

He didn't answer for a long time, but she continued to watch him. Finally, shifting in his seat, he looked away from her. "I was a member of the board of directors of Pals. That was the program that paired kids who needed an adult role model with men and women who could give them some time and attention. Eleanor was on the board, too."

"I remember reading about that program." Her voice was filled with wonder, and he squirmed in his seat. He should never have opened this can of worms in front of her. "You were one of the people who got it started here in Chicago, weren't you?"

"Yeah," he admitted. "I got all the glory and everyone else did the work."

"I don't think so. Why do you let people think you're such a hard case when you're not?"

He turned away abruptly and started the car. "Because I'm not like that anymore. Things have changed in the last two years. I'm not the same person I used to be."

"Oh, I don't know about that," she whispered softly.

He risked a glance over at her. It was a mistake. The look on her face definitely wasn't there for Luke McKinley, the brutal cop who beat defenseless drunks. He could almost believe it was for Lucas McKinley, a decent man. Only he knew it wasn't, because that man didn't exist anymore.

He drove down the street, staring blindly at the people in the other cars and on the sidewalks. He wouldn't ever be Lucas McKinley again. His scars had healed into a tough outer shell, and it would be too painful to peel it away. He wasn't sure if he could bear that kind of pain, not in this life, anyway.

He glanced at the sidewalk and slammed on the brakes. Julia jerked forward and bounced, held in place by her seat belt. "What was that for?" she cried, gripping the armrest next to her and looking at him.

He nodded toward the sidewalk, not taking his eyes off the boy standing there. After a moment she said, "Isn't that Piotyr, that boy you talked to the morning after your office was bombed?"

"Piotyr Bernowski," he said grimly. "And do you see who he's talking to?"

"It looks like just another kid."

"It may be just another kid, but that kid belongs to the Demons."

She shifted and turned to look at him. "How do you know? Do you know him?"

"I don't have to. See what he's wearing? That orange-and-green coat and baseball hat are the Demons' colors. They're as good as wearing a sign on his head."

"What are you going to do?" she asked, still watching the two boys.

"I don't know. I was afraid this was what was going on with Piotyr, but up until now I didn't have any proof." He shifted back into gear and pulled away from the curb. "But I'll have to do something, fast. Once the Demons get their hooks in, it can be tough to get them out."

"That poor woman."

"Who, Mrs. Bernowski?"

She nodded and he glanced at her, surprised. "Why should you feel sorry for Mrs. B.? She was downright nasty to you."

"Only because she was trying to protect you. How can you criticize loyalty?"

"Even loyalty can go too far," he answered. "Blind loyalty can be very dangerous."

"Not when it's for your friends. Or your family."

Her voice was fierce, and he looked over at her. Never had a woman felt that way about him, and for a fleeting moment he longed for some of that unquestioning support for himself. What would it be like to have a woman like Julia Carleton feel that way about him?

He would never know, he told himself savagely, because that could never happen. And it most definitely wouldn't happen with Julia Carleton. He knew better than to fall for her. He glanced over at her. Didn't he?

Chapter 10

Julia sat down gingerly on the king-size bed and looked around the room, nerves curdling her stomach. "Are you sure it's necessary for us to share a room?"

He didn't even look up at her. "It's necessary. We haven't seen much of our shadows in the past couple of days, and it's making me nervous. And when I'm nervous, I like to circle the wagons."

"Couldn't we circle them around two rooms like we did last night?" she muttered to herself.

He must have heard her, because he looked up. "If you're worried about your virtue, don't be. I plan on sleeping on the floor."

"That hardly seems fair."

"Okay, you can sleep on the floor."

She clamped her lips together on the retort she wanted to make. Instead, she changed the subject. "Are you going to call Raul and see if he's found anything out?"

Apparently he didn't want to discuss their sleeping arrangements any more than she did, because he stood up and went to the phone. "I'll do it now."

The conversation was cryptic and one-sided. When Luke hung up the phone and turned to her, excitement gleamed in his eyes. "It looks like luck is finally turning our way. They're meeting tonight, and Raul was able to find out where. Now we just have to figure out how to get me in there."

"What do you mean, get you in there?" She watched him prowl the room, fear congealing in her blood. "If the Demons are meeting with the cops from your old precinct, they'll recognize you in an instant. There's no way you can try to infiltrate that meeting."

"Then what do you suggest we do, ask them for an invitation? We may not get another chance like this for a long time."

"I know." She stared at him, an idea forming in her mind. "They don't know me," she said slowly. "I've never interviewed any of them. I've deliberately stayed away from everyone who's a suspect. So if they see me hanging around tonight, no one will recognize me."

"No woman would be hanging around at night near the place the Demons are meeting," he stated, his voice harsh. "Trust me on this."

"Oh, some women might," she said, giving him a sultry smile. "Women who were practicing the world's oldest profession might find it a very attractive place to ply their trade."

He gave her a shocked look. "Are you saying you want to masquerade as a hooker so you can get close enough to find out what's going on at that meeting?" he demanded.

Thrusting her chin out, she said, "Can you think of a better plan?"

"I can and I will," he said furiously. "Yours is the most absurd thing I've ever heard of."

"Fine. I'm all ears."

She folded her hands in her lap and watched him pace the room. Shooting her a black look, he said, "I'll think of one, don't worry. No way am I letting you do something so dangerous."

"But it's okay for you to do something both dangerous and stupid? At least they won't recognize me the minute they see me."

"Eddie has seen you before." It sounded as if he were grasping at straws.

"Two years ago. And I wouldn't look the same if I was pretending to be a prostitute. I suspect I would have to dress a little more flamboyantly than I normally do."

"I suspect you would," he mocked as he stared at her, incredulous. "You're serious about this, aren't you?"

"As serious as...as the Demons. I don't see that we have any alternatives."

"I'll think of an alternative. There's no way you're going to flaunt yourself on a street corner to get some information. It's just too dangerous."

"We don't have any choice, Luke. I have to do it."

"Over my dead body."

"Are you almost ready in there?" Luke's voice came through the closed bathroom door, and Julia took one last look at herself in the mirror. It was a good disguise, she thought, her heart beginning to pound. She almost didn't recognize herself.

She'd let her naturally curly hair dry without trying to style it or tame it into submission. Now it curled wildly around her face, making her look like a temptress. Her carefully made-up eyes were enormous in her face, and the eye shadow she'd chosen made them look startlingly green. Not that anyone was going to get close enough to be able to see them, she assured herself.

Smoothing her hands down the clothes she'd bought that afternoon, she licked her lips and opened the door. Show time.

The look on Luke's face when she emerged from the bathroom told her all she needed to know about her costume. He looked as if he'd been poleaxed. She almost wanted to laugh, until she saw the expression in his eyes.

It was hot and hungry, raw with need. For her, she realized with shock. Slowly she looked down at herself. The tight red leather miniskirt exposed too much of her legs, and she had a sudden urge to cross her knees. The black lace chemise she wore as a blouse was perfectly decent, but it clung to every curve on her upper body. Resisting the need to fold her arms over her breasts, she said lightly, "So what do you think? Is it going to work?"

"Hell, yes, it's going to work." He moved slowly toward her. "It's going to work too damn well. Don't do it, Julia." He reached out and grasped her shoulders, drawing her closer to him. "It's too dangerous for you to go to that meeting place looking like this. You're going to attract too much attention."

"I'll be a part of the background, Luke." Her heart was thudding against her chest and her mouth was dry, but fear had nothing to do with it. It was because of the way he was looking at her. "They'll see another hooker on the corner, and that's all they'll see."

"Like hell they will," he muttered, pulling her closer. "They'll see just what I do, a woman so beautiful and so desirable that they can't think of anything else. A woman they'll want, regardless of the consequences."

"And what are the consequences, Luke?" she whispered. Blood roared in her head and the world shrank down to include only him.

His eyes glittered with desire and need. "I don't care," he whispered back. "Right now, I can't think of anything but you."

Then his mouth was on hers in a hard kiss. There was no tenderness, just a deep, searing possession. His hands slid down her back to cup her hips in the red leather, pulling them closer.

She melted against him, her heart hammering and fire dancing through her veins. She didn't care about consequences, either. Not now. Not while Luke was holding her, branding her with his kisses, insinuating himself into a place deep within her heart.

"Luke," she moaned, and she felt his tongue swirl into her mouth. She was hot and weak with need, with desire for him. "Please..."

Her words were devoured as he claimed her with his lips. Sliding her hands up his back, she found his muscles were as hard and tense as steel. When her fingers drifted lower and caressed his hips, he twitched once and drew her into the vee of his legs. He was as aroused as she was.

Dragging in a ragged gulp of air, he trailed a line of kisses down her throat to the neck of her chemise. When his fingers closed over her breast, her breathing hitched and she arched into him.

"Oh, Luke, I want..."

She felt him tense at the sound of her throaty whisper, then his mouth brushed over hers again as he sighed into her ear. "I want, too, Julia. Too much. But this isn't the time or place."

Luke wrapped his arms around her and held her tight. The throbbing need slowly subsided, replaced by an aching loneliness. She suspected there never would be a right time or place as far as Luke was concerned. He had his armor on, and he was determined to let nothing pierce it. She wondered what he was protecting himself from, and realized with a stab of sorrow that she would probably never know.

Edging back a little, he leaned his forehead against hers. "You know I don't want to stop this, but we have to go."

She disengaged herself gently. "I know. They're not going to wait for us to put in an appearance."

The hunger in his eyes made her reluctant to turn away. His face was all hard angles and planes, the flush of passion not yet fading. "It's not too late to change your mind, Julia. You know that, don't you?"

"We don't have any other choices," she said, turning to pick up the red leather shoulder bag that matched her skirt. "Let's get going."

The ride to the Humboldt Park neighborhood was a silent one. When they began seeing the Demons' graffiti spray painted on the walls of garages, Julia felt her stomach contract. This was really going to happen. She was really going to stand on a street corner and pretend she was a prostitute, not fifty feet away from the place where the Demons and the cops from Luke's old precinct were meeting.

"What are you going to be doing?" she asked Luke.

"I won't be far. You won't see me unless you have trouble." He glanced over at her, then surprised her by reaching for her hand. "But I'll be here."

The wave of relief that washed over her was enormous. She'd known that Luke would be close by, but hearing him say it somehow made her feel much better. Her fingers curled around his hand, and she clung to him until the car stopped along a dark, deserted street.

She licked her suddenly dry lips. "I take it we're here."

"No, but this is as close as I intend to get. And in case of trouble, I know a shortcut back to this spot."

"There's not going to be any trouble," she answered with a confidence she was far from feeling. Looking out onto the streets that represented every modern urban nightmare, she tried not to let Luke see that her hand was shaking as she tried to open the car door.

His hand on her arm, pulling her closer, stopped her. "Hell, Julia, there isn't even a place in that outfit where we could put a wire. One more time, this isn't necessary." His voice, low and intimate, surrounded her in the darkness of the car. All she wanted was to melt into the safety of his arms, to turn her back on the deserted street outside the car window.

"I think it is, Luke."

He sighed in the darkness. He was so close that she felt his breath stir her hair just above her ear. "You are one stubborn woman. And one brave one." His voice softened. "I don't know of another person who would have been willing to do this."

The admiration in his voice made her throat thicken, but she tried to shrug off his praise. "It has to be done, and I don't think you'd make a very good hooker."

"Julia."

He leaned forward, and she jumped backward and bumped her arm on the door. "Let's get this show on the road." If he kissed her now, or even touched her, she'd curl up into a ball in his arms and beg him to take her away from this place. So she opened the door and stepped outside.

It was a mild night, even for early May. At least she wouldn't be standing on the corner shivering. Or at least not from the cold, she thought wryly. Luke materialized next to her, holding a dark plastic bag in his hand, and said, "The meeting place is a couple of blocks away. Let's go."

It was the shortest two blocks she'd ever walked. They didn't meet a soul on the street, and only the occasional light shone out of a window along the way. It was as if the neighborhood was a ghost town, completely devoid of life.

As they turned another corner, Luke slowed down and pointed to a tall two-flat that had lights burning from the second floor. "That's the place," he whispered into her ear.

She stared at the building. The blaze of light made it seem like a welcoming oasis on the dark and quiet street. It was hard to believe that such an innocent-looking place could hide so much evil.

Turning to Luke, she resisted the impulse to move into his arms. The gangway where they'd stopped was too narrow to prevent their bodies from accidentally brushing together every time they moved. The contact was undermining her will, making her want to forget why she was here tonight. Biting her lip, she forced herself to look away from him again and concentrate on what she had to do.

"Where do you think I should stand?"

He looked around, his gaze assessing. "That corner over there, I think," he said after a while.

Looking where he indicated, she saw that the streetlight above the sidewalk was burned-out. "Will I be able to see them in the dark?"

"You'll see them better once your eyes are used to the dark, and they won't be able to see you as well."

"But wouldn't a real hooker stand under the streetlight, where she could be seen?"

She could feel him scowl in the darkness. "Probably. But don't worry about it. They'll think you're new to the neighborhood and you're being careful not to encroach on someone else's turf. Believe me, Julia, you'll be much safer in the darkness. We don't have to carry reality to that extreme."

"I just want this to work."

"It's going to work." There was grim determination in his voice, and she could almost believe that his will alone could prevent any mistakes. "Don't forget, I'll be close by. If anything starts to go down, just get away."

"Nothing is going to go down, Luke," she answered, trying to make her voice sound firm. "Nobody is going to pay any attention to me."

"Not bloody likely," he muttered. "Do you have the camera?"

"Right here in my purse."

"And you know how to use it?"

"You were right there while I practiced! Everything is going to be fine, Luke. Don't worry."

"I can't help it," he whispered fiercely. "Do you know how it makes me feel, knowing the danger you're going to be in?"

Slowly she shook her head. With a savage oath, he pulled her to him and kissed her, dragging his fingers through her hair to hold her mouth under his. When he finally let her go, she stumbled backward, her mouth tingling.

"I won't let anything happen to you, Julia. Remember that."

He eased back into the shadows and disappeared, and she took a deep breath to steady herself. Adjusting the purse over her shoulder, she strolled out of the gangway primping her hair, as if she were getting ready for a night's work.

Her legs were unsteady but she managed to sway over to the spot where Luke had told her to stand. Once there, she sagged against the lamppost and drew in a trembling breath. When nobody yelled at her or materialized out of the darkness to challenge her, she straightened and willed her shaking legs to stop their quivering.

After a while, she began to relax. Nothing had happened so far. And Luke was close by, even though she couldn't see him. Comforted by that thought, she opened her purse and took a cigarette out of the brand-new pack. Placing it in her mouth, she got out the small camera that vaguely resembled a cigarette lighter and brought it up to her face. If she positioned it just right, she could get a clear shot of anyone who approached the entrance to the two-flat.

As she was fiddling with the lighter, a car that seemed to appear out of nowhere pulled up in front of the house. Fumbling with the camera, she got it into position just as a man stepped out of the car. It wasn't anyone she recognized, and as she snapped a picture of him in the pool of light from a streetlamp, she felt a wave of massive disappointment.

Had Raul somehow gotten the wrong information? Was this the wrong house, and were she and Luke performing a ludicrous masquerade for nothing?

The man disappeared into the house, and she lowered the camera and leaned against the lamppost, trying to look bored. But another car pulled up a few minutes later, and she brightened. Maybe they were on the right track and the man whose picture she'd just taken was one of the Demons. She repeated her maneuver with the cigarette and camera, just getting a shot of another unknown man when a car stopped in front of her.

"Hey, baby, you interested in some action?"

A man leaned out of the window, and she could see that several other young men were laughing inside it. Fear slithered up her spine, but she forced herself to relax against the support of the lamppost. "I'm not into group things. Come back by yourself and we'll talk."

The men in the car hooted and shouted suggestions that made her face flame, but the car pulled away. She watched the red taillights fade into the distance, praying that the man in the car wouldn't take her suggestion seriously and come back.

Another car pulling up across the street claimed her attention, and this time when she raised the camera as if to light her cigarette, she froze. The man getting out of the car was one of the policemen from Luke's old precinct, someone on her list of suspects. She snapped several pictures, praying that the super-high-speed film they'd bought would be sensitive enough to give them good pictures.

She'd been right, she exulted as she slowly lowered the camera. The last several months of work and frustration had been worth it. She'd just nailed one of her suspects, and with any luck the rest of them would appear tonight.

Then she froze. What if Bobby showed up tonight? Luke was watching from somewhere. What if he saw Bobby and recognized him? What would she do?

When the next car appeared she almost didn't raise her camera. She was too afraid it would be her brother who stepped out of the car. But it was another of the cops on her list, and she dutifully snapped several pictures of him while waiting fearfully for the next car to arrive.

After another half hour she realized it had been a while since the last car arrived. Six of the suspects on her list were accounted for, but she hadn't seen Eddie Timmons. Or her brother Bobby.

Maybe they weren't going to show up tonight, she thought with a surge of hope. No one had arrived at the building now for at least fifteen minutes. Unless there was a back way into the place.

Suddenly she had to know if Eddie or her brother had managed to sneak in the back door. The only way to do that was to go around the building and see if there was a way in that couldn't be seen from the street. Slipping the tiny camera back into her purse, she pushed away from the lamppost and walked across the street. She hoped she looked like what she was supposed to be, and for good measure tried to add a little more sway to her walk.

No one challenged her or even seemed to notice her. The two-flat was still a few houses away when she spotted a gangway between two buildings. Ducking into it, she emerged next to a garage that faced an alley. The gate hung open on broken hinges, and she stepped into the dark alley.

Pushing her fears aside, she moved toward the meeting site. Perhaps she could kill two birds with one stone. While she checked to make sure Bobby wasn't in the building, she might be able to hear some of the group's plans.

As she stepped into the yard of the two-flat building, someone emerged out of the shadows. Thinking it must be Luke, she moved toward him with relief.

She stopped abruptly when she came face-to-face with a teenager holding a gun in his hand. "What do you want?" he asked in a low, guttural voice.

Backing up, never taking her eyes off the gun, she said, "Obviously I'm in the wrong place." Out of the corner of her eye she saw another darker shadow flit behind the boy with the gun. Bracing herself for another accusing face, she was surprised when no one emerged to stand next to him.

She saw the boy's eyes travel slowly from her hair to her shoes and back again, and when he spoke there was an excitement in his eyes that made her stomach turn. "Maybe you're not in the wrong place."

"I think I am. This isn't the kind of reception I was expecting. My..." she paused delicately "...customers don't need guns."

He shoved the gun into the waistband of his baggy pants and showed her his empty hands. "No gun. So how about it, honey? I could show you a real good time."

What did she do now? she thought frantically. What would she do if she really was a hooker? She smiled what she hoped was a seductive smile. "Do you have what it takes?"

"I've never had any complaints, honey," the boy said, leering at her.

"I'm sure you haven't." She let her eyes run down his body, and was horrified to see the bulge under his fly. "But money is what it takes to show me a good time."

The kid's smile faltered for just a moment, then he grinned at her. "I've got plenty of that. My car is in the alley. Let's go."

Panic rose in her chest and she wondered where Luke could be. What if this boy pulled that gun of his and insisted that she go with him? She had to stall. "We're not going anywhere until I see the color of your money."

"My money's just as good as anyone else's," he said, stepping closer to her.

"Only if it's in my hands." She took a step backward and held out her hand. "Haven't you ever heard of payment in advance?"

His hungry eyes stared at her for a moment, and for the space of a heartbeat she thought she was going to have to use one of the moves she'd learned in self-defense class years ago. She tensed her muscles in anticipation.

Finally he pulled out a wallet and removed a twenty-dollar bill. "This'll be a down payment."

She shook her head slowly. "I don't think so. I don't have a credit plan. And I don't work for peanuts."

He took another step forward, and she backed up again. She was almost in the alley. She couldn't outrun him, not in the red high-heeled sandals she wore, but she might be able to outmaneuver him.

Just as she was poised to take off, a figure in black emerged from the darkness of the garage behind her and stepped close to her side. For a moment, she was afraid that one of the boy's friends had decided to help his buddy out, and terror filled her mouth with the coppery taste of fear.

Then the figure slipped his arm around her shoulder, and she realized it was Luke. She glanced over at him, and had to stop herself from letting her mouth fall open in surprise.

He'd changed his clothes since she'd seen him last. The black T-shirt and jeans had been replaced by a flowing black silk shirt and baggy pants made out of some shimmery material. Four or five heavy gold chains hung from his neck. She could see them so easily, she realized, because his shirt was unbuttoned halfway down his chest. His longish dark hair had been slicked back and pulled into a ponytail at the base of his skull. He'd disguised his dark blue eyes with sunglasses that he now pulled off slowly, with menace in every movement.

"Is there a problem here, baby?" He spoke without looking at her, although his hand on her shoulder tightened reassuringly. He kept his gaze fixed on the boy in front of them, who now backed up a step.

She nodded at the boy. "He seemed to think I'd take twenty dollars as a down payment."

Luke's arm tightened around her, a silent comfort in the darkness. Then it dropped away as he advanced toward the boy. "Nobody messes with one of my girls." His voice was so low she had to strain to hear him. She couldn't miss the threat in his tone, however. Judging by the expression on the boy's face, neither could he.

"I wasn't messing with anyone." The boy's voice rose, and his hand hovered over the gun in his waistband. "It's a free country. We were just negotiating."

"Nobody negotiates with one of my girls, either. You want some action, let's see your money."

Luke took a step forward, but the boy stood his ground. "I don't have to pay for it," he blustered. "I can get it free any time I want."

"Like you said, it's a free country. As long as it's not one of my girls, you're welcome to get it free any time you can."

For a tension-filled minute, Luke and the boy stared at each other. Finally, hearing a noise from the two-flat behind him, the boy turned and disappeared into the darkness of the backyard. Luke stood listening for a while, then turned back to her. "Come on, baby. There's no action around here tonight." His low voice was just loud enough for someone to hear if they were standing in the shadows and listening.

Draping an arm over her shoulder, he steered her out of the alley and around the corner from the two-flat. Staggering slightly beside him, she tried to remember that, until they were back in the car, she was a hooker and he was her pimp. What she wanted to do was throw herself into his arms and never let go.

They were in the car and blocks away from the two-flat before he spoke. "What the *hell* were you doing back there?"

"Trying to get a closer look," she said defensively. "I was doing such a good job blending in that I figured I might as well try to see or hear more."

"You almost got yourself raped in an alley." She heard the fury in his voice. "Dammit, Julia, why did you do something that stupid?"

It wasn't stupid to try to protect her brother, she told herself passionately. "It didn't seem stupid at the time," she finally murmured.

He shot her a look. "It was a damn good thing that I was there. Do you know what could have happened to you?"

"I know self-defense," she answered, looking out the window. But remembering how she'd felt in the alley, she wasn't sure she would have been able to use it. She'd been almost paralyzed with fear.

The car suddenly swerved into a deserted parking lot, and he threw the car into park and reached for her. The single streetlight cast an orange glow over the front of the car as he pulled her against him.

"Don't ever do anything like that to me again, Julia," he said into her hair. His hands roamed over her back, as if he were trying to assure himself that she was still in one piece. "I almost died when I saw the way that kid was looking at you." His hands tightened, pulling her closer. "Another few seconds and I would have choked him with my bare hands."

She let her arms settle around his neck and closed her eyes. "I'm glad you were there," she admitted. Now that they were safe and the fear was slowly dissipating, she could tell him how scared she'd been. "I was getting a little nervous."

She felt him smile against her hair. "You could have fooled me. And you sure as the devil fooled that kid." Slowly he pulled back and looked down at her, still smiling. "You did a hell of a job tonight, Julia. And it took more guts than most people have to do it." His smile faded, replaced by an oddly diffident look. "I realized, standing in the shadows watching you take those pictures, that you're not the person I thought you were. I'm glad you asked me to do this job for you, Julia. I'm glad I got to know you."

Slowly she brought her hand up to cup his face. His beard felt rough against her palm, and he went very still when she stroked her hand down his cheek.

"I'm glad I got to know you, too, Luke," she whispered. "You're not at all the person you want the world to think you are."

His eyes shuttered and he turned to look out the windshield. "And what's that?"

"You want the world to think you're a real hard case, a man who doesn't look back and never takes any prisoners. But I know now that's not true. I'm glad I got to know the person underneath the surface."

"You don't know anything about the person below the surface, Julia. Don't make the mistake of thinking that you do." He turned back to her, and his eyes were cold and bleak. "I told you before, don't make me into something that I'm not."

She had to thaw the ice in his eyes, and she wasn't even sure why it was there. "I'm not," she answered softly. "But I think maybe you are."

The look he gave her was filled with self-derision. "I don't have to make myself out to be bad, Julia. I'm already worse than anything you could possibly dream up."

She shook her head stubbornly. "You're not, Luke."

"I am, Julia," he mocked. "The Luke McKinley you're trying to conjure up simply doesn't exist."

"Well, then, maybe I'm talking about Lucas McKinley."

He turned away from her abruptly and twisted the ignition key. "Don't kid yourself. Lucas McKinley died a long time ago. Luke is the only one home anymore."

Sliding as close as her seat belt would allow, she reached out and touched his arm. "Not to me, Lucas," she whispered.

He took his eyes off the road for a long moment to stare at her. When he looked back at the street in front of him, he said quietly, so quietly she almost couldn't hear him, "I wish I could be Lucas for you, Julia. I wish I could, but I just don't think I can."

Chapter 11

Neither of them spoke on the way back to the motel. When they arrived, they walked quickly into the building and up the stairs to their room. Julia helped Luke check the room for intruders, inspecting all the little traps he'd laid. When he nodded curtly after a couple of minutes, she slid the chain on the door behind her and slumped down into a chair.

"What do we do now?" she asked, brushing her hair back from her face, trying vainly to tame the springy curls. "We know for sure that at least five of the men from your precinct are involved with the Demons, but a few photographs aren't going to convict them."

"We have to catch them in the act of taking money from the gang, and I think we'll be able to do just that."

He turned to face her, grim determination on his face. "Three days from now another big shipment of coke is due. It's brought in by laundry trucks to a warehouse in Humboldt Park. I suspect Eddie and his buddies will make sure they get their cut before the Demons are allowed to sell it."

Shooting bolt upright in her chair, she stared at him, fear washing over her again. "How do you know that?"

"It's amazing what you can hear at keyholes. They were just getting to the interesting part when I heard you down in the alley."

"What?" She actually felt the blood drain from her face. "Are you saying you sneaked up the back stairs of that building and heard what they were saying?" When he nodded, she jumped up from her chair, fear combining with anger to propel the words that came spilling out. "Do you realize how easily you could have been caught? And what would have happened to you if you were?"

"But I wasn't," he said, shrugging.

That casual, indifferent shrug fanned the flames of her temper. "Only because I was stupid enough to try to do the same thing and fortunate enough that the guard stopped me in time. What were you thinking about, Luke?" She advanced on him and grabbed the billowing material of the black silk shirt, crushing it in her fists. "Don't you care at all about yourself?"

"We had to have more information, Julia. I didn't see any other way of getting it."

Still holding on to his shirt, she tried to shake him. "There were lots of other ways. Raul probably could have found out for us. You didn't have to risk yourself like that."

Slowly his hands came up and gripped her shoulders. "You were taking just as big a risk, Julia."

"No I wasn't," she insisted. "They don't know me. And I wasn't listening at their back door."

His grip on her shoulders tightened. "Why are you so upset? This is what you hired me for, isn't it?"

"I didn't hire you to get yourself killed," she cried.

"But you hired me to get proof of the cops' involvement, and with this information we can do just that. You should be happy that I was willing to take the risk. There's no reason for you to get so bent out of shape. Is there, Julia?"

Her eyes locked with his. She tried to look away, but his fierce gaze held her mesmerized. "Is there, Julia?" he repeated, his voice a low caress against her cheek.

"Yes, there is." She swallowed past the ball of fear lodged in her throat. "I don't want you to get hurt."

He continued to watch her, and she felt as if the words were ripped from someplace deep inside her. "I care about you, Luke," she whispered. "Please don't take any more foolish chances."

His grip on her shoulders loosened and shifted, and suddenly his hands were cupping her face. "Now you know how I felt when I found you in the alley with that horny kid. I would have died if anything had happened to you." His voice dropped to a husky growl. "I couldn't bear it if you got hurt and I couldn't protect you."

"But you did protect me, Luke. You were there when I needed you." She stepped closer to him, close enough that she could feel the heat from his body. "Is there anyone you can count on when you need help?"

Sliding his hands back to her shoulders, he closed his eyes, but not before she'd seen the desperate hunger she knew he wanted to hide. "I don't need anyone. Not even you." When she began to protest, he brushed his fingers over her mouth. "I don't want to hurt you, Julia. And believe me, I will if you give me a chance."

"I'm willing to take that chance, Luke. And you should be, too."

He opened his eyes again, and she could see the battle he fought. "You don't know anything about me, Julia." His voice was hoarse and strained, torn from his throat. "You're seeing only what you want to see."

"And you're giving yourself a lot less credit than you deserve." She reached out for him, needing to draw him close, then stopped, curling her fingers into her palms. What was she doing? She'd never thrown herself at a man, ever. Usually she ran as fast as she could in the opposite direction.

"I'm sorry, Luke. I shouldn't have said any of that." She backed away, but it was too late. His eyes blazed with need, and she could see the passion he'd banked down come roaring back. His hands tightened on her shoulders and he pulled her close, murmuring her name.

"I'm glad you did."

He took her mouth in a kiss that swept away all her restraints. Desire sprang to life inside her, consuming her with its fire, and she forgot all the reasons she shouldn't be here with him. Wrapping her arms around his neck, she kissed him back. She was home, where she belonged, and the rightness settled over her like a cloak, warm and enveloping.

He slid his tongue along her lips then dipped his mouth to the hollow of her throat. He groaned as he tasted her, sliding his hands down her back to linger at her waist. When she put her hands on his chest she could feel his heart pounding under the silk, beating against her palm.

Slowly he pulled away from her. With one shaking hand he brushed the curls away from her face, looking into her eyes. "I don't want to stop, Julia, but I need to know if you're sure. Is this what you want?"

She licked her lips and nodded slowly. "Oh, Luke. I know I shouldn't, and I know it's wrong, but I can't help myself. This is what I want."

Without a word he picked her up and laid her on the bed. Then he stretched out next to her, the baggy shirt hanging open so she could see the dark hair covering the sleek muscles of his chest. He leaned over her and she opened her mouth for his kiss, but to her surprise all she felt was his hand tangling in her hair.

"Why don't you leave your hair like this all the time?" he asked softly.

She opened her eyes to see him looking at her, his concentration fixed on the curl he was twining around his finger. She shifted self-consciously. "It's too wild and out of control. Who would ever take me seriously with hair like that?"

"I take you very seriously, Julia Carleton." He lowered his mouth to hers and nipped at her lower lip. "Hair and all. Tell me, which is the real Julia?" He let his mouth slide over her cheek and nibble at her ear. "The buttoned-up, hair-in-control, suit-wearing investigator?" His tongue dipped into her ear, and she shivered uncontrollably. "Or the wild-haired, miniskirted, passionate temptress?"

She couldn't answer. All she could do was turn to him, needing to feel his mouth on hers. She needed to feel his hands on her body, holding her. She needed to touch him, to be sure he was real and not part of a fantasy.

"Who are you, Julia?" he repeated, shifting so his leg covered hers. "You try to hide, but I need to know. I've needed to since the minute you walked into my office." He bent to kiss her again. Just before his lips touched hers, he murmured, "Tonight I'm going to find the real Julia Carleton. Which one are you?"

She wasn't sure if she knew herself. No one had ever made her feel like this before. She had felt desire, had been moved by passion, but never had she wanted to twine herself around a man and never let go, to get so far inside him that she couldn't be sure where he began and she ended. Never before had she wanted to melt into a man until she'd filled all the empty places in his soul and erased all the dark corners in his heart.

"I don't know," she whispered.

His hand brushed over her scalp and stroked through her hair. Just that slight touch made her quiver. "I have my suspicions," he murmured against her temple. "But there's only one way to find out."

He moved from her temple to her mouth, kissing her with a drugging sweetness that took her breath away. She opened to him helplessly, craving the taste of him. His tongue swirled through her mouth, caressing her with an urgent rhythm that had her arching to get closer to him.

Breaking the kiss, he trailed down her neck to the edge of the black chemise. She remembered how she'd wanted to cover herself earlier when he'd looked at her, and now she panicked momentarily, thinking about the revealing garment she wore.

He trailed a finger down the neckline of the chemise, pausing for a moment to dip into the valley between her breasts. "You look sexy as hell in this," he murmured, as if he could read her mind. "But you really drove me crazy that first day in my office. I could see the lacy thing you wore under your business suit, and all I could think about was what you would look like without that blouse."

He bent his head and dipped his tongue under the neckline of the chemise, his mouth leaving a trail of hot, wet fire across the top of her breasts. When she shifted against him, the hard length of his arousal burned into her belly, even through their clothes.

Raising his head, he stared down at her. Slowly he pushed the strap of the chemise off one shoulder. "I need to look at you, Julia. May I?"

She nodded, holding her breath as he pulled the silky fabric lower and lower. Every inch of skin tingled, and the silk brushing against it aroused her almost unbearably. Her nipple scraped against the lace at the neckline and caught, and he bent his head and took it into his mouth.

She cried out as he suckled gently, and arched against him. "Luke," she said in a high, thin voice she hardly recognized. "Luke, please..."

When he raised his head she saw that his blue eyes were almost black. Hot and glittering, they showed a man holding on to his control by the merest thread. Staring into her eyes, he pulled down the other side of her chemise until she was bare to the waist. Only then did he look down at her.

"Julia," he breathed. Reaching up with one hand, he caressed her almost reverently, his hand sweeping around her breasts and cupping them in his palm.

She ached for him, throbbed for his touch. When he finally bent down and took one nipple into his mouth, she gasped his name and wrapped her legs around him. He groaned, deep in his throat, and she felt his hips thrusting against her.

As he moved from one breast to the other, she reached down and pulled his shirt out of his waistband, then slid her hands over the hot satiny skin of his back. He froze, then lifted his head and took her mouth again.

The thread by which he'd held control had snapped. His kiss was deep and wild, his tongue possessing her and thrusting into her as he mimicked the movement of his hips.

She clung to him, feeling her body tightening and coiling inside.

Suddenly he reached down and shoved the leather miniskirt up over her hips. When he touched her through the lace panties she wore, she stiffened in stunned surprise, then began trembling as he stroked her through the material. Exquisite sensations coiled through her, winding more and more tightly, and she reached for him blindly and began unbuttoning his shirt.

When her fumbling hands couldn't push the buttons through the tiny holes, he pulled the shirt over his head. His muscles rippled in the dim light, and she watched as he reached down and unbuttoned the black pants and peeled them off.

Before he could bend over her again, she rose up on one arm and pushed him back to the bed. "Now it's my turn to look at you," she whispered, letting her gaze travel down his body. He was magnificent, from his broad shoulders to his narrow hips and long, lean legs. Her fingers tangled in the soft hair on his chest then trailed down the thin band of dark hairs that arrowed down his belly. When her hands crept below his waist he grabbed them and pulled them away.

"Not this time," he rasped. "If you touch me I'll explode." Kissing her hands, he let her go and swept the leather skirt and the chemise down her legs and tossed them on the floor.

Sliding over her, he braced his elbows on the bed and cupped her face in his hands. "I wanted to make it last forever for you," he whispered. "But I don't think I can, this time." He lowered his mouth to hers, and she could feel every muscle in his body straining with the effort it took to hold himself back.

"I don't want to wait," she said into his mouth. "I need you, Luke. Now."

With a groan he slid his hands down to cup her hips, and she rose to meet him. One smooth thrust and he was inside her. His hips twitched once, then he lay still.

She felt complete, as she never had before in her life. Wrapping her arms and legs around him, she reached up to kiss his mouth.

The touch shattered whatever remained of his control. Arms tightening around her, he began to move inside of her. Sensations she'd never felt in her life overwhelmed her, swirling through her and taking over her body and soul. Holding on to him, crying out his name, she tumbled over the precipice and felt herself falling, floating through space.

His hold on her tightened and he whispered to her, going rigid in her arms. As she slowly returned to reality, she wondered if she had really heard him correctly or if her imagination was supplying what she wanted to hear.

They lay on the bed together for what seemed like eternity, arms tight around each other. Luke's head was buried in her hair, and her cheek was against his chest. The steady *thump-thump* of his heart gradually slowed down, but she refused to loosen her hold on him. She never wanted to let him go. *Julia, love.* The words he had whispered as he shattered inside her filled her heart and sang to her soul.

Luke had to struggle to free himself from her arms, but he was afraid he was crushing her. Shifting his weight off her, he rolled over and pulled her close to him. His heart was still pounding, and when he rested his palm on her breast he found with satisfaction that hers was, too.

"Julia," he whispered. He wanted to say more, to tell her how he felt, but the words froze and caught in his throat.

"What, Luke?"

His heart was threatening to burst, but he pressed her closer and stroked one hand down her back. He had to distract her from what he was afraid he had said aloud. When he could trust his voice, he murmured, "Tell me about it."

"About what?" She curled into him, pressing a kiss against his chest.

"Why were you afraid?"

He felt her stiffen beside him but he just held her tighter. After a moment she sighed. "It's ancient history. Something that happened in the past. Something that has nothing to do with us."

"It does or you wouldn't have mentioned it earlier," he answered quietly.

He didn't think she was going to answer, she was quiet for so long. Finally she shifted in his arms and looked up at him. "I've always sworn I wouldn't get involved with anyone I worked with. That's all I meant."

"Why not?" He wasn't sure he wanted to hear, but he needed to know. If it affected Julia, he had to know about it.

She sighed and looked up at the ceiling. "It's not something I'm real proud of. Who would be if they'd been played for a fool?"

"Tell me, please. I have to know what ghosts I'm fighting."

She turned back to him then with a tender smile on her face. "You've erased all the ghosts from my life, Luke. None of it matters anymore, but if you really want to know, I'll tell you."

"I want to know."

She paused as if marshaling her thoughts. "When I was first with Internal Affairs, I fell for a detective," she began. "He was handsome and charming, and tried real hard to convince me he was crazy about me. I believed him for a while," she said, a hint of bitterness in her voice. "I even thought I was crazy about him, too."

"Until," he prompted, anger churning in his gut. There always was an "until" in this kind of story, but he couldn't bear the thought of it happening to Julia.

"Until I found out that he was a good friend of someone I was investigating in another precinct. I tried to convince myself that it had nothing to do with us, until one night at my apartment." She closed her eyes to the memory, and he tightened his arms around her. He had to bite his tongue to keep himself from telling her to stop. He didn't want to hear about her with another man, but he'd asked her and now he could damn well listen to her.

"I went into the bedroom to change my clothes. I had closed the door behind me, but I remembered something I wanted to ask him. I opened the door and stuck my head out, and I saw him in my briefcase, looking at my files."

"I'm sorry, sweetheart." He felt helpless to take away her pain, and the feeling made him even angrier. He burned to know who the man was, to avenge Julia's hurt.

"I wasn't sure if I was more angry or more humiliated. Ever since then, I've refused to get involved with anyone even remotely connected with my job." She turned to him. "That's why I said it was wrong. Because I was breaking my own rule. Not because of you."

Honesty made him force the words out. "Maybe it's wrong because of me, too. You should be careful, Julia. I can hurt you far too easily."

She gazed at him with trust in her eyes and he could barely stand to watch. "You won't hurt me, Luke. I know that."

"Not on purpose. But I don't have a sterling record when it comes to relationships. And I haven't given a damn about anyone or anything for the past two years. Those aren't very good odds."

"I'll take them. I think they're better than you give yourself credit for."

Closing his eyes, he rolled away from her and sat up. "You're making me into someone I'm not and seeing things that aren't there. Don't you have any self-preservation instincts at all?"

"I guess not." She didn't sound too upset at the idea. "Don't you have anything good to say about yourself?"

He opened his eyes to find her sitting up next to him, the sheet clutched above her breasts. "Yeah. I'm a real good bastard."

A look flashed in her eyes momentarily, then they softened. If he didn't know better he'd think she was angry. But not at him, he realized as she smiled at him, slowly and seductively. "There are a few other things you're good at, Lucas McKinley. Do you want me to demonstrate a couple of them?"

He forgot the look in her eyes as heat flared in his groin and he felt himself hardening again. "Be my guest. I'm all...ears."

"Okay, we'll start with them." She leaned over and bit down delicately on his earlobe. All the blood in his body pooled just below his waist. Groaning, he reached for her, but she backed away and grinned at him.

"We're just beginning, remember? There are a few other things I have in mind."

"Am I allowed to make suggestions?" He shifted his hand so that it rested on her thigh, and when he felt her muscles quiver under his fingers a blast of desire hardened his whole body.

She tilted her head as if considering. "I liked your suggestions earlier. Go ahead."

He pulled her close and murmured some sexy words into her ear, inhaling the faint scent of her soap that rose from her heated skin. He felt her tremble in response, and tried to pull her down onto his body.

She braced herself above him and pressed her knees into his ribs. "We have a long way to go before that," she said, leaning over him so that her breasts just brushed his chest. "A long way. And in the meantime..."

Her tongue swirled around one of his nipples, and he thought he would explode. But every time he tried to grab her, she just laughed and slipped away to torture him with her mouth somewhere else. By the time he rose up on his elbow and leaned over her, unable to wait another second, she was as breathless and aroused as he was.

When he slipped into her, she cried out his name and convulsed around him. He tried to hold on, to prolong the pleasure for her, but he couldn't contain himself. The next instant the waves of ecstasy overwhelmed him, and he stiffened in her arms. He barely had enough energy to roll over and pull her on top of him. The last coherent thought he had before sleep overtook him was how right she felt, curled into him. He felt like a drowning man who'd just been handed a precious lifeline.

Luke slowly opened his eyes, reluctant to wake up. He was nestled in softness, surrounded by the scent of Julia Carleton, and he didn't want the dream to end. But the light filtering through the geometric pattern on the window curtains burned his eyes, and he struggled to shake off the hangover of sleep.

Trying to throw back the covers of the bed, he realized his dream had been real. Sinking back into the too-soft mattress, he looked at Julia, snuggled next to him. Her leg had slipped between his legs, and his arm was tucked around her chest, lightly cupping one rosy-tipped breast. As he watched the regular rise and fall of her chest, slow and steady in sleep, he remembered everything that had happened the night before.

Unconsciously he pulled her closer to him as his blood surged in response. In the cold light of day, maybe making love with Julia had been a mistake, but his body sure didn't think so. In fact, his body was shouting for an encore.

Carefully he tried to disentangle himself from her. If he could get out of bed and into the shower before she woke up, he had a much better chance of pulling off the casual approach. As he tried to slide to the edge of the bed, she stretched and rolled over, opening her eyes and smiling lazily at him.

In the early morning light her eyes were the deep green of the sea and just as magnetic, pulling him closer almost against his will. "Good morning," she murmured in a low, husky voice.

As if it had a will of its own, his hand reached out to touch her face. "Good morning to you. How did you sleep?"

She sat up in bed, pulling the sheet up to cover her breasts. "I had a wonderful night. How about you?"

Her smile was full of satisfaction, and he closed his eyes to block the sight of her. How could he have asked such a stupid question, one guaranteed to provoke a discussion of the night before? It was the one thing he didn't want to talk about.

"Great," he answered, his voice too hearty. "I was just going to take a shower."

He practically sprinted for the bathroom, shutting the door behind him and leaning against it. Turning on the tap with a vicious twist of his wrist, he stepped under the stinging-cold needles of spray and felt the guilt sluice over him along with the water.

He had been happy last night. He had made love with another woman, an experience like nothing he'd ever even imagined before, while Linda was lying in a box in the ground. Put there because of him.

Bracing his hands on the wall, he leaned forward and let the cold water beat the fever out of him, the fever to take like a greedy child what Julia offered. He wanted to let himself drown in her eyes, to lose himself in her sweet body, to look at Julia and think of nothing but her.

But he couldn't. Every time he looked past her shoulder, he saw his wife. Lying in a smashed car, covered with blood, motionless and limp. Himself helpless to get to her, trying to pull aside the crumpled metal with his bare hands.

The bathroom door opened with a click. Turning his head, he saw Julia standing beside the shower, easing open the glass door. "Care for some company in there?"

Without waiting for an answer, she stepped inside, flinching as the first blast of freezing water hit her. Jumping backward out of the shower stall, she looked at him, puzzled.

"Why on earth are you taking a cold shower?"

"It's a time-honored method of taking care of certain problems," he answered tersely.

She stared at him for a moment, then smiled. He'd never seen such an alluring expression on a woman's face before. "There are other ways of solving that particular problem," she whispered. Reaching to the front of the shower, she adjusted the handles and waited for the water to warm up. Then she stepped into the stall with him.

"In fact," she murmured, reaching for the soap, "I'm surprised you didn't think of some of them yourself. I thought you were a pretty smart guy, McKinley."

Not smart enough, obviously, to get out of the shower now, while he still could, he thought sourly. He watched as she ran the soap slowly down her chest, feeling his loins tighten helplessly in response.

Guilt swirled with need in his gut, and he tried to push the guilt aside. For now, until this case was over, he needed to have Julia with him. It was a matter of her survival. And he was no more able to turn away from her than he was able to stop breathing. He'd deal with the guilt later. Right now he'd take what she was offering, and damn his soul to hell.

Roughly he reached out and pulled her against him. His throbbing arousal pressed against her belly, and she dropped the soap on the floor and wrapped her arms around him. "I've thought about plenty of things this morning, Julia, believe me," he muttered, nuzzling her wet hair away from her ear. "And every one of them involved you."

Then as she lifted her mouth to his, everything but Julia was forgotten. Even the guilt, never far from the surface, disappeared into the darkness, banished by the power of her kiss. While he held her, he could pretend that nothing was important except for her.

A long time later she stirred on the bed next to him. He hadn't slept, but had held her tightly, staring up at the ceiling. With any luck, in three days it would all be over. He could go back to his life and send Julia back to hers. He would pay his penance for his few stolen hours of joy and get on with his life.

"I'm starving."

He looked down at her and found her grinning up at him. "I'm sorry, I know that isn't the best way to greet your lover after incredible lovemaking, but I can't help it. If I don't get food soon I'm going to start gnawing on the furniture."

He strained to match her teasing tone. "We'd better find you some food, then. The stuff in here is bound to give you indigestion." Sitting up in bed, he searched the floor until he found his shorts. After he'd pulled them on, he stood up.

She'd slid off the bed on the other side, dragging the sheet with her. Wrapping it around herself like a toga, she rummaged in her bag for clean clothes. When she stood up with a pair of jeans and a sweater clutched in her hands, she noticed him watching her and flushed a delicate pink.

"I've seen everything that sheet is covering, and more than once," he drawled, even as he asked himself why he was doing this. It would be much better to let her keep her distance from him. But, perversely, he was determined that there be no barriers between them, at least for the next few days. He might as well be hanged for a wolf as a sheep.

Her color deepened and her hold on the sheet tightened. "I'm not used to prancing around naked in front of men."

He was oddly moved by her modesty as he watched her. Abruptly he turned around. "It'll be kind of hard to get dressed while you're holding that sheet in place. How about if I promise not to peek?"

Behind him he heard the whoosh of the sheet dropping to the floor and had to stop himself from turning around. Now he could spend the day thinking about when he could take those clothes off her again.

Another minute and she said brightly, "I'm all set."

He turned around to find her trying to brush the curl out of her hair and deliberately not looking at him. Her sweater rose up as she raised her hand to attack her hair again, and a flash of white skin showed at the top of her jeans. He felt such a rush of tenderness that he had to fight the urge to go to her and gather her close, to feel her heart beating against his. Looking away, he pulled a clean pair of jeans and a flannel shirt out of his duffel bag and threw them on, then grabbed his gun off the night table.

He avoided her while he set his traps. Finally, opening the door, he permitted himself to look at her. "I can hear your stomach grumbling from here. Let's go get something to eat."

Chapter 12

Julia looked at Luke as the car slid to a halt in front of his old precinct house. He'd been too silent during breakfast, avoiding her eyes and making it clear he didn't want to discuss what had happened the night before.

That was fine with Julia, because she didn't much want to discuss it, either. The joy and the incredible sense of rightness that she'd experienced were overlaid by the knowledge that she hadn't been completely honest with Luke about the case they were working on. She hadn't told him her suspicions about Bobby, her horrible fear that he was somehow involved.

"I'm going to park around the corner." His voice interrupted her thoughts, and she looked up at him, startled. "I don't want anyone to walk out the door and spot me. No one knows for sure that I'm working for you, and I want to keep it that way."

"Okay." She licked her suddenly dry lips and nodded. They were back to business. "I'll get the time sheets and meet you at the car."

"Remember, don't ask to see the sheets for this week. But get a look at them."

"You've told me that five times already," she snapped, then bit her lip. "I'm sorry, I guess I'm just nervous."

He reached out his hand and cupped her face. It was the first time he'd touched her since they'd left the motel room. "I know. But this is the easy part. You have every right to those records, and you have surprise on your side. No one's expecting you. They're going to hand them over to you, and you're going to walk out that door and get back in the car. Then you're going to tell me who's on duty two days from now. And I'm willing to bet a lot that it's the six guys you saw last night, plus Eddie."

She turned to kiss his hand, feeling the ridges and calluses of his palm against her lips, letting her face rest there for a moment. Then, reluctantly, she drew away. "Okay, I'm ready to face the bad guys." Squaring her shoulders, she got out of the car and walked up the steps, careful not to look behind her as Luke pulled away. Already she felt desolate without him next to her, and he was only as far away as the next street. She forced herself to concentrate on what she would say to the desk sergeant.

And on what she would do if Bobby's name was on the duty roster for two nights from now.

Smoothing her hands self-consciously down her jeans, regretting that she wasn't wearing one of her business suits to make her feel more in control, she opened the door and walked in. The familiar smells of stale coffee and stale sweat surrounded her, and she felt herself calm down. This was her job, and she was good at it.

Strolling over to the desk, she resisted the impulse to look into the squad room. She was afraid that if she saw any of the men that had been with the Demons last night, her face would give her away. They'd know immediately that she knew. And she particularly didn't want to see Bobby.

"Can I help you, miss?" The gray-haired man at the desk looked at her politely.

"Julia Carleton from Internal Affairs," she answered briskly, showing him her identification. "I need to see your duty rosters for the last couple of months."

He gaped at her. "Duty rosters? What for?"

"I'm afraid that's classified information." She softened the words with a smile, and the man flushed and turned around.

"I'll get them." Fumbling in a drawer, he eventually turned back to her with a sheaf of papers clutched in his hand. He laid them on the counter, and she began to page through them, pretending to check that every week was accounted for.

"The last two weeks are missing," she finally said, looking up to find the older man watching her with a worried look.

"They're probably still on the board," he answered quickly. "I'll go get them."

That meant that this week's list would be on the board, too, she thought, her heart sinking. It was one thing to ask for records properly, at the front desk. How would she manage to get hold of a list that was posted in the squad room?

The old man hurried back, holding several pages in his hands. "Here you are. I just grabbed everything off the board. I hope this is what you want."

At the bottom of the stack was this week's list. She looked up at him with a brilliant smile. "This should do it. If you could just make me a copy of these?"

"Sure thing, Ms. Carleton." He grabbed the thick pile of papers and disappeared behind a door.

Julia reached for the current week's list but it was gone. The desk clerk must have taken it, too. Praying fervently that he would copy it along with the others, she shifted from one foot to the other and tried to look inconspicuous.

"Hey, Skinny," came a voice from the other room, and she froze for a moment, then turned around slowly.

"Hello, Bobby." Her voice was muted and she avoided looking at her brother's eyes, afraid of what she might see.

He strolled over and enveloped her in a bear hug, then set her down and held her at arm's length. "What's up, sis? Looking for me?"

His gaze was as bland as his voice. She met it briefly then looked away, shriveling inside at the guarded expression in his eyes. "Not this time, Bobby. I'm here on business."

She was sure no one but her would have noticed his infinitesimal pause, the almost imperceptible tensing. Stepping backward so he was forced to let her go, she caught a glimpse of his haunted eyes and tried to swallow around the hard lump of fear and despair that swelled in her throat. She turned blindly back to the desk, willing the desk sergeant to appear. *Please hurry,* she prayed silently. She had to get away from Bobby, to have time to think about what to do next.

"Here are those time sheets, Ms. Carleton." The desk clerk seemed to appear out of nowhere, handing her a thick sheaf of papers.

"Checking to make sure all our overtime is on the up-and-up?" Bobby's voice was just a little too hearty, and she nodded mutely.

"Something like that," she managed to answer. Looking at the clerk, she muttered, "Thank you," then turned and hurried for the door.

"Hey, hold on, sis." Bobby was in front of her, holding on to the door. "Why don't you come on back to my desk and have a cup of coffee? We didn't get much of a chance to talk the other night."

Julia looked around him, trying desperately to disguise her pain and anger. "Sorry, Bobby, not today. I've got a meeting scheduled for ten minutes from now. Maybe next time."

"Sure, Skinny." He stepped aside. "I'll catch you next time."

Mumbling a goodbye, she slipped through the door before it opened completely and ran down the steps, tripping on the next to last one. Catching herself on the rusty metal railing, she clutched the papers to her chest and hurried to the street where Luke would be parked. She didn't look back, although she could feel her brother's gaze on her until she'd turned the corner.

Luke was parked halfway down the block. He'd been watching for her, because she heard him start the engine before she reached the car. Sliding onto the front seat, she fumbled with her seat belt, then leaned back against the cushion.

"Did you see the roster?"

She shook her head, unable to answer. Fear for her brother, pain at his betrayal clogged her throat. If she spoke now, she was afraid she'd burst into tears.

Luke slammed his fist into the steering wheel. "Dammit to hell!" he exploded. Jerking the gear lever viciously into reverse, he maneuvered the car into traffic and pressed down on the accelerator.

As the car shot down the street, she swallowed several times and finally managed to croak, "But I got a copy of it."

"Thank God." He relaxed slightly, leaning back into his seat. "Who's on it?"

"I don't know." She tried to moisten her suddenly too-dry mouth as she held the papers more tightly in her hand.

"Well, look now, for crying out loud."

The papers rattled together as she looked through them slowly. She prayed he wouldn't notice how her hands were shaking, or that if he did he'd think it was because she was anxious to read the list. She found the sheet with Monday's date and pulled it from the pile reluctantly.

It made no difference now what other names were listed for the evening shift in two days. She knew her brother's name would be one of them. Glancing down the list, she wasn't even surprised when the name Bobby Carleton jumped out at her.

Closing her eyes, she willed the churning in her stomach to stop and cleared her throat. If she didn't read these names to Luke, he'd take the paper away from her and read them himself.

"Here they are," she began, then stopped, appalled at how shaky her voice sounded.

Luke had relaxed his grip on the steering wheel when she told him she had the list. Now he glanced over at her, a small smile on his face. "It's okay to be nervous. I'm shaking, too. That's the final nail in the coffin that you're holding in your hand."

He didn't know how true his words were. Clearing her throat, she began reading. "Joe Molloy, Les Gruber," she started, listing six names in all. It was every man they'd seen at the Demons' two-flat.

With two additions. She couldn't force the name Bobby Carleton past her lips, but after taking a deep breath, she added, "And Eddie Timmons."

"That's it. Those are our guys." He reached over and squeezed her nerveless hand. "Good job. Two days from now this case will be history."

She shuffled the paper back into the pile and nodded, staring straight ahead out the window. What should she do? Luke was bound to find out, sooner or later. She had to tell him. How could she get to her brother before Friday night, keep him away from that warehouse? How could she convince him to do the right thing? And what was the right thing, anyway?

She caught the flicker of motion out of the corner of her eye just as they started through the intersection. So did Luke, because he stomped savagely on the brake and twisted the steering wheel as the black sedan barreled toward them.

There was a stop sign in front of the black car, but the driver didn't even slow down. Julia froze, unable to move, as the grille of the car rushed toward her. Luke must have spun the steering wheel again, because at the last moment they skidded and the car spun in a semicircle. There was a sickening crunch behind her, a slashing pain on her forehead, then the seat belt caught her as the impact propelled her toward the windshield.

Her head snapped back and the whole world began to spin, slowly and sickeningly. Somewhere, far in the distance, she heard the squeal of tires and Luke's voice, high-pitched with panic, calling her name.

His hands were on her face, touching her shoulder, feeling for a pulse in her wrist. Her name was a chant on his lips. "Julia. My God, Julia, answer me. Answer me, dammit. Tell me you're all right. Tell me you're not hurt."

His hand tightened on her wrist, and she wanted to turn to him and tell him she was okay, she would be fine if only the world would stop its nauseating spinning. She opened her mouth, but no sounds came out. She tried to turn her hand to grasp his, but another wave of nausea swamped her and she closed her eyes. Maybe it would be better to sleep until this horrible churning in her stomach had stopped.

Luke saw her slump back against the seat, her skin bleached of color, and felt a deep and spreading panic. This couldn't happen to him twice in one lifetime, could it? Fumbling for his seat belt, he ignored the man who leaned in the window and asked, "Can I help you? We've already called the police and an ambulance is on the way."

Luke wrenched open the car door and pushed past the Good Samaritan, ignoring his worried, "Maybe you shouldn't move until the paramedics get here." He staggered around the car and tried to pull open the door next to Julia, but it was impossible. The impact had come right behind her door, and the metal was crumpled and crimped together. There was no way he could get her door open.

He reached in the shattered window, ignoring the shards of glass that lined the window frame like glittering knives. "Julia, you're going to be fine." He heard the frantic, pleading note in his voice but was powerless to subdue it. What he wanted to do was scream out his fear and his rage, beg and plead with her not to die, to open her eyes and look at him and tell him she was fine.

Her curly mass of hair had fallen forward, covering her face. With a trembling hand he brushed it back behind her ear, and froze in shock when he saw the dark red blood streaming down her face.

The night of his wife's accident played in slow motion inside his head, and suddenly it was as if it had happened yesterday. The crumpled car, his pregnant wife so ominously still, crushed between the steering wheel and the seat, the door of the car that wouldn't open and allow him to pull her out, pull her to safety.

Linda's face merged with Julia's, and he began tearing at the car door, desperate to get Julia out. If he could get the door open and get her out of the car, she wouldn't die like Linda had. He wouldn't have to stand here and watch her slip away, powerless to do anything to help her.

He never heard the sirens or the voices of the paramedics until someone wrapped him in a bear hug from behind and held him tight while someone else pried his hands away from the now bloody glass shards on the window.

"Let me go!" He struggled wildly, frantic to get away from the restraining hands. "I have to get her out of there."

"Take it easy, man." Someone spoke in his ear, his voice obscenely soothing. "We'll get her out."

Slowly he was being pulled away from the car, away from Julia and his only chance to save her. From far away he heard another voice say, "Look what he did to his hands, the poor sap."

Another voice barked, "Get him over here so I can wrap his hands. Jeez, look at this mess. My God, he's lucky as hell he didn't slice an artery. Get him on the gurney, right now."

He fought the straps tightening around him, fought the surprisingly gentle hands that smeared something cool on his hands, fought the voice that tried to tell him everything was going to be fine. Nothing could be fine anymore, not when Julia was trapped in that car, bleeding, her life slowly seeping away. He fought until he couldn't fight anymore, until the blackness swirled over him and threatened to pull him under. Just as it closed over him he heard Julia's voice calling his name.

A siren wailed above Luke's head, the sound reverberating in his ears. Where the hell was he? Trying to sit up, he realized he was tied down. Straps circled his chest and his thighs, and he couldn't get his hands free to untie them. As he began to struggle, a hand pushed him back down.

"Take it easy, pal. We'll be there in a couple of minutes."

"Where is there?" he croaked, the sound grating on his raw, aching throat.

"The hospital. You're not going anywhere until the doctors get a good look at you."

The accident. The pictures came swarming back. "Julia?" he asked frantically. "Where is she?"

The paramedic nodded his head toward the gurney on the other side of the truck. "Right there. We got your wife out of the car a couple of minutes after you passed out."

The word *wife* made a knife turn in his gut, but he ignored the pain. "How is she? Is she alive?"

The paramedic gave him a look, understanding mixed with pity. "Yeah, she's alive. I'm no doctor, but it looks like she's going to be fine." He grinned. "She asked about you, too, before she wanted to know what was wrong with her." His face sobered. "The two of you are damned lucky. If the impact had been another foot farther forward..." He shrugged. "You're real lucky."

The ambulance stopped with a jerk and the back doors were thrown open. Hands reached in and pulled out the two gurneys, first Julia's, then his. Before he could direct the nurse pushing him to follow Julia, he was in a cubicle with the curtains pulled around him and a young woman bending over him, shining a light in his eyes.

"Untie these damned straps, will you?" he barked at the woman, who ignored him as she continued to examine him. "Dammit, I feel like a Thanksgiving turkey trussed for the oven," he exploded. "Can't you at least untie my hands?"

The young woman smiled at him and slipped her tiny flashlight into her pocket. "Only if you promise to stay right here, Mr. McKinley. No jumping off the cart and running off to look for your wife."

Had the damned woman read his mind? "Where is Julia, anyway?"

"Just down the hall. As soon as Dr. Lynne finishes examining her, I'll let you know what he found."

"What am I doing tied down here, anyway? I wasn't hurt in the accident. The car hit Julia's side."

"You injured your hands." Her voice was infinitely gentle. "Besides checking for any other injuries, I have to make sure you don't need to be sutured."

Hands? How the hell had he hurt his hands? He tried to lift his arms to look at them, but they were still tied down. Peering at the name tag on the woman's white coat, he said, "Dr. Wright, please untie me. I promise to behave."

She looked at him for a moment, then nodded. In another second the straps were removed, and he slowly sat up, staring at the white bandages cocooning both his hands. Looking back at the young doctor, he said, "How did I hurt my hands?"

The look she gave him was filled with pity. "You were trying to get your wife out of the car. You cut them on the broken window."

He stared down at the bandages that covered him from the tips of his fingers to midway up his arm. "She's not my wife," he murmured. "I couldn't save my wife." Lifting his head, he watched the doctor as she unwound the gauze around his hands. "Do what you have to do, Doctor, but make it snappy. I need to get to Julia."

A half hour later, ignoring the voices raised in protest behind him, he strode into the cubicle where Julia lay on a gurney. She was wide-awake but lying motionless, flat on her back. Hearing him enter the room, she turned and smiled at him, her face full of relief. "I was worried about you," she said softly.

"There's nothing wrong with me," he answered brusquely, moving to stand next to her. "How are you doing?"

"Fine, I think. They took some X rays a little while ago, and they're just waiting for someone to look at them."

Her face was still too white, and there was a wide piece of gauze covering the right side of her forehead. Raising his hand, he smoothed the tip of one finger over the skin below it. "What's this?"

She shrugged, wincing with pain. "A cut, apparently from a piece of glass. It's nothing. They've already sutured it."

"Mr. McKinley, only relatives are allowed to stay with our patients. You must leave at once. You can't come barging in here like this." A middle-aged nurse bustled into the room, trying to shoo him away.

He moved closer to the gurney, closer to Julia, and he felt her slip her hand into his. Before he could open his mouth to answer, Julia did.

"I want him to stay with me. If he leaves, I'm going to get up and leave, too."

The nurse's mouth dropped open with astonishment. "You can't do that," she sputtered. "They haven't read your X rays yet."

Julia squeezed his hand and smiled at the nurse. "Then it's a good thing you're going to let him stay, isn't it?" she replied sweetly.

The nurse opened and closed her mouth a few times, glared at both of them, then spun around and stalked out the door. When Luke turned back to Julia, he found her staring at the bandages on his hands.

"What happened?" She raised her eyes to his. "How did you get hurt?"

He wanted to hide his hands behind his back, but couldn't bear to let go of her. "I cut them on some broken glass," he answered gruffly.

She looked at him questioningly, and he could see her getting ready to ask why there was broken glass on his side of the car. Someone cleared his throat behind them, and he spun around, grateful for the interruption.

"I've looked at your X rays, Ms. Carleton, and everything looks fine," the doctor said. "I imagine you'll have some soreness in your neck and shoulders for a few days, but there's nothing broken or dislocated. I've written you a prescription for a mild painkiller, and you need to see your own physician in ten days to have the sutures in your forehead removed. Otherwise, you're all set. You can leave whenever you're ready." He paused and smiled. "You were very lucky." He glanced over at Luke. "You, too, Mr. McKinley."

He left the room, and Luke turned to Julia. "Do you want to go?"

"Is the pope Catholic? Let's get out of here."

She tried to sit up, but he saw her bite her lip with pain. Slipping his arm around her shoulders, he eased her to a sitting position, then squatted to put on her shoes. Wrapping one arm around her waist, he eased her off the gurney and steadied her when she closed her eyes.

"Are you all right?" he asked, fear in his voice. "Should I call the doctor back?"

She opened her eyes and smiled at him. "I'm fine. I was a little dizzy at first, but it's gone. Let's go."

Walking slowly out to the desk, he asked the receptionist to call them a cab. When he eased Julia down onto a small couch in the waiting room, he pulled her close to him and she rested her head on his shoulder. He didn't want her any farther away from him than this. He needed to reassure himself that she was alive and that she was all right.

When they climbed into the cab, Luke told the driver to go to the nearest car rental office. They pulled up outside a familiar black-and-yellow sign a few minutes later, and after a surprisingly short time they were in a brand-new gray sedan, driving back toward the hotel.

Neither of them said more than a few words until they were back in their room. They'd stopped once, to fill Julia's prescription, and as soon as he'd checked the room Luke went into the bathroom, filled a glass of water, and handed her two of the pills.

She took one of them and swallowed it with the water. Luke scowled at her and said, "Take both of them, dammit. You're going to be sore in a few hours."

Curling his fingers around the other pill, she shook her head. "We can't afford for me to be that groggy. I don't hurt that much, honest. I'll be fine."

"We can afford to let you sleep for a few hours. Nothing is happening until the day after tomorrow, after all."

A shadow passed over her face and was quickly gone. "There must be something we can do between now and then."

"Dammit, Julia, forget about the case for a minute." He heard himself shouting and tried to lower his voice. "You were almost killed." The words felt as if they were torn out of him.

Smiling at him, she stepped forward and laid a hand on his chest. "But I wasn't. And it was because of your quick reflexes. If you hadn't managed to turn the car..." Her smile slowly died. "He would have hit me directly and I doubt if I would be standing here right now."

He couldn't hold himself back for another second. Closing his eyes, Luke reached for her and wrapped his arms around her. Rocking her back and forth, he whispered, "Oh, God, Julia, I thought you were dead. I thought I had killed you. You were so white, so quiet, and you wouldn't answer me. There was so much blood, and I couldn't get you out of the car." Pulling her close, he whispered again, "I thought I'd killed you."

Her arms encircled his waist and held on tightly. "You didn't kill me, Lucas McKinley, you saved me. If you hadn't reacted so fast, if you hadn't spun the car around, I might have died. But I didn't. You saved me." She unwound her arms from him and reached up to cup his face. "You saved me, Luke," she repeated. As she stared into his face, he saw the understanding flash into her eyes.

"You weren't able to save your wife, were you?" she whispered. "You tried, but you were too late."

"Oh, God, Julia," he cried, "I thought it was happening all over again." Closing his eyes against the hot press of tears behind his eyelids, he buried his face in her hair and breathed in her scent.

Julia pressed her cheek against his chest, hearing the steady beat of his heart. She wanted to absorb his pain, just as she was absorbing his heat and his comfort. "Do you want to talk about it?" she whispered.

He didn't answer for a long time, and she was content to stand and hold him. Finally she felt his mouth kiss her hair, and he shifted in her arms. "I should have been with her that night. If I had been with her, it might not have happened." His whispered words were pure pain, dredged out of the deepest recesses of his soul.

"You don't know that," she protested. She tried to lean back, to look at his face, but he held her more tightly.

"I do know that. She was coming home from a movie, by herself. I was supposed to go with her, but at the last minute Eddie set up a bust on a case that I'd been working on for months. By the time I found out, it was too late to stop it. The irony of it all is that the bust went bad."

"Why did you go on the bust instead of going with your wife?"

His arms tightened almost painfully, then he thrust her away from him and whirled, striding over to look out the window. "That's the sixty-four-thousand-dollar question, isn't it?" The words were spoken with a resigned pain that made her want to run to him, to hold him until it went away. But she stayed where she was, waiting for him to tell her.

"Do you want the truth? It was because my work was more exciting, more interesting, and more important to me than my wife." He whirled and stared at her. "We had a fight and she ended up insisting on going by herself. I was relieved, Julia. I let my pregnant wife go out alone to a movie because I would rather be working than spending time with her."

She looked at him, genuinely puzzled. Bits and pieces of the testimony from his case, two years ago, played in her mind. "I don't understand. Everyone said you were completely devoted to your wife. You almost killed a man and got fired from the job you loved because of her." Remembering what had happened a few nights ago, she flushed but forced herself to say, "You still keep a picture of her next to your bed. How can you say those things?"

"I can say them because they're true." He whirled and looked out the window again. "She was my first girlfriend. We were sixteen when we met, and we thought we were madly in love. We got married when we were twenty. By the time I realized that there was supposed to be a lot more to marriage than we had, it was too late."

He turned and faced her, and the agony on his face was almost too much to bear. "I think she loved me. We were married for eleven years, and that's all I can say. I think she loved me. I never knew what she was thinking, what she wanted, what she dreamed of. But I don't know if it was her fault. I've asked myself that a million times in the last two years. Why didn't I know her better? Why didn't I try harder?" He sank down on the bed. "Why was my job so much more important than my wife? So much more important that she died because of it?"

She said the first thing that came into her mind. "She didn't die because of your job, she died because of a drunken driver."

Raising his eyes, he slowly shook his head. The look he gave her was implacable. "It doesn't matter who hit her. I should have been with her."

Easing herself onto the bed next to him, she took one of his bandaged hands in hers. "Surely you must have loved her a little. One of the only things you took out of your house was her picture."

The look he gave her was grim. "I keep that picture where it can remind me what I did, what I was responsible for. So it can never happen again."

Her heart moved in her chest, tightening with pain. Sliding closer to him, she bent and kissed his bandaged hand. "Whatever was wrong with your marriage wasn't entirely your fault, you know. The guilt needs to be shared with your wife."

"She's paid the price. She's dead." His voice was flat.

"And you're not. Is that what's really bothering you?"

"You don't understand, Julia." His voice was desperate. "For eleven years I couldn't give her what she needed. Then, when she needed me most I wasn't there at all. That's a stain on my soul that won't ever come out."

"Most stains fade with time, if you allow them to," she murmured. "Did you ever think about the fact that your wife didn't give you what you needed, either?"

"It doesn't matter. I failed her. Nothing you can say can take away that guilt."

"Especially if you don't want to let it go. Is that what you use as a shield, to keep yourself from feeling again, to keep yourself from being hurt again? Let it go, Luke. Forgive yourself. Do you think that's what your wife would want, for you to wallow in self-pity for the rest of your life?"

He turned to her, furious. "What right do you have to say that to me? You can't make yourself into God and tell me I'm absolved of all responsibility."

She felt her heart crack at his words, but forced herself to answer. "Isn't that what you're doing, playing God? Taking all the responsibility onto your own shoulders? And I'll tell you what gives me the right. You couldn't save your wife two years ago, but you saved me today. Don't you think that brings your guilt full circle?"

All his anger disappeared and he reached out to touch her hair, letting his hand drop at the last minute. "Guilt and redemption. Is that what you're saying, Julia? That by saving you I've redeemed myself for what happened with Linda?" His voice was utterly weary, and she moved closer to him.

"I think you need to forgive yourself, Luke. You can't heal until you do."

"What if I don't want to be healed?"

"You need to let yourself heal, Luke," she whispered. "For me. For us."

At that he turned to her. "Is there an 'us,' Julia? Is there more between us than this job and this bed?" His voice was low and urgent.

Slowly she reached out and touched his face. "Do you want there to be?"

He grasped her arms and pulled her closer, so close she could feel the heat from his body, pulsing at her in waves. "I know I want you. Is that enough?"

Something moved inside her chest, grew and swelled until there was no room left for pain, for guilt, for regret. There was no room left for anything but Luke and how he made her feel, how she needed him. "It's enough for now," she answered, pulling his mouth down to hers.

Chapter 13

He answered with a kiss that was almost desperate in its need. As they tumbled backward on the bed, their tongues tasting and twining together in a dance as old as life, his hands were everywhere. Stroking down her face, pausing to smooth gently around the bandage on her forehead, brushing down her chest, his touch set off explosions under her skin. Desire roared to life, a raging inferno that threatened to consume her.

"Luke," she gasped. "I can't..."

He froze, then slowly disengaged himself from her. "I'm sorry, Julia. I forgot all about your injuries." His hands smoothed the hair away from the bandage and he bent to kiss the side of her neck.

Lying on the bed, looking up at him, she saw the tenderness in his eyes and wanted to weep. Why wouldn't he acknowledge all he had to give? As she watched him gaze down at her with a worried frown, fear behind his eyes, she felt her lips curling up in a smile.

"That wasn't what I was going to say. I guess that painkiller worked, because I forgot all about them, too."

"Then what were you going to say? You sounded like you hurt."

She smiled again. "I did. I do. I hurt from wanting you. I wanted to tell you I couldn't wait." Reaching up, she twined her arms around his neck and pulled him closer.

He followed her down to the bed, but eased himself over to her side. "I'm glad you stopped me," he whispered. "There's a time for wild, out-of-control lovemaking, and there's a time for something a little easier, a little more gentle."

He bent to trail kisses over her face, and she sighed as she turned her mouth to his. "I thought out of control felt pretty good just now."

"Hmm," he agreed, nibbling on her earlobe. "But this time, you're going to lie back and let me do all the work."

His hand found her breast, and she pressed into him with a low moan. He lingered for a moment, cupping her through the soft sweater, and then he slid his hand down and slowly pushed the sweater up to her shoulders.

For what seemed like hours, all she felt was his warm breath on her belly. When she opened her eyes and looked down at him, she saw that he was staring at her, the sweater crumpled in his hand.

"Is something wrong?" she whispered.

He slowly looked up at her and let go of her sweater, brushing his hand down over her lacy bra. "You look wonderful in lace," he murmured, slipping one finger under the top edge of the bra and trailing it along the top curve of her breast. "And all of my fantasies lately seem to feature it in a prominent role."

"What a coincidence," she gasped as he edged down and circled her nipple. "I wear it frequently."

He fumbled with the front clasp of the bra for a moment, and then it snapped open, leaving her breasts naked to his touch. His eyes darkened as he looked down at her, then he bent his head and flicked his tongue down the valley between her breasts. "I noticed," he murmured, his voice thick with passion.

His arm encircled her, pulling her closer, and his muscles were rock hard with the effort he was making to go slowly. When she reached up to unbutton his flannel shirt, he poised above her, motionless, until she tried to pull it down his arms. Then he leaned away and pulled it off, throwing it across the room. Sliding off the bed, he quickly shucked off his pants and then stretched out beside her again.

Slowly and gently he removed her sweater and jeans, being careful not to jar her or move too quickly. When they were both completely naked on the bed, she reached for him but he took both of her hands in one of his bandaged ones, kissed her fingers and then leaned over her. "Not yet," he whispered. "Not nearly yet."

He caressed and kissed every inch of her body, bringing her to the brink of release time after time, only to retreat and start all over again. She whispered his name, aching for him, but he silenced her with a kiss and continued his staggering seduction. He held her as if she were glass in his hands, fragile and valuable, as if one wrong touch could shatter her into a million pieces.

Finally, when the throbbing in her body became almost unbearable, when her blood was heated to the boiling point by his clever hands, she wrapped her arms around him and pulled him to her.

"I can't wait another moment for you, Luke. I need you now," she moaned.

She felt the almost uncontrollable trembling of his muscles as he held himself above her. Gently, so that he didn't jar her neck or head, he eased himself into her. When she arched up into him and wrapped her legs around him, she felt his control snap.

Sliding his hands around to cup her buttocks, he thrust into her time and again, her name a litany on his lips. She rose to meet him, holding him tightly, until she suddenly exploded, crying out his name.

"Oh, Julia," he gasped, gripping her more tightly, holding her against his sweat-slicked body. Then he surged into her one last time and collapsed onto her, still cradling her head gently in his hands.

After a long time he stirred and shifted his weight off her. "Did I hurt you?" he whispered into her hair.

"No," she answered. She had barely enough energy to raise her hand to his hair and let its silk slip through her fingers. "No one has ever treated me like that before, like I was something precious and fragile."

He raised himself up on one elbow and looked down at her, a rare smile crinkling the corners of his eyes. "I'd say you were hanging around with the wrong crowd, then."

"I'm beginning to realize that."

She watched his eyes darken, saw him begin to pull away, and she reached up and brought his mouth down to hers. They might only have this time, now, here in this anonymous motel room. In two days this case would be over, and he might walk away and never look back. But until that time, she could pretend that they had forever. For the next two days, they belonged to each other, and she would try to make him forget everything else but her.

He hesitated for a heartbeat, then he answered her kiss with one of his own. Passion swept over her again, and she let it pull her under. She didn't intend to waste a minute of their time together.

Another day and two nights had passed when Luke woke up with the early morning sunshine streaming over his face. Julia was curled around him, her leg wedged between his legs and her hand pressed against his waist. She slept so close to him that he could feel the soft rise and fall of her chest against his back. Desire slammed into him with the force of an engine barreling down a track.

He turned slowly and looked at the woman who lay so trustingly next to him. The past day and a half shimmered in his memory like a dream, a vision of perfection that mortal man could never hope to attain. Except for a couple of quick trips to get food, they'd spent the whole time in this room, in this bed. The memory of exquisite lovemaking wove in and out of the dream like a shining thread of gold, but even more precious was the way Julia had shared herself.

She'd talked about her childhood, growing up with three brothers, and what had made her go into police work. She told him about her training at the police academy, where she'd developed her aversion to guns. So she'd never been a beat cop, preferring instead the investigative work of the Internal Affairs Department. They'd talked of everything and nothing, from their favorite movies and books to their preferred restaurants.

Never once had she pressed him to tell her about his marriage to Linda. As a result, he'd found himself telling her more than he'd ever told anyone, even Eddie. And all the time she'd listened and held his hand, wrapping her arms around him and resting her cheek against his back while he spoke.

He couldn't remember ever feeling more at ease with a woman, or ever wanting anybody more. They'd made love countless times in the past couple of days, but as he watched her sleep he found that he wanted her even more than he had before they'd made love the first time.

He didn't want to look at his watch, because this was the day. Tonight, if he was right, Eddie and the others would meet with the Demons. Julia's case would be solved, over, and the two of them would leave this motel room and go back to their lives. Their separate lives.

The thought of his empty house and squalid, ruined office seemed unbearably lonely now. For a moment he tried to imagine Julia there in his house, her smile lighting up the hallway when he came home, her presence erasing the darkness from his life.

Maybe, just maybe, the bonds he felt forming and strengthening between them were real. Maybe it would be different with Julia. Never in his life, even at the height of his hormone-crazed teen years with Linda, had he ever felt the kind of passion that he and Julia had shared. Never before, even with his wife, had he wanted to share himself like he did with Julia.

"Hi there," he heard her say, her voice low and incredibly sexy. Her hand crept around his waist and lingered on his belly. "What are you up to so early in the morning?"

He swooped her up and pulled her close, letting her feel exactly what was up this morning. "What do you think?" He nibbled on her ear and felt her answering shiver. "There's only been one thing on my mind the last couple of days, and that's been you. And whenever I think about you, this is what happens."

"That's funny." Her breath tickled his ear as she spoke, and he felt her lips against his neck. "Because the same thing happens to me. Do you think we've got some kind of phenomenon here?"

"Mmm, could be." Turning her head, he drew her lower lip into his mouth and felt her moan vibrate against his lips. "Let's experiment."

A long time later, he sat up in bed and pulled her with him. She tugged the sheet along with her, and he grinned as he watched her. "How long are you going to do that?"

"Do what?" She looked at him, puzzled.

He nodded at the sheet. "Cover yourself up like that."

She glanced down at the sheet and her cheeks turned a delicate pink as she smoothed it self-consciously. "I guess I'm just not used to sitting around naked with a man."

"Hey, it's okay," he said, leaning over to brush a kiss across her lips. "It makes it more fun to peek that way." Easing himself off the bed, he stood up and stretched, enjoying the way she looked at him. Grinning at her again, he said, "It's time to get up and get something to eat. And with any luck, that sheet will slip when you get out of bed."

Yanking the sheet out from under the blanket and wrapping it around herself, she rolled off the bed and grinned back at him. "Don't count on it, McKinley." With a jaunty smile she disappeared into the bathroom, and he stood staring at the closed door for a moment.

Could this be the woman he had hated for the past two years, the woman he'd blamed for losing the job that he loved? The woman he'd labeled an ice princess, a hard, uncompromising person who had no softness in her soul?

Julia Carleton wasn't like that at all. Then what did that say about what she'd done to him two years ago? He shied away from the question, unwilling to examine it. His wife had been killed by a drunken driver and he'd done what anyone would have done in the same circumstances, he told himself. Julia had simply made a mistake in that long-ago hearing room.

And he didn't have time to think about that right now. He gave himself a mental shake. He needed to concentrate on what they had to do today. Reaching into his duffel bag, he pulled out the last of his clean clothes. As if he needed a reminder that everything was ending, he thought grimly.

He'd finished dressing and was standing at the window, scanning the parking lot, when Julia came out of the bathroom. He felt her come up behind him, smelled the tart aroma of the motel soap mixed subtly with her own scent as she pressed against his back.

"See any bad guys out there?"

He shook his head but continued to look out the window. "Since one of the witnesses to the accident was able to get a partial license number of the car that hit us, maybe the police have been able to corral our shadow by now."

"But wouldn't they just send someone else to take his place?"

At that he turned and slid his arms around her. "Not necessarily. We're not talking about rocket scientists here, Julia. Maybe no one knows where we are. Maybe when we got the rental car we lost them. I don't know what happened, but I haven't seen anyone out there for the last couple of days, and no one's tried to get into our room. I think we can assume that we're safe here."

He felt her shiver in his arms, then burrow deeper. "I think I would feel safe wherever I was, as long as you were with me."

Such a simple statement, but he felt his heart expanding at her words. Trust. It had been a long time since anyone had given him such a precious gift.

His arms closed around her, binding her to him for the space of a heartbeat, then he stepped away, breaking the mood. "If we don't get some food soon, I can't be held responsible for my actions."

"Let's go, then. I'm afraid to see what might happen." She shifted easily into an impersonal, bantering mood that made him want to grasp for the moment he'd just left behind.

But instead of sweeping her into his arms and onto the rumpled bed, he picked up his gun from the nightstand, checked it and slid it into his shoulder holster. It was time to get back to business.

An hour and a half later they walked back into the motel room. The maid had been there in their absence, cleaning up all traces of the way they'd spent the last thirty-six hours. Luke looked around at the impersonal room and felt a coldness settle in the pit of his stomach. Was it really that easy to erase all signs of what had happened between him and Julia? Would the same thing happen after tonight, the two of them separating and all traces of the passion that had flared between them evaporating like mist in the sunlight?

Julia touched his arm and he looked down at her smiling face. "How long do you think it'll take us to make it look like it did when we left?"

She watched him steadily, holding his gaze, and he felt a weight shift off his soul. "Two minutes, tops." Bending down, he brushed his lips over hers and felt her immediate response flare into life. Pulling her closer, he held her for a moment, then stepped back. "Hold that thought. I should call and get my messages, make sure no one's been trying to get in touch with me."

She swallowed and nodded, a shadow passing over her eyes. "Tonight is the night. Luke, I..."

"What is it, Julia?"

She watched him for a minute, troubled, then opened her mouth just as the telephone rang. They both froze. Luke stared at the phone for a moment, then strode over and picked it up.

"Yes?" he barked.

"Mr. Jones?" a timid voice on the other end of the line asked.

"Yes, this is Mr. Jones."

"We, uh, that is, the motel has a policy about extended stays." The clerk's voice drifted away, and Luke could hear him clearing his throat. "That is, when someone stays for more than three days, we need payment for the room before we can let them stay another night."

Luke relaxed and smiled reassuringly over to Julia. "No problem. I'll be down in a few minutes to take care of it."

He hung up the phone and turned to her. "They want us to pay for the room, since we've been here for three nights already. I guess their usual clientele make a considerably shorter stay. It sounds like anything longer than a couple of hours makes them real nervous," he added with a grin.

Julia smiled stiffly and watched as he headed toward the door. "I'll be right back," he promised.

When he walked into the room a few minutes later, he headed for the telephone. Julia stood by the window, but it didn't look as if she were watching the parking lot. Her gaze was unfocused as she stared out at the buildings behind the motel.

"I'm going to make a few phone calls, and then we'll talk about our strategy for tonight."

She turned around quickly, but he had already picked up the phone and dialed the number to his house. He listened to the message on his answering machine, then tapped in the security code that would allow him to hear his messages.

The tape clicked on, and Eddie's voice came over the line. He could almost see his ex-partner's cocky smile as he said, "How you doing, buddy? Just calling to see if you can get together tonight. A bunch of us are going to be at the Half Moon at about eight o'clock. Meet us there if you can."

Before he could think about Eddie's message, the tape beeped and another message began to play. "Luke, this is Raul." His voice was low and urgent. "Please call me. I have some information for you." There was the soft click of the receiver being replaced in its cradle, then silence until the tape beeped again. The tape stopped, and Luke pressed the buttons that would reset the machine, then slowly lowered the phone.

"There were two messages," he said to Julia. "One from Eddie and one from Raul."

Her eyes dilated with fear, and she moved away from the window to stand in front of him. "What did they want?" she whispered.

"Raul wants me to call. Eddie..." He paused, letting the pain wash over him, letting himself taste the regret and bitter betrayal completely. "Eddie wants me to meet him tonight at the Half Moon Bar. At eight o'clock."

Her forehead furrowed. "Why would he ask you to do that? Do you think that means that their plans have changed? And what would Eddie be calling you for, anyway?"

"Maybe Raul has found out something about the meeting. But I doubt it's been changed. They've gone to too much trouble to make sure everyone involved is on duty tonight."

"Then why would Eddie ask you to meet him in a bar when he knows that he won't be there?"

"I doubt if I would have made it to the bar," he answered grimly, trying to bury the pain deep inside himself. "The Half Moon is in a real seedy neighborhood. I have a feeling I would have met up with a mugger before I made it as far as the bar."

She stared at him, shocked. "Eddie is supposed to be your friend. He wouldn't do anything like that. Would he?"

"There's a lot of money involved in this, Julia. And Eddie sure seems to enjoy his new life-style."

"Maybe he just wanted to make you wait there for him while everything was happening somewhere else."

"This isn't a cop show on television, where the hero doesn't get hurt and everything turns out to be a misunderstanding." His voice was harsh and cold. "This is real life, where people get killed every day. A loser ex-cop P.I. found with a knife in his ribs in an alley wouldn't even make the newspapers, Julia."

"What are you going to do?" she asked.

"Ignore it, of course." His answer was immediate. "If Eddie thinks I'm wandering down dark streets to the Half

Moon, he won't be worrying that I'll show up when his deal is going down."

She watched him with her huge green eyes, and he wanted to go over and kiss away the fear that shadowed them. He wanted to tell her that everything was going to be all right, but he wasn't so sure anymore. Raul had sounded worried, and he needed to know why.

"I'm going to call Raul. It might take a while to track him down."

But the artist picked up the phone on the very first ring, almost as if he'd been waiting by the phone for Luke's call. "Raul, it's Luke. I got your message."

He heard a small sigh at the other end of the phone. "Thank goodness you called, Luke. I have heard some information that I think you might need." He quickly sketched in the details of the meeting for tonight, and the place and time where it was taking place.

Luke lowered himself onto the bed, feeling himself relax. He'd been afraid that something had gone wrong, that perhaps the meeting had been moved and that they'd miss their chance tonight. "Thank you, my friend. This confirms information I had already heard. I've made plans to be there."

"I'm glad, Luke." Luke could hear Raul exhaling on the other end of the phone. "These eight policemen must be caught and punished. They are destroying my neighborhood and seducing the children of my friends into dangerous and immoral acts."

"I'll stop them." Luke lowered the phone and eased it into its cradle as a coldness spread in his chest. Eight policemen. There had only been seven on the list that Julia had read to him. Who was the eighth? Was is someone so high-ranking that he wouldn't be listed on the duty roster? How high into the precinct chain of command did the sickness extend?

He swung around suddenly, scanning the room. "Didn't the policeman at the hospital give us a bag with everything from the car?" he asked Julia.

"It's right over here." Julia walked over to one corner of the room and handed him a plastic bag. "What do you need from it?"

"The duty rosters. Raul said something that bothered me."

Julia froze in front of him, fear enveloping her like a black cloak. She forced herself to speak. "Luke, before you look at that, there's something I have to tell you."

But it was too late. He looked up from the current week's roster and stared at her, fury and betrayal in his dark blue eyes. And buried far below that was a slashing pain that made her shrivel up inside.

"Luke, I can explain," she said desperately.

"I don't think that's necessary." His voice was silky smooth. "All the explanations I need are right here in front of me."

"I would have told you," she cried.

"When, Julia? When your brother Bobby was standing over me with a gun?" he said bitterly. "When I walked into a trap because I didn't know all the players?"

"I wouldn't have let you do that." She reached out for him, but froze when he flinched away from her. "I wouldn't have let you get hurt."

Something shifted in his eyes and she felt the wall spring up between them. "No? You have a funny way of going about it, Julia." He stared at her, and it was as if some stranger looked at her out of Luke's eyes. Never before, even two years ago when he'd thought of her only as his enemy, had he looked at her like that. As if she'd ripped away his most precious possession.

"I was going to tell you," she repeated, refusing to accept the closed shutters on his eyes.

The look he gave her now was filled only with scorn. "When, Julia? When were you going to tell me?"

"I tried to tell you earlier, before you talked to Raul."

"Not very hard, apparently. All it would have taken was a simple, 'Luke, I have to tell you something.'" He stared at her, implacable, and she felt something delicate and fragile shattering around them.

"You have to believe me, Luke. I was going to tell you." Even to her own ears her plea sounded weak, and one look at Luke told her it was futile.

Ignoring her plea, he asked harshly, "How long have you known, Julia? Did you know when you came into my office and asked me to betray my best friend? Were you protecting your brother then, too? When did you first find out that your brother was a dirty cop?"

"Maybe he's not," she said in a rush. "He's only a rookie. He's been at the precinct for only six months, and this has been going on for a lot longer than that."

"And maybe he was just real quick to get on the gravy train." His expression was unyielding. "But that doesn't matter, does it, Julia? Regardless of whether or not he's involved, his name was on that duty roster for tonight and you didn't tell me."

"I'm sorry, Luke," she whispered. "I should have told you, but I couldn't. When I saw his name, I was so scared. I didn't know what to do."

For just a moment, she saw his eyes soften. She took a step toward him, and he stood up, his look freezing her in her place. The hard man was back, and he wasn't going to give her an inch.

And she didn't deserve one. A voice in her head reminded her that she *had* betrayed his trust. She *should* have told him immediately. She opened her mouth to tell him, but he spoke first.

"Tell me, Julia, when did you first suspect your brother was crooked? Have you known all along?" He paused, and she could see him remembering. His eyes darkened even more. "Is that why you didn't want me to join you and Bobby for dinner that night? Were you afraid of what I might find out?"

She wanted to tell him no, but her face betrayed her. As he watched her, she saw the scorn fill his eyes. "Is that why you hired me, Julia, because you knew I had fantasized about you for two years? Did you think I wouldn't notice your brother was involved if you used your body to distract me?" He leaned closer to her, close enough that she could see not only the anger, but the agony, deep down. "Does Bobby know that you sold yourself for him?"

"That's not true, Luke," she whispered. "Whatever we shared was only between us. Bobby had nothing to do with it."

"I'd have an easier time believing that if you'd told me about him in the first place." He jumped up and stepped closer to her, the pain now clearly drawn on his face. "Was it all a lie, Julia? All the sweet words, the way our bodies fit together so perfectly? Was it all only a game to you, a way for you to control me and keep me away from your brother?"

"No, Luke, it wasn't a game." She tried to meet his gaze, but the pain in his eyes was almost too much to bear. "I swear it wasn't. It was real. All of it."

For a moment the anger faded from his eyes and he stared at her with a yearning that made her want to cry. "I wish I could believe that." His words were spoken so softly that she could barely hear them. "I wish like hell I could believe that." He gave her an almost pleading look. "Could you believe it, if you were in my shoes?"

She wanted to shout, *Yes, I would believe you.* She wanted to tell him everything she felt inside, the way she was alive only when she was with him. But she looked at him again, and knew it was too late. He couldn't believe her now, because she had let him down. The cold started in her chest and spread to every inch of her body. She hadn't been there for him, just like his wife hadn't been there for him. She had committed the ultimate betrayal. She hadn't been honest with him.

Turning away, she stared blindly around the room. Her belongings were mixed with his in a painful mockery of the intimacy they'd shared for the past two days. Moving slowly, like an old woman, she began to gather her things and stuff them into her suitcase.

"What do you think you're doing?" His voice, harsh and impersonal, came from behind her but she couldn't turn around.

"Leaving. I'm sure you don't want me around now."

"You're not going anywhere."

For a moment, she was riveted to the floor with joy. He didn't want her to leave. She spun around, looking for forgiveness in his face. All she saw was impersonal regard. He stared at her as if she were a stranger he was forced to spend time with. A stranger he didn't much care for.

"What do you mean?" she faltered.

"Do you think I'm going to let you run to your brother and tell him what's happening tonight?" He smiled at her, a curving of his lips that was completely without humor. "I'm not that slow. It may have taken me a while to catch on, but I've figured it out now. No, Julia, you're staying with me until this is all over."

"I wouldn't tell him anything," she said, desperate to get away. She couldn't bear to feel his scorn for the rest of the day.

His gaze flickered over her once, then he picked up the duty roster and sat down on the bed to study it. "You'll understand if I don't believe you, won't you?"

He didn't even bother to look at her as he spoke, and he didn't seem to expect an answer. Feeling her soul shriveling inside her chest, she slowly sank down on one of the hard chairs. This wasn't the way she had planned to spend their last hours together. She stared at him, silently pleading with him to look at her, but he continued to read the sheets of paper in front of him. It was as if she no longer existed.

Chapter 14

Julia faced the television blindly, not seeing the old black-and-white movie that played in front of her. She was vividly aware of Luke's presence behind her, but she couldn't bear to turn around. In the hours since he'd discovered the truth on the duty roster, he hadn't once looked at her or spoken to her. He sat on the bed, gazing into space and occasionally jotting something down on the back of the roster.

She desperately wanted to ask him what he was doing, but she knew that he wouldn't tell her. And she didn't want to see the distrust in his eyes when she asked, or feel the weight of his suspicion crushing down on her.

She couldn't just sit here, though, feeling his indifference, especially not in this place where memories of their lovemaking still shimmered in the air. She had to get out of this room. Jumping up, she turned off the television and spun around. "I'm getting hungry. Do you want me to run out and bring back something to eat?"

He glanced up at her from the sheets of paper in his lap, and his look sent a shaft of pain through her heart. He was watching her as if she were an unwanted intrusion that he longed to get rid of, but didn't quite know how to. After a moment, he set aside the paper and stood up.

"I'll come with you."

Unshed tears gathered in a huge ball in her throat. "I wouldn't try to call Bobby, Luke."

"No, you won't." His voice was impersonal and implacable. "Because I'll be there to make sure of it."

"I give you my word," she said desperately. "I will not call Bobby."

He stared at her for a second, and she wanted to wrap her arms around herself and shrivel up into nothing. The scorn in his eyes would haunt her for a long, long time. "Just how much do you think your word is worth, Julia?" he said softly.

He didn't bother waiting for her to answer. Picking up his gun, he checked it again and shoved it into the holster he still wore. He opened the door into the hall, checked it in a routine that had become second nature to her, then waited for her to leave the room. Locking the door behind them, he led the way down the stairs and into the car. She trailed behind him, her heart constricting in her chest and her soul weeping bitter tears of regret.

He chose a fast-food restaurant, and they sat in silence and ate their hamburgers. The food tasted like sawdust and sat in a heavy lump in her stomach. Getting away from the motel room had seemed like a good idea, but it was far worse to sit in public with Luke and have to pretend that everything was all right. At least in the privacy of the room she didn't have to sit across from him and see his glance pass over her and dismiss her, or feel the cold dislike when his gaze did settle on her.

"Are you finished?" he asked abruptly.

She nodded, even though half of her food was still lying on the tray in front of her. The motel room that had been so confining earlier now seemed like a haven from the scorn in his eyes, and she couldn't get back there fast enough. At least there she wouldn't have to sit close enough to him to feel the waves of distaste that rolled off him whenever he looked at her.

The trip back to the motel was equally silent. Clenching her teeth, she looked out the window and tried to tell herself that she had to endure only for a few more hours. After they caught the policemen with the Demons, the case would be over and she wouldn't have to see Luke ever again.

The lump of tears that had been threatening ever since Luke discovered her deception slid down her throat and lodged in her chest. How long would it take to forget about him and get on with her life?

An icicle pierced her heart at the thought. She wouldn't ever forget him. There might come a time when she would be able to function, to put on a normal face for the rest of the world, but it would all be a cruel facade. Without Luke, there wouldn't be anything alive inside her.

When they got back to the motel, Luke got out of the car and came around to open her door. The small, unconscious gesture made the tears threaten to fall, but she ducked her head and didn't look at him as she followed him up the stairs to the third-floor prison. Once they were back in the room, he picked up the papers he'd been working on and cleared his throat.

"The meeting is for ten o'clock, so we're going to get there at seven-thirty. You are going to do everything I say, when I say it. Is that clear?"

He was going to take her along? Her spirit soared, but crashed to earth a second later when he added, "I don't have any choice but to take you. I can't let you go so that you can run to your brother, and I can't leave you here unless I tie you up." For just a second a look of pain passed over his hardened features. "No matter what you've done, I can't do that to you. So you'll just have to come with me. But if you try to influence this in any way, I won't hesitate to stop you." The momentary softening was gone from his face. "Is that clear?"

She nodded. "I won't do anything or get in the way."

She didn't want to be there to see Bobby arrested, but he wasn't giving her a choice. Bobby. She'd tried to avoid thinking about him, but now memories came flooding back. He was her baby brother, the one she'd always felt responsible for. She was the one who'd rescued him from scrapes when they were children, keeping his escapades from her parents. When they were teenagers, he would go to her for help, knowing she would give it unconditionally.

And when he got older and started running with the wrong crowd, she was the one who'd convinced him to try police work as an alternative. She'd shared his triumphs and his problems at the academy, and no one had been prouder than her on the day he'd graduated. Her heart had felt as if it would burst at the sight of him in his uniform, standing tall and proud alongside the other rookies.

What could have gone wrong in six months? Why had he chosen the path of easy wealth over honor and justice? Julia bit her lip. Had she helped her brother out of one too many jams, made him think that someone would always be there to rescue him from trouble? Was she the one to blame for his lack of responsibility?

"You might as well get your stuff together." Luke's voice interrupted her thoughts. "If everything works out tonight, we won't have to come back here."

What he really meant was that he didn't want to have to think about her for any longer than necessary, she told herself bitterly, choking back a response. She didn't know that a person's heart could hurt so much. Standing up too quickly, she stumbled once as she walked over to her suitcase. Out of the corner of her eye she saw Luke instinctively reach out for her.

She righted herself by grabbing the chair, and he curled his fingers into his palm and let his hand drop. Just as well, she told herself, squatting next to her suitcase. If he touched her right now she would probably humiliate herself by begging him to forgive her, and she didn't want to have anything else to torture herself with during the lonely months and years ahead.

Packing slowly and carefully, she tried to concentrate only on the task at hand, deliberately erasing from her mind any other thoughts. By the time she'd finished, Luke had his duffel bag packed and was sitting on the bed, waiting for her.

"Ready to go?" he asked.

She nodded, not looking at him. Stripped of all their belongings, the room looked sterile and impersonal once again. There was no trace of the passionate lovemaking they'd shared. The bed had been made neatly by the maid, the sheets, blankets and pillows replaced where they belonged. Would it be that easy for Luke to erase his memories of what they'd shared, she wondered.

She glanced over at him. It looked as if he already had. The glance he gave her was completely cold and impersonal, and she picked up her suitcase and waited for him to open the door.

"I paid for another night, so if something goes wrong we can always come back here," he surprised her by saying.

"Nothing's going to go wrong." She heard the desperate tone in her voice, but she didn't care. Just the thought of spending another night in this room with him, in that bed with all the memories, made her insides clench into a hard, painful ball.

"Something can always go wrong," he said as they got into the car. She felt his eyes on her, but couldn't look at him. She knew she would see only accusation in them.

Taking a deep breath as he started the car, she waited until they were headed for Humboldt Park before asking, "What are you planning?"

He didn't answer, and for a moment she thought he wasn't going to. Then he surprised her by saying, "The meeting's for ten o'clock. They're sure to have some people there early to stand guard, but I'm hoping they won't be there yet. I'm going to check out the building, make sure I know where all the exits are, then find a place for us to hide."

She allowed herself to look over at him. "How are we going to arrest them ourselves? You have a gun and I have a badge, but aren't we going to need some help?"

Shifting in his seat, his hands tightened on the steering wheel and he nodded curtly. "We might. Once I check the place out, I'll decide if I should call the captain."

"We're pretty sure he's not involved, but how can you be certain?"

He looked over at her, his mouth grim. "I can't. But I may have to take that chance if I don't think I can handle it myself."

"Surely there's something I can do."

His lips tightened. "Your job is to keep your butt where I tell you to put it and keep your mouth shut. That's it."

She wanted to protest, but knew it would be useless. It was more than clear there was no way he was going to trust her with any part in his plans.

And anyway, she asked herself with a stab of pain, did she want him to? Watching Eddie Timmons and the others get arrested would make up for the months of work she'd done on this case, but did she really want to be there while someone handcuffed her brother and shoved him into a police wagon?

"You won't have to worry. I'll do exactly what you tell me to do."

"Damn straight you will."

He didn't even glance at her. They were approaching Humboldt Park now, and she could feel his tension gathering in the closed atmosphere of the car. The neighborhood was beginning to take on the ghostly appearance it had the other night. No one stayed out on these streets after dark if they could help it.

"Here we are." Luke spoke abruptly, and she looked up with a start. They drove past an old warehouse, gray and neglected in the fading light. All the windows were dark, and there were no cars in the parking lot next to it. It looked abandoned and unused, another casualty of urban blight and job flight to the suburbs.

"It doesn't look like anyone's used it for quite a while," she ventured, turning her head to watch it as they drove past.

"That's probably why the Demons chose it. I imagine it's been like that for years. It's just another abandoned building in a city full of them."

He drove several blocks away from it, then parked the car on a residential street. As they sat in the car in the gathering dusk, she felt his eyes on her.

"Julia," he said, "I wish..."

She waited for him to finish, but silence quivered between them for what seemed like a long time. Finally he muttered, "I wish I didn't have to bring you with me."

It wasn't what he'd begun to say, she was sure of it. But it didn't matter anyway, she told herself. The only thing that mattered was getting through this night, one minute at a time. She couldn't bear to think any further ahead than that. The loss of Luke and her brother at the same time was too overwhelming to contemplate.

"Come on," he said in a low voice. "I've got things to do."

It was more dark than light as they walked the blocks back to the warehouse. Remembering what had happened the last time they were in this neighborhood made Julia want to press closer to Luke, but she forced herself to keep a distance between them. In a few minutes, the gray shape of the warehouse loomed up in front of them.

Luke stopped suddenly, reaching out and grabbing her arm so she would stop, too. He dropped it as soon as she'd halted, snatching his hand away and jamming it in his pocket. She looked down to where her skin still tingled on her forearm and wondered if he'd felt it, too.

If he did he wasn't paying any attention. He'd pulled her into the shadow of the building next to them, and now bent over to whisper, "There's someone in front of the warehouse. I didn't think the Demons would have someone here so soon. We'll have to go around to avoid him."

They hurried across the street, sticking to the shadows. Walking past the warehouse quickly, they turned and doubled back, slipping past the rusting gate across the entrance to the parking lot to stand in the shadows next to a window.

They stood there for a long time. Julia braced herself for the sound of someone coming, for a yell that would tell them they'd been discovered, but there was nothing but silence. Finally Luke stepped over to the window and looked inside. Julia expected to hear a hail of bullets in answer, but there was no response from inside the dark building.

When he moved away from the window, he stepped close to her and whispered into her ear, "I can't see much because there's a pile of boxes in front of the window, but I don't hear anything from inside. Let's go and see if we can get one of the doors open."

He led the way out of the parking lot and around to the big door in front of the building. There was no one in sight, and she stood and watched nervously as he tried to open the door. The huge wooden panel was just beginning to creak open when Luke froze.

"What are you doing?"

It wasn't Luke's voice that spoke, and slowly she turned to look at the boy who was sticking a gun in Luke's back. There was something familiar about him, and as she stared at him, Luke turned around to face him.

"Piotyr?" he said, his voice incredulous. "What are you doing here?"

Even in the dim light Julia could see the boy pale. "Mr. McKinley," he breathed. "They never said you would be here."

"Who never said what, Piotyr?"

The boy shook his head, the gun wobbling in his hand. "You've gotta leave, Mr. McKinley. If they catch you here, we'll both be in big trouble." He sounded desperately frightened.

Luke glanced down at the gun in the boy's hand. "Give me the gun, Piotyr," he said, his voice infinitely gentle. "It's dangerous to wave it around like that."

"I can't." The words came out in a croak as Piotyr looked around with haunted eyes. "This is my initiation. I'm supposed to take care of anyone that comes snooping around." He looked back at Luke, pleading with him. "Just leave, Mr. McKinley. Okay?"

"I'm not going anywhere, Piotyr. I guess you'll just have to shoot me."

Julia gasped, but Luke didn't even look at her. His gaze fixed on Piotyr, he stood perfectly still while the boy stared back at him, the gun waving wildly in his hand. When he finally lowered the gun so it pointed at the sidewalk, Luke reached out slowly and pried it out of his fingers.

"What are you doing here, Piotyr?" Luke drew him away from the door that had opened a crack and around the corner into the shadows. "How did you get involved with the Demons?"

Piotyr Bernowski looked both sullen and scared. "Everyone else made fun of me because of my English. They were the only ones at my school who were nice to me."

"And now you want to join the gang?"

The sullen look disappeared from his face, and now he only looked like a frightened child. "No," he whispered. "I don't. But all of a sudden they were telling me I could join, and I didn't know what else to do. I knew if I didn't that I would be in big trouble and they would do something to me." He looked shamefaced. "I skipped school a lot and hung around with them. I guess I heard things I wasn't supposed to hear."

"What do you want to do, Piotyr?" Luke asked in a gentle voice, and suddenly Julia could see the boy's lower lip trembling.

"I want to go home."

"Do you know what's going on here tonight, Piotyr?"

Slowly Piotyr nodded. "I wasn't supposed to know, but I overheard some of them talking about it."

Luke put his hand on the boy's shoulder. "That makes you an accessory to the crime, you know."

The boy nodded, tears welling in his eyes.

"I'm supposed to turn you in, but I'm willing to make a deal with you. Are you interested in that?"

Piotyr nodded more vigorously, tears standing on the edge of his eyelashes. "Yes," he whispered.

"If you go home now and don't tell anyone about what happened here tonight, and promise not to have anything more to do with the Demons, I'll forget about seeing you here. Do you think you could do that?"

"Yes, Mr. McKinley," Piotyr blurted out. "I promise. I'll do whatever you say."

"Good. Now you go on home."

Piotyr looked around anxiously. "What if one of them sees me leave?" he whispered. "I'm not supposed to leave until the others get here."

"When is that going to be?"

"They didn't say. They just told me to stay here until they arrived, and kill anyone who was snooping around." His voice began trembling again, and he turned away and wiped his nose on his sleeve.

"You won't have to worry about killing anyone, Piotyr."

"And he won't have to worry about running into the Demons on the street," Julia interjected. "I'll drive him home."

Luke turned to her, and she could feel him assessing her reasons. "Do you have any other solutions, Luke?" she asked. "It's either that or let him go alone and hope he doesn't run into anyone."

"No," he said finally. "There isn't any other choice." He watched her for a moment. "And what about you, Julia?"

"I've already given you my word that I won't contact Bobby. What more can I do?"

He sighed. "I'll have to trust you, I guess, because I don't have any other choice. Go on, take him home. And as long as I'm letting you leave, stay away from here after you deliver him to his mother. There's no reason for you to be in the line of fire. I'll call for backup after you leave."

This was it, then. She probably wouldn't see him again. Her heart contracted as she stood on the sidewalk and tried to memorize his face. It was half in the darkness, but she could swear there was regret and something more in his eyes, something he tried very hard to hide. Staring at him for a moment, longing to tell him how she felt and that she was sorry about the way things had happened, she began to speak when Piotyr touched her arm.

"We should go now," he whispered. "The longer I am here, the more dangerous it is for all of us."

"All right." With one last look at Luke, she turned to go. He stopped her with a touch on her arm, and she spun around, hoping to see forgiveness in his eyes.

Instead he handed her the gun Piotyr had pointed at him. "Here, take this. It's four blocks back to the car, and you may need it."

She hefted the unwelcome weight in her hand and watched as he vanished into the shadows. After a moment, she turned and led Piotyr away.

Luke stood next to the dilapidated building and watched them go with regret, anger and desire together churning a hole in his gut. In spite of the fact that she had used and deceived him, he still wanted Julia Carleton with a desperation that infuriated him. He wanted to run after her and tell her to wait for him, that he would let the cops have their dirty money and let the Demons have their drugs. He was willing to betray his honor for Julia Carleton, and he had to force himself to watch them disappear.

Shocked at himself, he slid farther into the shadows and tried to concentrate on what he had to do, but Julia's face kept appearing in front of him. She was pleading for him to forgive her, to understand, and he almost reached out to pull her closer.

His fingers closed around a handful of air, and he clenched his fist and let it drop to his side. Julia had made her choice, just as he'd made his. He couldn't let his emotions interfere with the job he had to do.

And his job right now was to get inside this warehouse and scope out the situation. If he was going to call the captain and tell him to send some men over, he'd have to do it soon. Finding Piotyr here had really messed up his schedule.

When he looked at the street in front of the warehouse, he saw that it was deserted. The door was still cracked open, just wide enough for him to slip through. After one last look around, he ducked into the building, then stood there for a moment as his eyes adjusted to the dark.

But it wasn't as dark as he'd expected, and his pounding heart slowed as he looked around. There were several skylights in the ceiling, and although the glass was dirty and streaked, they let in enough light for him to find his way around the building.

One side of the building was piled high with the boxes he'd seen through the window. Some stood on pallets, some on the floor, and none of them looked as if they'd been disturbed for years. Cobwebs and dust covered them so completely that he couldn't read what was stamped on their sides. The rest of the building was open, with a loft running around the entire perimeter. Several rickety staircases led up to it, but he wouldn't have trusted a dog's weight to the old wood, let alone a person's.

As he moved through the empty, dimly lit building he saw something moving out of the corner of his eye. Dropping to one knee and spinning to face it, he pulled out his gun with a fluid motion and aimed it with a steady hand.

No one shouted at him and no shots cracked the silence of the empty warehouse. Focusing hard, he finally realized that what he'd seen was the flapping of a sheet covering something on the far side of the building. Easing his gun back into his holster, he walked quickly over to inspect it.

A pile of boxes stood under a white sheet, and when he threw the sheet back, his lips tightened at the words stenciled on the sides of the four boxes. If they were labeled correctly, they contained automatic weapons. He'd heard about a theft of these guns from a local warehouse. They'd become the weapons of choice for many drug dealers, but he hadn't thought the Demons were that sophisticated.

Apparently the Demons were moving up in the world. Dropping the sheet back over the boxes, he hoped grimly that after tonight those weapons would be going nowhere except to an evidence room. Backing away from the boxes of guns, he noted another door behind them big enough to accommodate a truck and a smaller door in the third wall of the building. Two separate telephones hung on the back wall, their newness in sharp contrast to the decay around him.

The Demons had a nice little setup here. In this neighborhood, they could come and go and no one would call the police if they saw lights where there weren't supposed to be any. Everyone minded his own business in this neck of the woods.

There was no way he was going to be able to do this by himself, he realized grimly. There were too many ways in and out of the building, and too many places for the gang members to hide. He had no choice. He'd have to call the captain and have him send some men over. He had no time to come up with an alternate plan.

Hurrying to one of the telephones, he dialed the precinct and in a low voice asked for the captain. Thank God he was still there. In a terse voice, he outlined what was going on and gave the older man the names of the men he thought were involved.

"Thanks, McKinley," Captain Lewis said, exhaling quickly. The man sounded edgy. "I'd heard rumors, but no one seemed to know anything concrete. I'll get right on it."

"They're supposed to meet here at ten o'clock, so wait a while before you come in. They may not start on time."

"I've been doing this for a while, McKinley. I think I can manage." The captain's voice was sharp. "Now get out of there. We don't need any civilians screwing things up."

"No thanks, captain. I think I'll stick around." He hung the phone up slowly, disturbed by what he'd heard in the older man's voice. Captain Lewis hadn't seemed too surprised when he'd told him the names of the men involved. Was it because he already knew? And did he know because he was getting a cut of whatever they made?

There was no way he was leaving this place until every one of those cops and every one of the gang members was under lock and key, even if he had to do it himself. Grimly assessing the warehouse, he decided that the best place to hide was behind the piles of boxes that stood along one wall. Glancing at his watch and noting that it was almost nine o'clock already, he slipped between the rows and found a place to sit. As he waited in the silence broken only by the occasional car passing on the street, he watched the shadows of the warehouse as night gradually descended outside.

No more than a half hour later he became aware that he wasn't alone in the building. He hadn't heard any of the doors open, but he felt air currents that shouldn't have been swirling through the closed building pass over his face. Moving slowly, he raised his hand to the handle of his gun and let it rest there while he strained to listen in the inky blackness that had enveloped the warehouse.

Something scrabbled against the concrete floor on his right side, and he jerked his gun out of his holster and waited for whoever was there to come into view. There was a scraping sound next to one of the boxes directly in front of him, and the next second something small and light colored twined itself around his ankles.

A cat. Closing his eyes, he shoved his gun back into his holster, hearing the rasp of metal against leather as it slid home. He'd been spooked by a damned cat. Leaning down, he tried to shove the thing away from him, but the animal apparently had decided that Luke was his friend and wouldn't leave. Bending over to give it another push, he saw a pair of expensive Italian loafers on the floor in front of him and slowly straightened.

Chapter 15

"Don't even think about going for your gun, Luke." Eddie's voice echoed hollowly through the cavernous building. "Just stand up nice and straight and put your hands on your head."

Slowly raising his hands, Luke tried to look behind his ex-partner to determine the odds.

Eddie set his flashlight on one of the boxes next to them, casting a dim, shadowy illumination over the area surrounding them. "There isn't anyone else here, Luke, if that's what you're wondering about. I clean up my own messes." His voice hardened. "But before I do, I want to know how you found out about us. Was it that bitch from Internal Affairs?"

Luke clenched his jaw at Eddie's reference to Julia and stared at his ex-partner with hard eyes. "Do you see her anywhere? If it was Internal Affairs, don't you think they'd be here?" He allowed himself to smile coolly at Eddie. "Internal Affairs cleans up their own messes, too. No, this one is strictly personal."

"You always were distressingly straight, Luke. You cramped my style for a long time when we were partners."

Even in the dim light Luke could see Eddie's mouth harden. "But you were too straight for your own good. I laughed myself silly the day I testified against you at that hearing. I'd been looking for a way to get rid of you for months, and you handed it to me on a silver platter."

For a moment, Luke allowed the rage to burn through him. He tensed his muscles, prepared to spring at Eddie. Then he saw the expectant light in Eddie's eyes. His old partner was waiting for him to do just that.

Slowly he forced the rage back into its hiding place, deep in his soul. He wasn't going to give his old partner any convenient excuses to kill him. If Eddie pulled that trigger, it was going to have to be in cold blood.

"So when did this all start, Eddie?" He rocked back on his heels and spoke in a conversational voice, never taking his eyes off the man with the gun.

Eddie's eyes narrowed, and Luke saw his hand tighten around the handle of the gun. Then he shrugged and gave Luke a cold smile. "I suppose it doesn't matter now. You're history, McKinley. You might as well know what you missed out on."

Ignoring the taunt, Luke shifted closer to the boxes, speaking as he moved. "Is this just your game, Eddie, or are there other guys involved?"

"If you knew enough to be here, Luke, you know I'm not the only one. But I'm the one that makes the decisions."

Eddie always had been a braggart. Maybe Luke could use that trait to his advantage. "If you make the decisions, what made you pick a bunch of losers like the Demons to deal with? These guys are pathetic."

"Maybe they are, but they control most of the drugs coming into this part of the city." Eddie smiled again and shrugged lightly. "It was strictly a business decision. We went where the money was."

Luke edged over another half step and slowly lowered his elbow until it rested on the top of one of the dusty boxes. If he got an opportunity to use his gun, he didn't want his arm muscles trembling and weak because he'd had to hold his arms on top of his head for too long. "Tell me something,

Eddie," he asked in an even voice. "Did you even once think about the fact that what you were doing was wrong? Or does it feel good to be one of the scumbags?"

Eddie's face darkened and he took a step forward. Luke braced himself, watching Eddie's eyes as he prepared to lunge to the side. Eddie raised the gun, but just as Luke was tensing his muscles to move, Eddie relaxed and lowered the gun a hair. He gave Luke a twisted smile.

"You're too much of an idealist, Luke. I prefer to think of it as creative justice," Eddie explained, waving the gun around the warehouse. "Nine guys out of ten would agree. Hell, I got seven other guys in our precinct alone to go along with me." He stopped, realizing what he'd given away. After a moment, though, he shrugged and smiled again. The smile told Luke what Eddie had planned for him.

"I only did what anyone else would have done under the circumstances," he continued. "The department doesn't pay us enough to live on, and they expect us to risk our necks every day."

"They never told us anything different than that when we signed up to do this job, Eddie," Luke answered softly. Tomorrow, he knew, he would grieve for the man who used to be his friend. Right now, he just wanted to figure out a way to get out of this warehouse alive. He thanked God he'd sent Julia home with Piotyr, that he hadn't led her into this.

"You call this creative justice?" he asked, his voice echoing in the darkness. "These people are killing kids every day, Eddie. Where's the justice in that?"

Eddie scowled. "Who gives a damn if a bunch of drug dealers knock each other off? Makes our jobs easier. Besides, we've gotten a lot of them off the streets."

"I'll bet that doesn't go over real big with your buddies the Demons," Luke mocked.

"It's part of the deal and the Demons know it." Eddie's voice was matter-of-fact. "For every load we let them deliver, we arrest a few of the low-level dealers." He flashed his brilliant smile at Luke. "That's what I mean by creative justice. We're rounding up more of the dealers now than we ever have before."

"Is that how you've managed to avoid being caught until now, Eddie?" Luke felt sick to his stomach. The arrest statistics had actually been protecting Eddie and his buddies, but thank God Julia had been smart enough to see beyond them. "Pick up enough of the expendable kids, and no one will wonder why you never make the big bust?"

"You got it, pal. We've been doing a public service here. Have you seen my statistics?" he asked with pride in his voice. "Since you left and I haven't had to work behind your back, we've put away dozens of these guys. We cleaned up the streets and made some money for ourselves doing it. It's been the best of all possible worlds."

"But the drugs haven't stopped coming into the neighborhoods, Eddie. The kids haven't stopped dying. And you can arrest as many of the low-level scumballs as you want. There's always two more to take their place. Until you get the guys in charge, nothing's going to change."

"Who wants it to? Nobody's holding a gun to people's heads, telling them to buy the stuff. The Demons are just filling a niche. The law of supply and demand, McKinley. That's all it is."

"You're supplying death, Eddie." Luke's voice was hard. He didn't care whether he made Eddie mad. He'd heard enough. "Don't try to fool yourself. For every kid that dies of a drug overdose, you are just as liable as the Demons. More. You could stop it, but you haven't. You choose instead to buy your big-screen televisions and your exercise equipment."

Luke took a breath and edged closer to the box. Eddie wasn't smiling anymore. "Tell me, Eddie, what do you watch on that big TV? Do you watch the cop shows? You know, the ones where the bad cop is always caught in the end?" he taunted softly.

Eddie looked at him scornfully and clicked off the safety on his gun. "No one's going to catch me, Luke. And do you know why? Because I know you too well. You're Mr. Big Shot, Mr. I-can-do-it-myself. You didn't tell another damn soul about this meeting tonight." He must have misinterpreted the flicker in Luke's eyes, because he laughed softly.

"I didn't think so. And you know how I knew? Because that's the way you operated when we were partners. We were partners, but somehow you always got credit for whatever happened. You were the loner, never giving anyone else the credit they deserved."

"Looks like I was right, doesn't it, Eddie?"

Something brushed against one of the boxes behind Eddie, and he tightened his hold on the gun. Luke could see that it took all his effort not to turn around and look. "Is that you, Joe?" Eddie called.

Eddie's voice echoed in the silence, and there was no answer from the darkness beyond them. "It's probably that damned cat," Luke said casually, but he strained his eyes to see behind Eddie. Nothing moved in the inky blackness.

Eddie turned his attention back to Luke. "Do you feel like a hero, buddy?" he mocked as he raised his gun again. "Because the papers tomorrow morning are going to have a story about an ex-cop found dead in a real nasty area of town. There's going to be a lot of speculation about why you were here, Luke. And after everything's said and done, you're going to look real bad."

"And what about you, Eddie?" Luke kept his voice steady as he concentrated on the place behind his ex-partner. Something had moved back there, something that was darker than the blackness around them. "Do you think of yourself as a hero?" He laughed harshly. "The only person you're a hero to is the salesman who sold you all that fancy stuff you have in your house."

Eddie shrugged. "Like I said, I just did what anyone else would do in the same circumstances."

"Not a cop, Eddie." Luke stared at his former friend, and felt a vicious kick of satisfaction when he looked away. "I know there are dirty cops, but I figure they were never real cops in the first place. Maybe other people would accept money and look the other way, but a real cop never would. Cops are held to a higher standard." He continued to stare at Eddie as he lowered his voice. "A standard where justice is more than a word. A standard where justice actually means something besides a convenient way to justify what you're doing."

"I'm touched by your high ideals, Luke. Just look where they've gotten you." Eddie raised his gun to fire just as something came sailing out of the air behind him. Before he could pull the trigger, one of the dusty wooden boxes that were stacked all around them slammed into his head, knocking him to the ground at Luke's feet.

Luke kicked the gun out of his hand and watched it spin into the darkness between two stacks of boxes. Yanking his own gun out of his holster, he held it steady on the semi-conscious man while he searched him for another weapon. Finding none, he stood up slowly and saw Julia standing in front of him.

His heart leapt in his chest at the sight of her, then began to race. "Julia!" he whispered. "Where did you come from?"

She stepped up into the area illuminated by the flashlight and looked down at Eddie, still sprawled on the floor. She looked back up at Luke, but it was too dark to see the expression in her eyes. "I dropped Piotyr off and came back, of course. Did you think I'd leave you here alone?"

Joy expanded in his chest. In spite of the way he'd treated her, she'd come back.

"This is my case," she continued, and the joy withered to dust. "I'm going to be here to finish it."

"Thanks for showing up when you did." His voice was flat. "Eddie wasn't too happy about finding me here."

"So I heard." She moved to one side and looked down at the man lying on the concrete floor. "What are we going to do with him?"

"We're going to tie him up, gag him, and leave him here, then get the hell out of this warehouse. I called the captain and told him to send over the troops. They'll find him when they arrest all the others."

She stood gazing at him, her eyes still unreadable. Finally she said, "Is that what you were planning to do?"

He scowled. "I was planning on busting these creeps myself. I especially wanted to watch him—" he poked Eddie with his toe "—get thrown into the wagon personally. But there's no reason the uniforms can't take care of it. Let's go."

Slowly she shook her head. "Are you leaving because I'm here?" At his silence, her lips tightened. "Forget it, McKinley. I'm not going anywhere." She looked at him, and for an instant the soft light of the flashlight reflected off a shimmer in her eyes. "I have to stay and make sure."

Her voice had dropped to a whisper and he looked away, uncomfortable with the raw grief in her face. Suddenly he understood. Just as he'd had to be sure about Eddie, she had to be sure about her brother.

And with that thought came another, even more uncomfortable one. How different was what she'd done from what he'd planned on doing? Hadn't he taken this case thinking he'd do everything in his power to prove that Eddie wasn't guilty?

"Julia," he began, turning to her impulsively.

"Shh," she warned, freezing. "Did you hear that?"

There was a faint scraping sound coming from the other side of the warehouse, and Luke swore savagely to himself. It was too late to leave now, even if he wanted to. Someone was trying to open the door.

Grabbing the flashlight Eddie had placed on top of the boxes, he switched it off and pulled Julia down next to him in the darkness. Eddie groaned once, quietly, and he could feel Julia tense next to him.

"I'm going to gag him and tie him up," he whispered into her ear, and he felt her nod. Her scent drifted up to him, and he had to stop himself from reaching out to touch her. Even if he hadn't driven an insurmountable wedge between them, this wasn't the time. If he touched her just once, he'd forget all about why they were here.

"Do you have anything I can use?" he whispered, struggling to remove his belt.

After a moment, he heard her barely voiced answer. "I'm wearing a bodysuit. I'll take it off and you can use that."

He froze, holding the belt suspended over Eddie's hands, and listened to the soft rustlings in the blackness. She was taking off her clothes. He couldn't see a thing, but his imagination supplied all the details.

After a moment, he felt a soft piece of clothing dangling over his fingers. He crushed it in his hand, trying to resist the urge to bring it to his face and inhale her essence. It was still warm from her body, and his hands began to tremble as he tightened the belt on Eddie's hands, then used the soft cloth to tie Eddie's feet together.

"Do you need my socks?" she asked, and his whole body clenched at the thought of her taking off even one more article of clothing.

"No!" He spoke more harshly than he should have, and he felt her freeze.

"No, we won't need that," he made himself say more steadily. "All I need now is something to gag him."

"How about my hat?" she asked, tossing it in his direction. It smelled like her, too, but he grabbed Eddie's head and shoved the hat into his mouth. The less time he spent thinking about that, the better off they'd be.

The scraping sound came from the other side of the warehouse again, louder this time. Luke patted the floor around them, searching for Eddie's gun. When he found it, he stuck it in his waistband then touched Julia's arm. At least she had her shirt back on, he thought sourly.

"Let's move over here a little more. I don't think they'll come looking for Eddie right away, but I don't want to be near him if they find him."

She followed him without a word, and he settled them behind a stack of boxes closer to the other door. He didn't give a damn if she wanted to be here or not. If they had a chance, they were going to get the hell out of this warehouse.

The door across from them scraped again, and suddenly the warehouse was flooded with light. A truck engine idled on the other side of the door. He longed to look out and see what was going on, but knew he didn't dare. Realizing that Julia must be as curious as he was, he bent over and put his mouth to her ear.

"That's the truck they're using to bring in the coke. As soon as they get the door open all the way they'll just drive it right in."

"How do you know?" she demanded, carefully turning her head to look at him and moving her ear away from his mouth. He should be grateful, he told himself. Her pulse had fluttered wildly just beyond his lips, a hairbreadth away from his lips, and the scent of her warm skin was enough to drive all other thoughts from his mind.

"How do I know?" he repeated. "Because I've seen this dozens of times. Standard operating procedure."

"Where are the police?" She turned to look at him, and he saw the worry on her face. "Shouldn't they be here by now?"

"They're here. They're just waiting until all the players are in place." He prayed it was true. He glanced at her, not sure of how much to say. "They have to catch Molloy and Eddie and the others in the act."

She licked her lips and turned her head. "I know that."

Reaching out for her hand, he wrapped his fingers around hers. "It'll be all right, Julia."

She surprised him by returning the pressure of his fingers. Holding his hand desperately tight, she looked over at him, infinite sadness in her eyes. "We'll solve the case, Luke. But it won't be all right."

What could he say? He remembered how it had felt when she'd told him that Eddie was involved in this. How much worse would it be if Eddie had been his brother? Letting go of her hand, he wrapped his arm around her shoulders and pulled her close. She resisted for a split second, then let herself relax into the curve of his arm.

On the other side of the warehouse the door swung fully open with a groan and the truck rumbled in. Low voices mingled with the noise from the truck and the sound of footsteps entering the warehouse. Leaning forward, he strained to hear.

Julia shifted in his arms, throwing him off-balance, and he slammed into a stack of boxes. He grabbed frantically for them, but they tumbled down onto the floor in front of him.

The warehouse was instantly silent. Even the truck engine was switched off, and the sounds of their breathing became unbearably loud in the stillness. Then voices began murmuring again, getting louder as they headed toward the place they hid.

Pulling his jacket around him to hide his shoulder holster, Luke grabbed Julia and eased her onto the dirty floor. "We have only one chance to convince them," he whispered urgently into her ear. "Follow my lead."

He began kissing her, unbuttoning the top buttons of her shirt at the same time. She froze, resisting for a moment, but then wrapped her arms around him and drew him closer. When he ran his tongue over her lips she opened to him immediately, and he nearly forgot where they were and what was happening as he tasted her.

"What's going on? What are you doing here?" The voice came from directly above him, and he felt Julia stiffen in his arms and clutch her blouse together with one hand.

Rolling over slowly, he sat up and tried to shield Julia with his body. Behind him he could hear the rustling of her clothes as she fumbled with the buttons of her blouse.

"What the hell does it look like we're doing?" Luke snarled. He'd always believed the old saw about a good offense being the best defense. "Get out of here and leave us alone."

The gang member who stood over him with a gun couldn't have been any more than fifteen. He licked his lips nervously and looked over his shoulder toward the truck. "I think you're going to have to come and talk to the boss."

"And what if I don't want to?" Luke crossed his arms and stared at the kid, trying to intimidate him.

But apparently that was the wrong approach. The kid's gaze flew back to him and hardened, and the hand holding the gun steadied. Gesturing with the pistol, he backed up a step. "Stand up and get moving."

Never taking his eyes off the boy, Luke reached behind him and pulled Julia to her feet. As they walked slowly into the glare of the truck's headlights, he could see a group of figures standing around the truck. Tightening his hold on

Julia's hand for a moment, he finally dropped it and casually rested his fingertips in the pocket of his jeans. He needed to be ready to pull his gun.

"What did you find, Mongo?" someone called from the other side of the truck.

"These two were rolling around on the floor. He had his tongue down her throat and his hand in her blouse."

Crude laughter floated over to them, and Luke longed to reach for Julia's hand, but he didn't dare even look at her right now. He had to be ready to react in a split second.

"Don't you have a bed, lady?" another voice asked, accompanied by another burst of laughter.

"Get them out of here, Mongo," the first voice ordered impatiently, and Luke exhaled slowly. Without a word he turned to go, reaching for Julia's hand.

"Wait a minute." This voice came from in front of the truck, and Luke turned around slowly. All he could see was a silhouette in front of the truck, but he didn't like the tone of that command.

"That broad is the nurse we saw a few days ago. Remember? She was looking for someone in the neighborhood."

Dead silence filled the warehouse. He felt Julia move behind him and reached for her hand to warn her to stay silent. His finger itched to pull his gun, but they would both be dead in an instant if he did. He tensed, waiting to move.

"If she's a nurse then I'm a dancing horse." The voice came from the deeper shadows against the far wall, and Luke jerked his head in that direction. He knew that voice.

Joe Molloy, one of the detectives from Eddie's precinct, stepped into the light. His gun was steady in his hand and it was aimed right at them.

"The guy she's with is an ex-cop. I doubt if it's a coincidence that they're in here tonight. Where's Eddie?" Molloy looked around. "He used to be McKinley's partner. We'll let him deal with these two."

"Good to see you, too, Joe," Luke said. "What brings you to these parts?"

"Shut up, McKinley. Eddie!" he yelled. "Get the hell over here!"

After a moment someone shifted his feet, the noise shockingly loud in the silence. Luke reached behind him slowly and squeezed Julia's hand, waiting for the right moment. When most of the gang members were looking toward the shadows at the back of the warehouse, he shoved Julia to the floor and rolled on top of her, shooting for the headlights on the truck at the same time.

As the room was plunged into darkness he pulled her to her feet and headed for the door. Just as they got there the door burst open and a bright light was switched on, blinding them.

"Police! Freeze!" someone shouted, and Luke jerked Julia over to the side and out of the way.

The door behind the truck burst open a few seconds later, and another bright light illuminated the interior of the warehouse. The gang members and the cops inside the building were caught with their guns in their hands, frozen in place.

"All right, drop your weapons," Luke heard another voice command, and realized with a jolt of relief that it was Captain Lewis. As they watched the uniformed officers rounding up everyone in the warehouse, he pulled Julia into the circle of his arm and held her close.

"Are you okay?"

She gave a shaky laugh. "Other than having ten years scared off my life, you mean?"

He dropped a kiss onto her hair. "I'm sorry. I thought we had a better chance at bluffing our way out of here."

She leaned into him for just a second, pressing against his heart, and then stepped away so quickly that he wondered if he'd imagined it. "Don't be. You made the right choice," she said. "You bought us enough time for the cavalry to save us."

He reached for her again, to reassure himself that she was all right, but stopped when he saw that she was staring across the warehouse. The uniformed officers had the gang members and the cops who were dealing with them lying on the floor, their hands on top of their heads.

Julia was watching them intently, and with an ache in his chest he realized why. "Do you want me to check for you?" he asked gently.

She shook her head. "No," she whispered. "I have to do it myself."

Julia was halfway across the floor when she realized that she still held the gun in her hand. It was the one Luke had taken away from Piotyr and handed to her. She'd pulled it out of her waistband when he'd stood in front of her, facing down the Demons, and now she slowly shoved it back into place. The cold metal chafed against her skin.

Captain Lewis glanced over at her as she approached the men lying on the floor. "You did a good job on this case, Carleton," he said gruffly. "Why don't you go on down to the station house and wait for us there? We'll have a few questions to ask you later."

She didn't answer as her eyes scanned the prone men on the floor. Her heart began to lighten as she didn't see any bright blond heads lying in the dirt. Then, just before she got to the end, she saw him.

He was facedown in the dust, but her heart contracted when she saw her brother's profile. Stepping over to stand at his feet, she stared at him for a long time, feeling the hot lump of tears congealing in her throat.

"Bobby," she breathed.

It wasn't possible that he heard her above the din of noise in the warehouse, but her brother turned his head and his eyes met hers. They were filled with regret, pain and shame, and he looked at her only for a second before he turned away.

"Bobby, how could you?" she cried. "What made you do this?"

At that he turned around again. "Get out of here, Skinny," he said, weariness etched in every word.

"Don't call me that," she sobbed, feeling the tears streaming down her face. "Don't ever call me that again."

"Let's go," Luke's voice whispered in her ear, and his arm slid around her shoulders and pulled her close. "I'll take you home."

"No!" She resisted stiffly, pulling away from him to stand staring at Bobby, lying on the floor below her.

"Come on, Julia. You can talk to him later." Luke tried to pull her away, and she jerked her arm out of his grasp.

"Let go of me, Luke. You can't tell me what to do. I have to know why he did it. I can't leave until I find out why."

Luke slid his body between her and her brother, blocking her view of his humiliation. "He may not be able to tell you that," he answered gently. "Especially not right now. It'll be easier to talk to him later, when you're alone."

Alone. She grasped that thought to herself and turned away, heading blindly for the cool air rushing through the open door. Right before she stumbled through it she felt Luke at her side, but before she could tell him to go away she heard the captain's voice again.

"You two need to come into the station and tell us what happened. I'll finish cleaning up here and meet you there."

"Could we do it tomorrow, sir?" Luke asked.

"Tonight, McKinley," the older man barked.

The captain turned away, and Luke called after him, "You'll find Eddie Timmons behind those boxes over there. You'll want to collect him, too."

Then Luke steered her out into the clear night air. He didn't say a word, just wrapped his arm around her as he led her down the street to the rental car. Neither of them spoke as they drove through the night toward the police station.

Julia stared down at the cup in her hand, not seeing the brown sludge that seemed to be slowly congealing inside of it. It had been hours since she'd noticed the drab walls that surrounded her and the uncomfortable chair she was slumped in. All she could think about was Bobby, locked in a cell somewhere below her, and Luke, who'd disappeared as soon as they'd reached the station.

It was standard procedure, she knew, to isolate witnesses so they didn't have a chance to compare notes, but after three hours she'd finally realized that Luke was avoiding her.

"What did you expect?" she asked herself harshly, standing up abruptly and dumping the cold coffee into the drinking fountain. "That he'd be waiting for you with open arms?"

She'd hoped he'd come to take her home after they'd given their statements so that she could at least give him one final apology. Not that it would make any difference to him, she acknowledged sadly. She had failed him, just like so many of the other people in his life. Eddie, his wife, even the police department had failed him when he'd needed it the most.

It had been wrong to fire him. She knew that now. She'd merely been obeying orders, doing what she'd been told to do, but now she realized how wrong she'd been. And not only because his firing had been political. She'd broken the rules herself, trying to protect her brother. Had what Luke done been any worse? She didn't think so.

She should have challenged the department two years ago. Even though what Luke had done had been wrong, even though she'd followed the rules precisely, there were times when the rules had to be bent. And Lucas McKinley's case had been one of them.

She stood over the trash can and slowly crushed the paper cup in her hand. She couldn't change history. She couldn't even change what she'd done last week, although she'd give anything to do so. She should have been straight with him up front, told him that she suspected Bobby was involved.

But she hadn't, and now she had to live with it.

Prowling around the tiny room, she wondered if Luke was talking to Captain Lewis right now, or if he'd already left the station. Could he have walked right past the room where she waited and not even stop to say goodbye?

Remembering his face when he'd found Bobby's name on the duty roster, she knew it was not only possible, but likely. He'd felt betrayed and manipulated, and he wouldn't forgive that easily.

Dropping back down onto the hard chair, she buried her face in her hands and tried to hold back the hot tears that threatened to fall. She'd been afraid to trust him, and she'd ended up making sure he would never trust her.

Footsteps echoed in the hallway outside the door; she ignored them at first. People had been walking by the room all evening. But the steps slowed and stopped outside the door, and she looked up, her heart leaping with hope.

Maybe he had come for her, after all. Maybe he'd been able to forget what she'd done, and been able to forgive her. The doorknob turned, and she stood up as the door began to open.

Her brother Bobby stood framed in the doorway, his face etched with lines that made him look ten years older. "Thanks for putting up my bail," he said. "Come on, Skinny. I'll take you home."

Chapter 16

Julia paused on the sidewalk and stared up at the boarded-over windows of Luke's office. Was he up there? He hadn't been at home for the last three days, and she didn't know where else to look for him. The boarded-up, bombed-out rubble of his office was the last place to check. Nobody had seen Lucas McKinley since the night Eddie and the others had been arrested.

She didn't know if Luke had found out that they'd caught the kid who'd caused their accident. She didn't even know if he'd been home since the Bomb Squad had swept his house and found it clean. She wasn't sure if he cared. Not even Raul had been able to find him to share his good news about the scholarship.

She reached into her briefcase one more time to make sure the check was there. Running her finger over the stiff paper, she took a deep breath and pushed open the lobby door. It was as good an excuse to see him as any, she told herself. She had made a deal with Luke and she intended to keep it. And she wouldn't be sure he'd gotten the money unless she handed him the check herself.

The hallway was just as dingy as she remembered it, and the linoleum just as worn. But now there was a new smell in the corridor, the faint, acrid odor of smoke. Maybe he wouldn't be here, she thought, disappointment crashing over her. After all, how could anyone stay in a bombed-out office?

Shifting the handle of her briefcase to her left hand and tightening her grip on the warm leather, she raised her right hand to knock on the door.

"Come on in," his voice answered almost immediately from the other side.

Taking a deep breath, she ran one hand over her curly hair, then glanced down at her suit to make sure that nothing was out of place. Licking her lips, she opened the door and stepped inside.

The smell of burned wood hung in the air, stinging her eyes as she closed the door behind her. Luke had half risen from a chair over by the window, and as she watched him he slowly sank back into it. For just a moment, she'd thought that his eyes had blazed with happiness when she walked in the door. Now they were unreadable again as he slid down into his chair and stared at her in the semigloom of the office.

He broke the silence first. "What brings you to this neck of the woods, Julia?" he drawled, propping his feet on the table and folding his hands behind his head.

Something shattered inside her, crumbling into dust. Up until this minute, she'd been hoping that he would want to see her. In her heart, she'd been imagining an emotional reunion, the two of them falling into each other's arms and pledging undying love. Reality was more like a fist in the gut.

"I brought the money I owe you." She was pleased that she managed to keep her voice brisk and businesslike. "I have a check for you."

Fumbling in her briefcase, glad for the excuse to avoid looking at him for a second, she drew out the piece of blue paper and walked over to him. She placed it on the table that stood where his desk used to be, then turned and headed for the door.

"Julia, wait." She could almost imagine there was desperation in his voice, but that was ridiculous. Lucas McKinley had nothing to be desperate about.

Turning around slowly, she watched him as he swung his legs off the table and stood up, shoving his hair back off his face. The look he gave her was almost uncertain, and she bit her lip as her heart began to pound.

"Why did you come here, Julia?" This time his voice was soft, and she couldn't detect any sarcasm in his tone. It sounded as if he really wanted to know.

"I hired you to do a job, and I owed you payment for it," she said stiffly. "That's why." She would die before she let him know about her secret hopes.

"You could have mailed it."

"I didn't know if you were still using this office. I wanted to make sure you got it." It sounded lame, but she raised her chin and stared at him, daring him to contradict her.

"You know where I live. Why didn't you mail it to my house?" As he began to move from behind the table he stepped into the shadows, shielding his face. "I would have gotten it there."

"I wanted to be sure," she repeated stubbornly, and when he didn't answer she took one last look at him and turned to leave again.

"Julia, wait."

"I have to go, Luke." She spoke without turning to look at him. This was a mistake. She never should have allowed herself the indulgence of seeing him again, the futile exercise in hope. She felt as if someone had reached out and ripped off the scab that had been slowly forming over her heart, leaving it raw and bleeding again.

She heard him move behind her, and then he was standing between her and the door. Watching her with an unreadable expression on his face, he said, "Why didn't you wait for me the other night? I told you I would take you home."

It was the last thing she'd expected him to say. Staring at him, speechless, she finally managed to reply, "I thought you were long gone. I hadn't seen you, and I'd been waiting in that horrible little room forever. When Bobby came to get me, I just assumed that you weren't there."

"I was there," he said grimly. "I couldn't leave until I'd heard everything that Eddie had to say, even though it made me ill." Jamming his hands into his pockets, he looked away. "He'd been making deals with the Demons on the side almost the whole time we were partners. That bust that had fallen apart the night my wife was killed? That was his doing. When he found out I was going to be there, he called it off. He was afraid that we might grab someone too high up in the Demons' power structure, and then his little scheme would be over."

His voice was bitter, and impulsively she dropped her briefcase and reached out for him. "I'm so sorry, Luke." She touched his arm. "I know how you must feel."

He looked down at her hand on his arm, then back up at her. Slowly he took her hand in his, and held it lightly. Pain mixed with tenderness washed over his face. "Yeah, I guess you do. You've had a rough few days."

"At least Bobby is freely cooperating with the investigation and has given back every penny of the money. He was only involved for the past few months. If he's lucky, he won't go on trial. Maybe he'll even be able to stay on the police force. You had to find out that what Eddie did was even worse than you'd thought." Turning her hand in his, she gripped his fingers, trying to take away some of his pain.

For a moment, he clung to her as if he never wanted to let go, then he dropped her hand and moved away. Flinging himself onto the couch, he said, "The captain didn't give me many of the details, just that Bobby was cooperating. What happened?"

She walked over and sat down on the couch next to him. "He'd been at the precinct only for a few months when Eddie approached him. The seven of them had decided they needed someone in uniform on their side, and since Bobby was the rookie, they tried to suck him in."

She looked away from him as she continued, "Bobby has always acted before he thought. He claims that before he knew it he was in up to his neck. He wanted to go to the captain, but was afraid he might be involved, too. That night we had dinner together he intended to tell me, but he didn't trust you. Then I disappeared and he couldn't find me. So he continued to go along with them." She raised her head and looked at Luke, suddenly wanting to tell him what she hadn't confided to another soul.

"He said he never meant to get involved and just didn't know how to refuse, but what if that's not true?" She could hear the agony in her voice. "What if he joined Eddie and the others willingly, or even eagerly? I'm afraid that he might have spoken up so quickly only because he'd been caught."

He slowly sat up. "Maybe that is what happened, Julia." Luke's voice was infinitely gentle. "But he did the right thing in the end. Doesn't that make it all right?"

"No," she cried. "No, it doesn't make it all right. Why didn't he tell Eddie to get lost right away? Why didn't he go to the captain the minute Eddie spoke to him? I can't bear the thought that Bobby was involved, even if it was unwillingly."

"He's not a perfect man, Julia. But then none of us are." He closed his eyes for a heartbeat as a shadow flickered across his face, then opened them again and looked at her. "Maybe he's stronger now that he's seen how easy it is to get sucked in. Maybe this has been a wake-up call for him." He watched her for a moment, then reached out to touch her face. "Consider Bobby a lucky man. Not everyone gets a second chance in life."

It was now or never. Julia took a deep breath. "What about you, Luke? Do you get a second chance?" *Do we?* she ached to ask.

"I already did, but I was too thickheaded to recognize it." His voice was flat and devoid of emotion. "I don't deserve a third."

Hope began to grow in her heart, a tiny blossom still tightly furled, but there nonetheless. Looking down at the briefcase that stood on the floor, she said, "Have you seen the newspapers the last few days? Some of the reporters have gotten hold of what happened two years ago, and there's been a public outcry for your reinstatement."

"I know," he said. "The superintendent called yesterday and asked me to rejoin the force."

"And what was your answer?" she asked, holding her breath.

"I accepted, of course. It's all I've ever wanted to do."

She let out the breath she'd been holding. "Thank God. I was afraid you might be too stubborn and proud to go back."

He watched her with unreadable eyes. "I've learned that stubbornness and pride can have a very high price."

Her heart leapt in her chest, but she fumbled in her briefcase. She had to get through what she'd come to say. "I've reopened your case and asked that your file be reviewed. After everything that's happened it's just a formality, but I don't want any blemishes on your record. As the investigating officer, I'm going to recommend that the order to dismiss you be rescinded."

She felt him stiffen beside her. "Why did you do that, Julia?" he asked after a long moment.

She turned her head and saw him watching her closely, uncertainty in his eyes. "There are several reasons, Luke. I should have told you the first one long ago." She took a deep breath and bit her lip. "Your investigation was fixed. You know the drunk driver was the son of an alderman. Word came down from higher up that you were to be convicted and thrown off the police force. I tried to tell myself that you deserved it, that you had been brutal, but it really didn't matter what I thought. Your case had already been decided."

"Why are you telling me this now?"

She couldn't read the expression in his eyes, and she looked away. "Because I was wrong to go along with my superiors, and I'm ashamed of what I did. I've always tried to justify it to myself by saying that you were wrong and deserved your punishment, but I knew, deep down, that you didn't. I don't want there to be any more lies between us."

"Your superiors aren't going to be happy with you, Julia, if you go around saying that they fixed my case. You could lose your job," he said carefully.

"It doesn't matter," she cried passionately. "Don't you understand? I should have spoken up two years ago. I shouldn't have allowed them to use me to punish you. I told myself that you were wrong and I was right, but I think I was just appeasing my conscience. The whole city thinks of you as a hero right now, but in the back of their minds you're still the cop that got fired for brutality. I have to make sure they know the truth."

He closed his eyes and said, "It doesn't matter anymore, Julia. Like you said more than once, it's over and done with."

"No, Luke, it's not. The fact that I allowed myself to be pressured when I investigated you is just one of the reasons I'm reopening your case."

"You don't have anything to feel guilty about, Julia. You did what you had to do."

"Maybe I did and maybe I didn't. But I learned a few things during the past week. I learned that not everything is black-and-white," she answered honestly. "The way you handled Piotyr was a good lesson. You could have had him arrested, too, and you would have been perfectly justified if you had. He's a juvenile, he was carrying an unregistered weapon and he was working for the Demons. Most people *would* have arrested him, in fact."

Luke shrugged. "He's basically a good kid. And I think he's scared enough that he won't step off that narrow path again."

Julia shook her head. "He won't. We talked a lot while I was driving him home. He knows just how much trouble he could have been in, and he knows who's responsible for getting him out of it." She smiled. "He says he wants to be a police officer when he grows up."

He jumped up and paced around the room. "There are so many kids that could go either way. You see them on the street all the time. And all it takes is one little push in either direction. Sometimes you're lucky and you're in the right place at the right time to provide that push."

He stopped and looked at her. "That's what it was like with your brother Bobby, wasn't it?"

Shocked, she could only stare at him. "How did you know that?" she finally whispered.

His mouth twisted up in a grim smile. "I began to wonder why you just assumed that Bobby was guilty. And you did, or otherwise you would have told me about him. I still have a few friends in the department, so I managed to get hold of his juvenile record. It seems that Bobby Carleton had a few brushes with the law as a teenager. Nothing serious, but it could have escalated into that. And it was usually his big sister who pulled his chestnuts out of the fire." His face softened. "You felt responsible for him, didn't you? You were afraid that you'd steered him into police work and it was your fault that he'd gone bad."

Focusing on the briefcase, she tried to blink away the stinging in the back of her eyes. "I was so scared, Luke," she whispered. "I love him so much, and I was afraid that it was my fault." She looked up at him, swallowing the lump in her throat and feeling it burn down into her chest. "I'm sorry I didn't tell you. I wanted to, but I just couldn't. I kept telling myself that it was a coincidence, that he wasn't really involved, that once Eddie and the others were arrested everything would be fine. I told myself that you didn't know Bobby like I did, that you wouldn't understand that it was a coincidence."

"I would have gone after him like all the others."

She nodded slowly. "Like you should have. Like *I* should have." Sighing, she said, "I should have taken myself off the case when I realized that Bobby might be involved, but I couldn't do that, either." Taking a deep, shaky breath, she added, "And that's the other reason I recommended that you be reinstated. I understand now that emotions cloud what you do and affect your judgment. If a drunk had killed *you,* I might have done the same thing. Considering what had just happened when you beat that man, a suspension would have been a more just punishment. And if the drunk hadn't been politically connected, that's what would have happened."

"You would have been wrong."

She looked up at him, shocked. He stood over near one of the boarded-up windows, his back to her. "What do you mean?"

"I mean you were right that day at the hearing. Cops are held to a higher standard. The fact that he had just killed my wife was no excuse. Because I was a police officer, I had an obligation to handle myself according to department regulations. You did the right thing."

"Why do you insist on punishing yourself over and over for what happened, Luke?" she cried. "You've already paid the price."

"I'm not punishing myself again. If you'd asked me this four days ago, my answer would have been completely different. But Eddie said a lot to me in that warehouse. He said that anyone would have jumped at the chance to make some money and put away the low-level dealers. That's when I realized that police officers *are* held to a higher standard, that we *are* more responsible than the rest of the citizens. That's when I realized that what I did that night was wrong."

"It doesn't matter anymore. You've paid the price, and I'm going to make sure that your record is cleared."

"Why, Julia? Why are you doing this?" He turned around and faced her, his eyes intense.

"Because it's the right thing to do, Luke. Because it should have been done a long time ago. Because I know I was wrong."

"Does this have anything to do with what happened between us?"

It felt as if he'd taken a knife to her soul and sliced it open. "If you're asking if I'm reopening your case because we slept together, the answer is no."

"I didn't mean it like that, Julia."

"Then how did you mean it?" she cried, her heart crumbling to pieces inside her chest. "I love you, dammit. Don't you dare cheapen what happened between us by implying that I was simply overcome by sex."

She bent down and fumbled in her briefcase for a tissue. As she was blowing her nose she felt his hand on her arm, pulling her up to stand in front of him.

"I wasn't implying anything of the sort." He reached out to touch her face but stopped at the last moment. "Did you mean what you just said?"

"Yes, I love you." So what if she humiliated herself? she thought fiercely. She wasn't about to deny what she felt.

"How can you, after the way I treated you?" he whispered, his hands tightening on her shoulders.

"I hurt you," she said honestly. "Even though I loved you, I didn't trust you with the information about Bobby. You had a right to not trust me."

"It looks like neither one of us was very good at trusting."

Slowly she shook her head. "We were both afraid. But I'm not afraid anymore, Luke, because I realized that without you I'm not whole. That's why I came here today." She reached up and pushed a lock of hair off his forehead. "Remember those second chances we were talking about earlier? They don't come along too often. I'm willing to grab for this one. Are you?"

He pulled her into his arms and held her tightly. "Oh, Julia. I love you so much." He leaned away from her, cradling her face in his hands. "What did I ever do to deserve you?"

She gave him a shaky smile. "That's funny, I was just asking myself the same thing about you."

"I would have come after you, you know. I wouldn't have given up until you forgave me and admitted that you loved me, too."

"You wouldn't have had to work very hard. I'll admit that anytime. I love you, Luke. I think I've been a little bit in love with you for the past two years."

"Is that so?" he murmured into her ear as his hand caressed down her back. "That's quite a coincidence, because ever since I met you I've been seeing a lot of this wild red hair of yours in my dreams." He wove his other hand through the springy curls. "It irritated the hell out of me, too. I wanted to hate you, I really did, but all I could think about was what was under those trim little business suits of yours."

"I hope your curiosity is satisfied," she whispered, pressing closer to him.

"I don't think it ever will be." He kissed her, a long, lingering caress that made her ache for him. "Now that I know the person who lives inside this gorgeous body of yours, I'll never get tired of discovering new parts of you."

"Luke?" She had to be sure. Leaning back, she put her hands on his shoulders and stared at him intently. "Are you sure you can forgive me that easily? What I did was wrong, and it was dangerous, too. You could have been hurt because of Bobby."

As he watched her his lips curved into a tender smile. "You're not the only one who's been doing a lot of thinking the past few days, Julia. You would have told me before it got to that point."

She drew in a shaky breath. "Are you sure it's that easy, Luke? How can you know that?"

"I love you, Julia," he said gently. "I know you. You're too honorable a person not to have told me. You wouldn't have let me walk into that warehouse without telling me about Bobby."

"You have more faith in me than I have in myself," she said, looking at him with wonder.

"I have no doubts at all, Julia. You would have told me."

"I love you, Luke."

"I know," he whispered. "And I love you, too."

He bent to kiss her. What started as a gentle caress was a match that lit the dry wood in both of their hearts. She wasn't sure who moved first, but with a groan of desire he swept her into his arms and fell back onto the red leather couch.

Suddenly they couldn't get enough of each other. As she tugged at his shirttails with trembling hands, he unbuttoned the jacket of her suit. When he brushed open the lapels, he froze for a moment, then slowly looked up at her.

"Julia!" he managed to say in a strangled voice. "How could you walk down the street like this?"

She glanced down at the sheer teddy she'd worn beneath the suit jacket, then back up at him. "No one could see me." Slowly she bent down so the lace-and-chiffon concoction brushed over his chest and kissed his mouth. "I wanted you, Luke. I was prepared to fight dirty if I got the chance."

Bringing one hand to trace the pattern of lace across her chest, he murmured, "Maybe we're going to have to fight more often. I think I like this concept."

"I think I'd prefer to skip the fighting and go straight to the making-up part."

"There's a lot to be said for that approach, too," he agreed as he swept her jacket off her shoulders and tossed it onto the floor. His eyes darkened to the color of midnight as he looked at the teddy once more.

"Julia," he breathed. Suddenly he bent and took her mouth, and his kiss wasn't tender or sweet this time. It was wild with desire and possession, and she felt herself responding to the need in him. The yearning started in her heart and spread like wildfire through her soul.

Clothing disappeared, swept away by searching, trembling hands. Their bodies strained together, passion heating her skin and turning his touch into liquid fire. His hands were everywhere, giving her pleasure and stoking the flames higher.

She reached for him, desperately needing to feel his mouth on hers. As he kissed her, he pressed her down into the leather of the couch and she felt his heart booming against her chest. Her own pounded in an answering rhythm, and she gasped his name as he entered her.

His control disappeared as she began moving against him. Cupping her buttocks in his hands, he drove into her, gasping her name over and over. When she shattered in his arms, he let himself go and shuddered into her one more time. As the trembling slowed, he wrapped his arms around her and nuzzled his face into her neck. "I love you, Julia Carleton," he breathed into her ear.

She tightened her arms around him and pulled him closer, trying to hold the world at bay for another few minutes. If she had a choice, she would never let him go.

After a long time he stirred and rolled over, carrying her on top of him. "I knew this damned couch was here for a reason."

"Mmm," she agreed, wriggling against him. "It's a lot more comfortable than the floor."

Feeling his response to her movements, she bent down and kissed him. He moaned softly into her mouth, then cupped her face in his hands as he held her away from him and looked in her eyes. "We can't do this, Julia."

There was a note of desperation in his voice, and she sat up slowly. "Why? What's wrong?"

"Don't you realize what we just did? I didn't use any protection." Running his hands down her sides, rising up to kiss her, he added, "It's not the kind of thing I keep around the office."

Sliding down his body, she kissed him again and said, "Well, then, I guess this is as good a time as any to ask how you feel about children."

"I want them," he said promptly. "The thought of you, pregnant with our child..." He paused and, laying his hand over her belly, slowly lifted his head to kiss her abdomen. "It would be more than I ever dreamed of. But it has to be something we both want."

She covered his hand with hers, feeling his warmth burn into her over the place their children would grow. "I want to have babies with you," she whispered.

"There's only one little hitch," he murmured. "I'm an old-fashioned kind of guy, Carleton. If you want to have babies with me, I'm afraid you're going to have to marry me first."

She smiled at him, the love inside her shining out of her eyes. "I thought you'd never ask, McKinley."

"I got sidetracked a little earlier, but I'm asking now. Will you marry me, Julia?"

"There's nothing I want more," she whispered.

Sitting up, he pulled her onto his lap and kissed her again, a promise and a vow. Then, leaning away from her, he said, "Are you sure you want to be married to a cop? You know, more than most, the dark side of the job. You know what it can do to a marriage. I don't have to go back to the force."

"I want to marry you." She took his face in her hands and looked at him. "I would want to marry you no matter what you did." Her fingers trailed along his cheek. "You were meant to be a cop, Lucas McKinley. You're one of the good guys. I couldn't bear it if you gave that up for me. Besides, my love for you doesn't depend on what you do. I love you for who you are, and part of that is being a cop. Every job puts different kinds of strains on a marriage. We'll be strong enough, and we love each other enough, to overcome the problems we'll face."

"I think we'll be able to overcome anything, my love."

"I'm sure of it." She cuddled closer to him. "I will miss one thing about this office, though."

"What's that?"

She looked up at him, grinning. "This leather couch. It's beginning to hold a lot of memories." Leaning over, she kissed him again as she laughed softly. "And it may be the place our first child was conceived."

"We'll move it to the house," he answered promptly. Bending down, he kissed her again, a long, leisurely caress. "Traditions are very important for families. This can be our first one."

Still holding her close, he picked up her clothes from the floor and handed them to her. "But tradition or not, I can think of better places to have this discussion. Like at home, in bed. With you, for the next week or two."

Sliding the straps of the teddy over her shoulders, she watched as his eyes darkened again and he reached out to trail his fingers over her lips. Brushing a kiss over his mouth as she pulled on her skirt, she said, "You said something about a bed. Are you changing your mind?"

Never taking his eyes off her, he grinned as he threw on his clothes. "I wouldn't dream of it. I've spent the last three days imagining you in my bed."

Picking up her briefcase, she stood in the doorway and looked around the room. It had been a dusty, ruined office when she walked in, but from now on it would hold a shining place in her memory. Looking over at Luke, she saw the same truth reflected in his eyes. Picking up her hand, he kissed it as he opened the door.

"The old Lucas McKinley was incinerated in the fire in this office. You rescued me from its ashes and created the new one. How can I ever thank you for that?"

"By taking me home," she whispered.

Silently he held out his hand, and as she took it he pulled the door shut behind them. They walked down the stairs into the sunlight, holding each other tightly.

* * * * *

INTIMATE MOMENTS®

Silhouette®

COMING NEXT MONTH

#709 MADDY LAWRENCE'S BIG ADVENTURE— Linda Turner
Heartbreakers

He was the hero of her dreams...as if he were straight from the pages of a book! But to prim-and-proper librarian Maddy Lawrence, Ace MacKenzie was all too real and way too dangerous. Because sheltered Maddy now found herself on the adventure of a lifetime... and falling fast for one too-good-to-be-true man.

#710 HUNTING HOUSTON—Sandy Steen

Abby Douglass knew all about men like Houston Sinclair: risk-taker, pleasure-seeker...*possible killer*. And now her job—her very life—depended on how well she learned this man's secrets. But in hunting Houston, Abby found one very frightening truth: she was in love with a wanted man.

#711 UNDERCOVER COWBOY—Beverly Bird

If single mom Carly Castagne had learned anything, it was that men couldn't be trusted! And that included Jack Fain, the brooding cowboy who'd arrived at her ranch full of questions and long on charm. But what exactly did this man want, and how far would he go to get it?

#712 CHILD OF THE NIGHT—Lee Karr

Tyla Templeton knew Clay Archer was dangerous—she just didn't realize how dangerous until after she fell in love with him. But could she trust a man whose own daughter was afraid of him? Somehow Tyla had to discover the secrets hidden in the Archer family...or lose the man she loved.

#713 THE ONE WORTH WAITING FOR—Alicia Scott
The Guiness Gang

She hadn't seen him in years, but Suzanne Montgomery would never refuse Garret Guiness anything—especially after he collapsed on her doorstep from a gunshot wound! Now town spinster Suzanne found herself awakening to the only man worth waiting—or dying—for.

#714 THE HONEYMOON ASSIGNMENT—Cathryn Clare
Assignment: Romance

Newlyweds? That was the last role investigators Kelley Landis and Sam Cotter wanted to play. They'd come close once, but a tragedy had driven them apart, confirming their single status. That is, until their honeymoon assignment had them hearing wedding bells...for real!